THE
VIOLIN

ODELLA HOWE

"In the hands of a true violinist, the instrument becomes a mirror of the soul, vibrating with emotion and with the very breath of life." Pablo Casals

Prologue

Chapel Grove, 1923

The house stood as one of the earliest constructions in old Chapel Grove, an age echoed in its appearance. The paint was peeling, the shingles were worn, and the overgrown garden appeared to conceal untold secrets. The residence evoked a sense of foreboding in those who dared to approach, which perhaps explained why so few ever did.

Lucy was among the rare few. Her visits to the woman residing there, Ms. Knight, began at the suggestion of Reverend Bell. When Neil Bollen endorsed this suggestion, Lucy eagerly volunteered, drawing a look of admiration from Neil.

Recalling this moment, Lucy adjusted the ring on her finger. It had been the first real conversation between her and Neil, one that had blossomed into much more.

Despite this auspicious beginning, the visits to Ms. Knight had become a strain on Lucy. The woman was not unpleasant, just rather aloof. She seldom spoke, and although she welcomed Lucy without complaint, it never appeared that she derived any pleasure from the visits. Continuing felt futile, as it hardly seemed to benefit Ms. Knight at all.

Perhaps someone else could take my place, Lucy mused, *someone who might truly reach her*. With a wedding to plan and a life with Neil to prepare for, the time had come to end these visits.

She was resolute that this visit would be the last.

Still, she dreaded the conversation. Perhaps the discomfort wrought by the home was more about Ms. Knight herself. Though Lucy wasn't certain of her precise age, Ms. Knight was undeniably old and bore a distinct lack of warmth. From what Lucy knew, Ms. Knight had never married, had no children, and had lived in that house for as long as Lucy could remember.

Beyond this, Lucy knew little, for Ms. Knight was never forthcoming with personal details, even after months of visits. Lucy rapped on the door and noticed the ring's looseness on her finger, making a mental note to have it resized before it slipped off and was lost. "Come in," a faint voice called from inside, and Lucy obliged, bracing for the slightly musty smell within as she entered the sitting room just off the entryway.

Ms. Knight sat there in an armchair, her needlework nestled in a basket beside her, hands folded neatly in her lap. Her once dark hair was now fully grey.

"Hello, Ms. Knight," Lucy greeted her.

Ms. Knight looked exceedingly tired, dark circles shadowing her eyes. Her gaze followed Lucy, but she remained silent. "Hello, Lucy." Her voice was low and devoid of emotion.

"I've brought you some lunch," Lucy offered, the looming conversation settling around her shoulders like an uninvited guest.

"How kind of you," the old woman replied without enthusiasm. There was no sign of derision in her tone, merely a factual observation, as though she lacked the energy for anything more. This lack of enthusiasm was typical of their visits, making them somewhat burdensome.

"There is no one with whom I would rather share it," said Lucy, reasoning that a small white lie would do no harm. She arranged a pair of sandwiches and some cut fruit on the table between two chairs by the window, keenly aware of the ensuing silence.

"Come, it's ready," Lucy said. Looking up, she noticed Ms. Knight's attention fixed on the diamond ring on her finger. Lucy self-consciously brushed it with her thumb.

"It's beautiful," commented Ms. Knight.

"Thank you," replied Lucy. "Shall I help you to the table?" Startled, Lucy realized that Ms. Knight had tears in her eyes. "Ms. Knight, is everything alright?"

The old woman shook her head.

All this time, the woman Lucy had been visiting was so reserved, so stoic. The surprise of her emotion pushed the impending conversation out of Lucy's mind. "What happened? Are you alright?"

"Fine, fine, dear," Ms. Knight assured her. "Just the reflections of an old woman."

"What is it?" Lucy couldn't help but ask, for this was the most Ms. Knight's cold exterior had softened in all her visits.

Ms. Knight looked at her with eyes that sparkled with a youthful glimmer. "I was just reminded of my love," she said.

Her love?

Though Lucy was determined to inform Ms. Knight of her impending departure, curiosity overcame her resolve, and she sat down.

"Why don't you tell me about him?"

Chapter One

Chapel Grove 1871

It was a few days before my wedding to William that I discovered him lying motionless in his family's field. Beside him lay a rake, having slipped from his grasp during his work. Whatever had transpired caught him completely off guard. Overcome with shock at the sight, I screamed and rushed to his side in panic.

"William, my love." I murmured, rubbing his back in an attempt to rouse him. When my efforts proved futile, I tried to roll him over just as his mother arrived, alerted by my screams to the devastating situation. "Please, darling, wake up."

Even now, fifty years later, the events of that day are difficult to comprehend.

Dr. Bell was the town's physician in those days. When he arrived and declared William dead, I refused to believe it.

"Please," I asked, my voice quaking, "Surely it is only the excitement of our upcoming wedding that has overtaken him, perhaps the early summer heat and the exhaustion of working the fields. Surely, with a little rest in the parlor, he will regain his strength?"

Dr. Bell looked at me with such compassion that it nearly shattered my resolve. The heart-wrenching cries of William's parents echoed from the adjacent room. I pressed my lips together, determined to hold back my emotions.

"The three-day wake has fallen out of favor," Dr. Bell had said gingerly. "But under the circumstances, if it would make you feel better, I can allow it."

"Thank you."

I thought my faith would be justified within those three days.

It had to be.

Yet it was in the parlor of the Whittaker home, three days later, that a knock at the door caused my heart to sink. I knew it was Dr. Bell, and still, William's countenance remained unchanged, as if frozen in time.

"Please, please, wake up," I begged in a broken whisper, aware that time was slipping away. I could not bear the thought of losing him forever.

The door creaked open in the other room, but I kept my eyes fixed on his chest, praying it would rise. I gently placed a hand on his belly, hoping to feel some movement, any movement at all.

The dark features of his face were still blank like he was in a peaceful slumber. I longed to see his eyes once more, those lovely caramel-colored eyes which once sparkled when he looked at me. I drew a shuddering breath at the terrible thought that they might remain closed forever.

In the other room, hushed conversation drew nearer, making my heart race with dread.

"Please, William," I begged. "My love, if you seek to come back to me, now is the time." Nothing. I clasped his unmoving hand between mine. "Please, darling."

The murmurs which had moved to somewhere behind me stopped.

"We will give you a moment," a voice said from afar. Sumner, the undertaker, again, likely with his assistant.

Slow, deliberate footsteps padded into the room, the sound of which was instantly recognizable as my father's. They were steady, like the ticking of a clock counting down to the end of time.

Steady, though seemingly tentative. Reluctant, even.

I stayed focused on William.

Please stay with me.

My lips trembled.

I need you.

I pressed his hand to my cheek. His fingers felt icy to the touch.

The footsteps halted beside me. A familiar hand rested on my shoulder.

My grip on William's hand tightened, willing it to stir. I was uncertain what I hoped for—simply anything that might validate the faith I held onto.

"Elise, honey." My father spoke softly, as one would in church. *Or at a funeral,* my cruel mind supplied. I swallowed hard without responding. "Elise."

Helpless, I laid William's hand back down and tousled his chestnut hair. *Give me something, anything.* Still, nothing.

The hand on my shoulder squeezed gently. "It's time, darling."

A pause lingered in the air.

Tears blurred my vision as they began to spill, obscuring William's face further. I closed my eyes, trying to stem the tide down my cheeks.

"I'm so sorry," my father whispered.

"Just a few more minutes?" I attempted to keep the tremor from my voice, though my composure was slipping. "Please?"

Silence fell behind me, my father torn between my plea and the inevitable reality.

"*Lissie.*" His words neither affirmed nor denied, only urged acceptance of what could not be changed.

A sob escaped my chest.

"I'm sorry, love," repeated my father.

The truth was plain for all to see: my William had not come back to me. I glanced at his still face once more before turning to my father and collapsing into his arms.

William, my love, my husband-to-be, was dead.

Dead.

The word echoed in my head. My father guided me to the chaise on the opposite side of the room, allowing Sumner and his assistant the space they needed. William's stone-faced parents stood in the doorway, flanked by his siblings.

With methodical care, Sumner and his assistant swaddled William in burial cloths.

My father held me close while the men labored quietly.

Despite my fervent prayers, my desperate pleading, and my profound longing for his return, William's body lay before me—a hollow shell where once existed his vibrant, beautiful spirit. I observed in silent despair. The assistant had covered his face with a cloth, casting me a fleeting, furtive glance before turning back to his duties.

A hushed murmur stirred in the hall, creating a slight commotion that piqued my curiosity. My attention shifted.

"I don't know," said William's father. "I don't think we can afford one."

William's mother covered her face, stifling her sobs.

"He needs a casket," William's brother insisted. "He must have one."

A casket.

It felt as though the wind had been knocked out of me as I pictured William buried beneath the soil, unprotected from the earth around him by anything more than the burial cloth the undertaker had provided. The Whittakers did not have the money for anything more, nothing like the mausoleums of the wealthier residents of Chapel Grove which dotted its graveyard.

My breath came in shallow bursts as fresh grief washed over me.

"I would be obliged to craft a casket," my father said softly.

William's mother dissolved into fresh tears.

"Thank you," said William's father, holding his grieving wife.

"It is the least I can do," said my father.

Though grateful for my father's generous offer, in my heart I clung to the absurd notion that William did not truly need a casket; caskets were for the dead, and in my heart, William could not be gone.

He had seemed so alive till the very end, his cheeks holding color, a slight smile playing on his lips as I approached him. Earlier that day, his unresponsive silence to my every question had stunned me, for I wholeheartedly believed he would answer.

Sumner and his assistant carefully took my beloved's body out of the house. Feet first, as per tradition. Not wanting him to turn his eyes toward the house and bid any of us follow him. I would have, though. I would have followed William anywhere.

Watching William leave his family home for the final time, an unbearable weight of grief descended upon me, persisting in the oppressive haze of sorrow that followed in the days thereafter.

On the day of William's funeral, as I searched for appropriate attire, a specter from happier times confronted me. Instead of the somber black dress I sought, I was met with the sight of the gown Mrs. Miller had painstakingly crafted for me—a beautiful steel blue dress accented with cream-colored lace. It was the dress I had intended for the day I would become Mrs. Whittaker.

Hands trembling, I placed it at the back of the closet, and as I did, a realization struck with such force that I sank to my knees: William never saw this dress before he passed.

A caustic rage overtook my grief. This was the dress I should be wearing, I thought bitterly—not the garments of mourning.

Rising from that spot proved difficult without my father's aid, but I eventually collected myself enough to prepare for the funeral. My father walked with me to the church, which was a short walk along the creek road beside our house. We passed the cemetery on our way, a place suitably shrouded in mist and melancholy.

Upon arriving at the church, I faltered. My father gave my hand a reassuring squeeze, and with a deep breath, we proceeded inside. Entering, the muted conversations seemed to ebb, though whether this was reality or merely my own heightened self-awareness, I couldn't say. My gaze remained on the floor as my father and I took our places with the Whittakers in the front pew. William's mother offered me a wan smile before returning her gaze to the casket at the front of the church. Beside her, William's father sat with hands clasped, eyes closed in silent prayer. Beyond them sat William's younger brothers, and behind them, his sisters with their spouses and children.

Father Willard soon approached the podium.

Though I tried to find solace in his words, my mind wandered, for none could ease my heartache.

Perhaps God did simply give and take away, but reconciling the idea of a just, loving God with the loss of my William was difficult. For what reason would He give my William a deficient heart? Did he not deserve better than what he had received?

Dr. Bell had attempted to reassure me that nothing could have been done to save William, even had his condition been discovered sooner. But I struggled to accept that it had been simply his time. How could that be, with so many cherished plans left unfulfilled?

None of the comforting platitudes Father Willard offered could remove the black shroud of grief enveloping my heart.

Upon returning home, there was nothing more to be done but to retire to my room and weep.

Chapter Two

The remainder of June and most of July were largely spent, to my shame, confined to my bed, buried within my grief. I watched the sun rise and set on what would have been our wedding day, a day that felt like a second funeral—a quiet, solitary time for me to mourn the death of what could have been. I wore no special attire to commemorate the day, nor was there a gathering of mourners; it was just me in my nightclothes, wrapped in my quilt.

While watching a spider spinning a web in the corner of the room, memories drifted through my mind—those cherished moments shared with William, which assumed an overwhelming significance in his absence.

I recalled the times I would lightheartedly urge him to stop working and pay attention to me, wishing we could escape together and spend time nestled in the hay, a far more desirable activity than any farm chore he attended to that day.

"Lissie, you're nothing but trouble," he would say with a smile.

I never truly expected him to abandon his duties, though I secretly wished for it.

How I wished to see that coy, nearly tempted smile once more, to admire him once more for his dedication.

But the memories were nothing compared to the nightmares which haunted me throughout the night, preventing me from finding solace in sleep.

One nightmare featured William being buried alive. I was surrounded by the onlookers from the funeral, scraping futilely at the earth as William screamed within.

"I told you he was still alive!" I shouted to those around me.

His cries grew fainter as I furiously dug at the soil, unable to reach him.

"You've killed him!" I would accuse them, raging like an animal, waking with a start at the height of my despair.

Sometimes these nightmares were set in my own bedroom, where I would imagine waking to find William standing over me. I would rejoice, my heart rejuvenated, until I realized that his gentle brown eyes had turned to the red eyes of a feral cat, his fingernails transformed into claws. Just as I was about to scream, I would wake, too terrified to move, uncertain what was real and what was not.

Other, more subtle nightmares plagued me too, such as those where my father and I worked side by side in his workshop. Although benign at first, the dreams would inevitably shift to a more sinister event, such as my father slipping with a saw or gouge, inflicting a fatal injury on himself. A rapid succession of images would follow—his body being removed from our home, a funeral, and a burial.

Perhaps this stemmed from the unexpectedness of William's death, but being tormented by grief for unrealized losses felt exceptionally cruel.

Peculiarly, other disturbing dreams came as well, like one of a small child hidden in the shadows of my room One stormy night, I awoke, convinced I heard her giggling, and spent the rest of the night in the chair in our sitting room, wishing to be closer to my father but not wanting to disturb his sleep. I was unsure why this child unsettled me so greatly, but the reason was insignificant compared to its disturbing nature.

Some dreams started blissfully, only to turn cruel. In such dreams, I found myself standing on the shore of a sandy beach. In this paradise, my William stood knee-deep in the sparkling turquoise water. Overjoyed, I raced to him, throwing myself into his embrace. The warmth of the sun, the movement of the water, and the strength of his arms all felt so real. Even upon waking, just for a moment, I believed I was in a world where William had never died. Then, as ever, reality took hold again, settling back in like a bird returning to a familiar perch.

Occasionally, in a half-sleep state, a scent would rise to my awareness—the scent of William in his clothes after a day on the farm. I would look around hopefully, only to face disappointment.

It was as though the angel of death sought to extract every last ounce of hope from my emaciated spirit. My fractured mind refused to be quieted.

My despondent state deeply troubled my father, who coaxed me to eat as best as I could. With no appetite, my already fragile form became even more frail. He sought to remedy this by bringing meals to my room on a tray, looking at me with his kind eyes, silently imploring me. I would yield, taking a few bites of the tasteless food that offered no pleasure.

My listlessness made fertile soil for guilt, knowing that my father, too, had dealt with tremendous loss; my own mother, in fact, died from hemorrhage after my birth. During his grief, he had cared for me. Admirable as his actions had always seemed, I now understood and respected them on a more profound level. My father had raised me, taught me, and brought me up without a wife—a feat that must have been challenging, even with the support of Chapel Grove. Alongside my growing admiration for him came a deep sense of shame over my inability to escape my sorrow. I lacked the fortitude he had evidently possessed. Despite my desire not to burden him, grief had latched onto me like a demon.

On my darkest days, I felt the fervent desire to be buried with William myself, though lacked the initiative to make such a thing happen. I was listless, despondent, beside myself, and had shut myself away from those around me as they, too, mourned the loss - for, in hindsight, they surely were.

Many in Chapel Grove came to call during this period of mourning, but not wishing to speak of my loss, not wanting to hear any more trite explanations for why my love had been taken from me, I hid myself away instead of welcoming their compassion. For better or worse, my father became a buffer between me and these well-meaning visitors, sparing me from taking on more than I could bear. I often wonder how things might have unfolded differently if I had sought solace from those around me rather than isolating myself; perhaps it would have fortified me against the challenges that awaited.

Chapter Three

My misery was unexpectedly disrupted one day by my father's sudden entrance into the room. This was unusual, as it was not long after he had brought me some bread and jam. Aside from meals, he typically left me undisturbed.

"Is everything all right?" I asked, turning to meet his gaze.

There was a violin in his hands, his eyebrows arched with a hopeful expression. I straightened slightly, intrigue piqued.

"Everything is all right, love," he said, pulling a chair next to my bed. "Only I wanted you to be the first to see it." He sat down and rested the violin upright against his knee.

"It's lovely," I replied.

It was, truly. Its body was a rich bronze-brown, reminiscent of cinnamon. My eyes traveled from its body up the neck with its genuine ebony fingerboard. The scroll atop the violin was a work of art that evoked images of a seashell. I envisioned a late sunset over the bay, that moment when daylight has almost vanished, but the sky retains a sliver of crimson. My mind imagined the scent of salt in the air, waves swelling and receding. Perhaps the distant song of a siren, luring unsuspecting sailors into her embrace.

The allure of a brand-new violin tantalized me. How might it sound?

"Freshly stringed and ready to play," my father coaxed. Like a salesman, he gently rotated the instrument. Gorgeous, every inch.

I shifted to a sitting position in bed and glanced from the violin to my father. His blue eyes held a certain sadness, a hint of uncertainty.

"I'm not sure if I can." My voice sounded foreign to my own ears, having been so seldom used in recent days. My father tilted his head sympathetically, placing the violin across his lap, holding it with one arm while grasping my hand with the other.

"I understand," he said.

Tears welled in my eyes, and I buried my head against my knees, sobbing.

My father set the violin down on my bed and wrapped his arms around me, holding me close as sobs shook my chest. I found safety in his embrace, inhaling the smell of varnish and wood shavings on his clothing, his graying beard tickling my face.

"I would take the pain away if I could."

"I know," I whispered.

We separated, and as I wiped my eyes, I glanced again at the violin.

"Play it for me, Lissie."

My initial urge was to refuse. Getting out of bed was a daunting task, and though tempted, I questioned whether I had the strength to do so.

It then dawned on me that perhaps my father truly needed me to perform this small act. There was a flicker of hope in his expression. Surely watching his daughter in such distress had been a heavy burden, as was caring for her.

"There is no one else I would rather see play it first," he added.

My lips twitched in an unwilling smile. Doubts aside, there was ultimately no question of whether I would do as he asked.

"I would love to." I told him, eying the violin with a certain greediness.

Upon standing, my head swam, unaccustomed as I was to being out of bed.

"Steady, steady," my father cautioned, placing a hand upon my back for support.

"I'm okay," I assured him, carefully swinging my legs over the edge of the bed. My gaze returned to the violin in his lap. It really was a magnificent instrument, one which I was honored to christen.

"Whenever you're ready," he said.

I nodded in acknowledgment, then moved to my wardrobe, where my long-neglected violin case lay. I retrieved the bow and tightened the loosened horsehair. My thumb lightly brushed its playing surface, confirming it was adequately rosined.

"I'm ready," I said.

He handed me the violin.

"What would you like me to play?"

"You choose," he said.

"Okay."

The imagery of the ocean lingered in my mind. I lifted the violin to my shoulder and nestled it below my chin. The scent of fresh lacquer filled my nose, stirring something slumbering within me as I breathed it in.

The violin's potential was evident from the very first pluck of the G string. I bowed across it, checking its pitch.

With the G string tuned, I moved to A, which resonated warmly throughout the violin's body. The D and E strings matched its warmth.

By the time I was finished tuning, a sensation of warmth radiated through me, like snowcapped mountains thawing to expose timid spring blossoms. I glanced at my father.

"Ready?" I asked.

"Whenever you are," he replied.

I pondered my song choice, then settled on an old favorite: a folk song from my youth, affectionately known as Blackberry Blossom. I knew my father favored it, and it was one I knew by heart.

My fingers pressed against the strings, seeming to remember of their own accord what to do, where to go. The bow held in my other hand pulled across the strings—short strokes, long strokes, and everything in between. My toe tapped to the rhythm, keeping time.

My shoulders relaxed. My heart raced, my breathing harmonizing with the violin's ebb and flow. The longer I played, the deeper my desire grew to continue, to hear more of the instrument's buttery, rich, smooth sound. Playing the violin was like being reunited with a long-lost friend.

As I reached the song's final note, I drew it out, letting it linger in the air before gently resting the violin and bow at my side. Something like electricity coursed down my spine, awakening something that had been dormant. Music, which I had overlooked in its significance, awakened that latent part of my being.

My father's eyes shone.

"Beautiful," he said, after a hushed pause, "Just beautiful."

"Thank you." I beamed broadly, unable to hide my delight. It wasn't just a smile; it was an exuberant grin stretching from ear to ear.

"My pleasure." His blue eyes neared turquoise. I found myself giggling, despite myself, and my father's smile only widened in response.

I began to return the violin, but he folded his hands in his lap. "It's yours."

"Oh," I breathed, taken aback. "I couldn't." Nevertheless, I clutched the violin to my chest as though safeguarding a newborn.

"You must."

I glanced from the violin to him, my brow furrowing as I pondered the violin's worth.

"No," I said, though my resolve faded as I gazed at the violin, the fight losing oxygen in favor of another flame.

"I insist," he said firmly.

I looked back at him, somewhat guiltily.

"Thank you." I meant it sincerely, recognizing the sacrifice this violin represented, both in the time my father had spent on it and its material cost. "It really is an incredible instrument."

"It's no Vuillame, but it will do just the same," he said with a casual shrug, though his lips hinted at quiet pride.

"Give yourself due credit," I gently chided.

"It certainly comes to life with your playing."

"Thank you." Tears welled up, this time of gratitude. "Really... thank you."

He stood and took the violin from me, placing it on the bed, and wrapped me in a hug.

"I would do anything for you, Lissie," he whispered softly, and I entirely believed it.

The responsibility of owning my father's prized instrument spurred me to action, preventing me from succumbing to melancholy. A part of me had been revived by the act of producing music. That part of me demanded nourishment, and I saw no reason not to oblige.

As my mind engaged with the intricacies of finger placement and bowing for beautiful sound, there was no space left to dwell on the past. Each moment with the violin was an opportunity to temporarily escape my sorrow.

Sometimes, playing the violin purged the anguish within. When sorrow threatened to overwhelm, as if raked by nails from the agony of loss, music acted as an exorcism, banishing the misery back to its dark origin.

The music distracted me from my grief, a balm on the wounds inflicted by William's absence. Even my father noticed, mentioning it one day when we ate dinner together: the first meal for which I had been at the table in many weeks.

"I've enjoyed your playing," he mentioned over dinner.

"Thank you." I speared a potato with my fork, meeting his gaze. "You crafted a lovely violin."

"I would make you a thousand more if it brought you happiness," he said, busying himself with his meal as though he had said nothing of significance.

I paused, taken aback by his words. He didn't look up, perhaps out of shy humility. I allowed the moment to pass without further acknowledgment of his sentiment, simply replying, "Thank you."

After dinner, I returned to my practice.

After a few days of such fervent playing, however, my fingers became tender and painful. I knew calluses would eventually form, but I did not want to risk bleeding on such a fine instrument; nor did I wish to stop playing long enough to heal more significant injuries.

So, unwillingly, I allowed my fingers to rest, and my mind teetered on the edge without the music which had so comforted it.

Chapter Four

It was during this break in violin playing that my dear friend Rebecca came to visit.

"Elise?" she said as I opened the door, her voice tinged with surprise, as if she had not expected to find me.

"Becca!" I greeted her with a smile. "It's wonderful to see you. Please, come in." Having seen little of anyone in the weeks following William's death, her visit was a welcome surprise, especially under the circumstances. She stepped in, holding her long dress out of the way. Her chestnut hair was plaited down her back.

"Please, have a seat. Can I offer you something to drink?"

She sat but shook her head. "No, I don't wish to trouble you."

"Not at all," I insisted. "I'm truly glad to see you. How about some tea?"

She nodded. "That sounds lovely."

When I returned, I noticed Rebecca nervously picking at her nails and gazing out the window.

""Thank you, Elise. You're very kind," she said, as I poured tea into her cup. She added sugar and stirred it absently, lost in thought.

"How have you been?" I asked, trying to break the silence.

"I have been well," she said, smoothing her skirt against her legs. A strained silence followed once more.

"What is it?" I pressed, sensing there was more to her visit.

"I felt you should be the first to know…" Her voice trailed off.

"Know what?" I asked, bracing myself for some kind of impact.

"Frederick asked me to marry him."

"Oh." I glanced at the modest ring on her finger, which she quickly covered with her other hand. A swirl of envy and shame washed over me.

"We're planning to marry soon," she continued. "After everything with William, I suppose Frederick felt there was no time to waste." She smiled hesitantly, as if embarrassed to show her joy. "It made us realize… well, how short life can be." Her confession poured out in a flurry of words. "I'm so sorry. I just felt if I told you, then…"

Then perhaps I would not be caught off guard by the information, made to feel worse than I already did. In theory, knowing sooner was better, but the news still splintered my fragile spirit. "Don't be silly," I assured her, my voice quiet, avoiding her gaze. I forced myself to say, "Congratulations."

"Thank you." Her expression softened with relief, and she wrapped me in a hug.

My heart broke all the more. I wanted so desperately to be happy for Rebecca. Indeed, I *was* happy for her, but still, there was a beast within me that raged with jealousy, at the unfairness that she should marry her beloved and mine should be buried.

"We intend to marry in September. September 30th," she said.

"So soon?" I replied, surprised by the nearness of the date.

"Yes. We do not wish to wait longer than necessary."

"I can understand that," I said politely, my heart shattering all the more. Another wedding, so soon after William's death, so close within the proximity of when we should have been married.

What we spoke about thereafter I could hardly recall. I promised help with whatever she required of me. After she left, however, I found that the grief which had previously been my tormentor had not been eliminated, but only stagnated. I found myself pacing the sitting room, struggling to settle. I felt some kind of presence laughing at me as I struggled to throw off the crushing weight of despair.

Having once discovered the healing power of music, I vowed not to let grief overwhelm me again without a fight. I refused to succumb to inertia, though I doubted whether the violin's magic could revive my spirit a second time.

My grief had taken the form of a being which had pinned me in the corner of a room, trapping me like an animal. My heart palpating, I paced forward and back, worried that if I stood still, I would be overcome.

My never-ending footsteps must have caught my father's attention, for he came to check on me.

"I am all right," I reassured him, though uncertain myself.

He saw through my forced smile. "I was about to go out for some fresh air," he suggested. "I would love some company, if you'd oblige."

It was a ruse, I knew, but I agreed with a nod anyway.

Outside, we sat on the porch swing. I trusted my father to sit quietly with me, having mundane conversations, but did not wish to go farther, to risk conversation with anyone else.

The porch swing creaked beneath my father and me as he held my hand. Crickets chirped in celebration of the onset of evening, a completion of another day. The air became cooler, decisively autumnal. While my spirit was somewhat soothed by being in the fresh air, a sense of deep melancholy loomed as I discovered the world was still turning.

The world, even without my William, continued to move forward. Unabated. Careless. Without regard to me or anyone else.

Fall would come; winter would follow. Then summer, spring, and fall once more.

All of it without William.

Meanwhile, Rebecca and Frederick would marry, have children, and other couples would follow suit.

And what lay ahead for me?

I sighed.

"What am I supposed to do?" I whispered, not meeting my father's eyes as the question left my lips. It was directed more at the universe than at him, posed while I watched birds' flit from branch to branch.

My father gently squeezed my hand. "Life will go on."

I met his gaze, my lips pressed tightly together. His blue eyes mirrored the peach-hued light of the setting sun. "I know. I know it doesn't feel that way," he admitted, sighing. "But it does. It must. It will."

My lower lip trembled, and I dared not speak. Correct as he likely was, that truth did nothing to put my soul at ease.

He pulled me closer, wrapping an arm around my shoulder. I rested my head against his chest.

"Lissie," he began softly. I glanced at him, apprehensive. "Have I ever told you why I chose to become a violin maker?"

It struck me as surprising; the thought he could have been anything else had never occurred to me. "No," I replied.

"Entirely by chance, actually."

"What do you mean?"

"I was lost as a young man," he said softly. "Angry. Unsure of myself. My parents were destitute, my father unable "—he hesitated, clearing his throat—"perhaps unwilling to keep a stable job."

The porch swing swayed gently as I absorbed his words. My father rarely spoke of his youth or early adulthood.

"Thus, I left Chapel Grove in search of something, anything that would provide me a way forward. I found myself in the city, nearly penniless. Around that time, a Frenchman by the name of Jean Pelletier happened to be in town. I can hardly recall the reason, perhaps to search for new wood for his violins. Whatever the case, we became acquainted, and he took pity on me." His eyes glinted with mischief, and I tilted my head curiously. "I will admit, when I heard him speak of France and especially of Paris, I may have exaggerated my woodworking skills a bit…"

"*No.*" I laughed. It was hard to reconcile the image of this reckless young man with my steadfast father.

He nodded, confirming the truth of his tale. "Yes. He was kind enough to take me on as an apprentice," he reminisced, smiling. "It changed my life."

As he recounted these memories, there was a youthful sparkle in his eyes, something I cherished witnessing. I imagined what his life must have been like: the romance of Paris, the rich history, the art, the adventure. My imagination bathed it all in a rosy hue.

"France must have been lovely," I mused.

"It was," he said. "But it was not the thing I fell in love with."

"What was?" I asked, half-expecting a newfound tale about my mother.

"Violin making," he said. "I learned to love its blend of artistry and physics, the complexity of the craft. It felt as if I'd discovered something within myself that was missing until then. I was enthralled by the process, by how intimate it could be, I suppose. It demands more than just technical knowledge; it requires an understanding of the distinct qualities of each piece of wood and what each violin needs to reach its fullest potential."

"How so?" I asked, intrigued. Though I had been around his craft throughout my childhood, I had never heard this side of him before.

"Each violin is different, with its own… spirit, you could say," he mused. "Even two violins made from the wood of the same tree, created by the same person, would no doubt behave differently."

"Indeed?" I asked.

"Indeed."

"But…" I started, choosing my words carefully. "You returned. Why?"

"It simply wasn't to be," he said with a sigh. "It was a letter from my mother that did it. She informed me that my father, your grandfather, had passed on. It was a difficult choice to make, but I realized I could not allow her to be on her own."

"That was noble of you," I observed.

"I suppose so. I had wished to make a name for myself in France, but instead hoped, perhaps, I could make a name for myself as a great violin maker—the first great American violin maker." He sighed. "It never happened, but I am proud of my accomplishments, nonetheless. Had my violins come from the motherlands of France or Italy, they'd have fetched the proper price tag. Instead, I shall settle for the satisfaction of knowing their true value, I suppose." Then he added, "Though I never valued any of them more than the ones I made for you."

I raised an eyebrow, a bit skeptical. "Really?"

"Of course. In fact, I still recall the first violin I made you."

"Me, too," I said, thinking of the one he had given me when I was perhaps four years old. "I remember playing on it for hours."

He shook his head and laughed softly. "No, not that one."

"Which one, then?"

"Perhaps you were too young to remember. You wanted me to make you one so badly, but I worried a child so young—perhaps two, three years old at the most—would only damage a real instrument. I tried to ply you with a largely unplayable toy." He chuckled.

"I don't remember any such thing!"

"I admit, I am surprised," he responded, "considering the ruckus you made when you discovered it couldn't be played was truly unforgettable."

"I apologize," I said with a grin.

"There's no need for apologies," he assured me. "Because that incident led me to create your first real violin, and when I did, you took such excellent care of it that I knew I had made the right decision. Even when your music wasn't exactly conventional, it has always been my favorite sound."

I snuggled close to my father, feeling tremendously loved.

"But, my darling, the reason I tell you this story is that life always continues forward. For every opportunity lost, a new one will rise. Had I not left France, I would never have met your mother. Though I lost her, I gained you. And you, too, will find life has so much more to offer you, even if it doesn't feel that way right now."

I closed my eyes, fighting back the tears that threatened to escape once more. "I love you."

"Love you, too," he returned. He gave my shoulders a gentle squeeze. "More than you can fathom."

Chapter Five

The sense of calm that my father's words had instilled in me began to dissipate later that night. In the silent darkness of my room, the tormenting demons that had haunted me since William's death threatened to re-emerge.

Despite this, if the world was to keep spinning, then so must I. But how? I yearned for something new, something exhilarating that would give me hope for the future, even if just for the next day.

A new idea sparked forth in my mind, that of bringing my new violin to the cemetery to play for William.

Not so long ago, William would have gladly listened to my playing, making special requests and enjoying every note. The idea of sharing my rediscovered joy with him, even in this small way, illuminated my dark thoughts just enough to carry me through another night.

The next day, though my fingertips remained tender, they had healed sufficiently to allow me to play, if only briefly. The weather seemed inviting, with no ominous clouds on the horizon—for, despite my determination to play for William, it was unthinkable to risk damage to the violin in the rain.

Indeed, it was a beautiful day, one that William would have relished with me. Perhaps it was this thought which inspired me to prepare for the day as though truly expecting to see William. This was an illusion, of course, but one which seemed harmless to entertain.

After a refreshing bath, I styled my dark hair into a low bun to keep it neat and out of the way. I chose a plum-colored dress which William had once praised—*it brings out the bronze in your eyes,* he had remarked—making it perfect for the occasion.

While securing the latches of the case after packing up the violin and bow, the dinginess of my ring caught my attention. I polished it, lest William notice its tarnished state.

Encountering William was a fantasy, naturally, but one I wasn't yet ready to dispel as mere trickery of light.

The stairs creaked underfoot as I descended, alerting my father in the kitchen, who was savoring breakfast.

"Good morning!" he greeted, his voice tinged with pleasant surprise. "Can I get you something to eat?"

I shook my head. "No, thank you."

His eyes wandered to the violin in my hand. "Where are you going?"

With this question, my father had inadvertently shifted the light casting the illusion. My cheeks burned as my quest suddenly seemed too foolish to explain. Would my father find the whole thing silly, or perhaps worse?

Not wanting to worry him, I opted for vagueness. "I wanted to go play for a bit," I said. "Simply in a new place for a while."

"It's a lovely day to do so," he said simply. "Would you like some company?"

"No, not today." Perhaps another day, but this was a time for me and William.

"Next time, then."

"Next time," I agreed.

"Wait, before you go," he said, raising a hand and disappearing into the other room. Upon his return, he pressed some money into my palm. "In case you go into town. Get yourself something, okay? On me."

"No, really, you don't have to," I protested, attempting to return the money, feeling it could serve better elsewhere.

"I realize that. I insist." He pocketed his hands, leaving me no way to return the coins.

"Well, thank you." I could always give the coins back another time. I kissed him on the cheek and stepped out the door.

The air was cool and crisp, and the nearby trees' leaves had begun their transformation from lush green to pale yellow. The approaching splendor of autumn, usually a source of delight, instead felt like an affront. Nature seemed to belittle my halted world with its eagerness to progress to the next season.

With a sigh, I resolved to put the feeling aside. *William is waiting.* All other considerations were mere distractions which, if indulged, threatened to unravel me. The season of languishing in bed had persisted for too long already and so, despite the ache within my soul, I trudged onward toward the cemetery via the narrow path by our home.

Upon reaching the cemetery and passing through its gates, I was surprised by its objective loveliness. The grass among the tidy row of graves was well-groomed, and pops of asters and daylilies gave color to the fringes. So much life for such a dark place, I mused. The caretaker obviously took pride in his work. Mackenzie, I reminded myself. Rowan Mackenzie. A constant presence, the cemetery's caretaker for as long as I could remember. His fastidious care of the cemetery, and, by extension, of William, brought me great comfort.

William's final resting place was located near the back of the cemetery, in the newer section of burial plots. I trod carefully, respectfully past the other graves until I reached his plot, keeping my eyes on my feet, for it felt intrusive, somehow disrespectful, to look at the graves I was not there to visit.

Finally, I reached William's grave. It was so bare, so freshly dug that hardly a sprig of grass had begun to grow over it, but in the time since the funeral, his stone had been set. The engraving upon it read:

IN LOVING MEMORY.

WILLIAM DURANTE WHITTAKER

BELOVED SON.

REST IN PEACE.

6 MAY 1852 - 18 JUNE 1871

My heart thrummed at the sight of his death, so starkly etched in stone.

"William," I began slowly, striving to keep my voice steady. "I've brought my violin to play for you." I paused, as if awaiting a reply, then envisioned his response.

Oh, Elise—thank you. Please, play for me.

I smiled softly.

"I would be delighted to. Anything for you, my darling." Still crouched, I placed the violin case on the ground before his gravestone and unclasped it.

"My father made it," I explained, retrieving the violin from the case. "He gifted it to me."

It's lovely, he said, *one of his finest.*

"I agree."

There was a song William always loved, a Vivaldi piece, which came to mind as I tuned the violin. My imagining of William's presence was so vivid that I fancied I could catch his scent on the breeze. Illusion or not, the thought comforted my soul.

"Ready?" I asked.

Of course, my love.

And with that, I launched into the Vivaldi piece that William adored, feeling my spirit begin to lift with every note. It was as though the violin itself was drawing out my sorrow. As the final note resonated, I gazed at William's headstone, envisioning his presence beside it.

Bravo, he said, applauding. *Beautiful, Elise.*

"Thank you," I said, my heart swelling with warmth.

Do you have time for an encore?

"For you, always."

I continued in this manner, playing and conversing with my beloved William, perhaps for hours. In my mind, time ceased to exist, enveloping us in a personal sanctuary where the outside world held no sway.

Eventually, however, my stomach clamored, protesting its prolonged neglect.

You must be famished, my love.

"I am hungry," I admitted. My fingers, tender from playing, had grown numb, promising aches later, but this seemed insignificant at that moment.

Go and have supper. I will be here whenever you return.

I know you will. I love you, darling.

"I love you, too."

Chapter Six

As hard as it was to walk away, it was comforting to be with William once again. The question remained where to go next. I absently fingered the coin in my pocket, thinking of the delicacies it could procure in town. Though it had been my intention to return home and give it back to my father, it occurred to me that spending more time out of the house would perhaps encourage my father that I was getting better.

With that in mind, I left the cemetery and resumed the path along the creek to town, where it led to the main road of Chapel Grove. From there, it was a short jaunt to the deli run by Rodney Nash. Through the shop window, I could see Rodney behind the counter, his presence bringing a wave of comforting familiarity despite the surrounding upheaval. I approached his establishment, grateful to reconnect with an old friend.

The bell above the door chimed as I entered, announcing my arrival. Rodney turned to greet me with a warm smile, which faltered the moment our eyes met.

"Oh, dear," he murmured. "Dear, it's so good to see you."

His sudden change in attitude drew the attention of other patrons. Conversations halted as they watched us.

I felt my cheeks warm. "You too."

"Oh, darling. Mary and I were so sorry to hear what happened. Such a tragedy."

"Thank you," I replied softly.

Maybe this outing had been a mistake. I had simply—perhaps foolishly—hoped that this outing could be as before, but the sobering reality was that nothing would ever be the same again. *I ought to have gone home for lunch.*

Rodney hadn't done anything wrong, of course. My struggle stemmed from the realization that I would never again be the Elise who existed before William's passing. In this state, discussing William's absence or ignoring it would equally unsettle me. It was the dramatic shift in my life that rendered everything uncomfortable.

Even so, leaving so soon after my arrival would seem rude, and, as I said, no one had done anything wrong. To avoid offending Rodney, I took a seat at the counter and browsed the menu, aware of eyes on me.

When Rodney returned, I placed my order. "Eggs, please. Fried, with toast."

"Much obliged," Rodney replied.

My discomfort diminished slightly as conversations resumed within the deli. Nevertheless, I felt a growing restlessness to return home. I lightly pressed my sore fingers against the wooden counter, replaying the music I had practiced when a voice spoke behind me.

"Excuse me, Elise," it said. I turned. "Is this seat taken?"

It was none other than Abel Sinclair, son of Chapel Grove's mayor. Though we had exchanged greetings in passing, our social circles rarely intertwined. Indeed, even his knowledge of my name was surprising to me.

"No, it isn't."

"Would you mind terribly if I took it?"

I shook my head. "No, not at all."

"Thank you," he said politely.

I focused on my restless fingers, aware of Abel watching me, his hands resting on the counter.

Rodney passed at that moment. "Abel, good to have you in," he said, offering a menu, which Abel declined with a gesture.

"Not today, thank you," Abel replied. Rodney nodded and fetched a carafe of coffee.

"I heard you playing the violin this afternoon," said Abel.

"Did you?" I shifted uneasily, feeling somehow caught. I opened my mouth, about to apologize, perhaps, for disrupting his day, but Abel spoke first.

"It was lovely," he said softly.

His unexpected compliment thawed my unease. "Thank you,"

Rodney placed a plate before me, looking between myself and Abel quizzically, but said only, "Your meal, miss."

"Thank you," I replied, sprinkling salt over the eggs and picking up a fork.

"Where did you learn to play?" Abel asked.

"My father—I'm sure you're familiar with him." I gestured vaguely in the direction of my house "He has made violins since before I was able to walk. I just kind of picked it up."

"Amazing," he said, shaking his head in—was it wonder? "A natural talent."

"Thank you," I responded. "Those were some of my favorite songs. Some of them are from sheet music I found in my father's collection," I thought of the Vivaldi which had been William's favorite, "But others I toyed around and came up with myself."

"Is that so?" he asked, intrigue shining in his gray eyes.

"Indeed."

"Beautiful," he remarked. "A natural talent."

My face warmed. "That's very kind of you."

"Only the truth." He caught Rodney's attention as he passed, handing him money. "Mr. Nash, for Ms. Knight's meal."

"Oh, you needn't—" I made to object, but Rodney accepted the payment with a nod and moved to another customer.

"It's already done," said Abel.

"Well, in that case," I replied, "Thank you. That was very generous."

"I am pleased to do so. I'll leave you in peace, but I hope to hear you play again soon?"

"Perhaps," I said.

"I hope so."

After he left, I finished my meal and returned home along the road by the creek once more.

Having grown up in Chapel Grove, I never imagined anything could make me feel like an outsider. Yet, being at the diner reminded me of how drastically things had changed since William's passing. William and I had been inseparably intertwined, our futures bound to one another, so his absence left me fragmented, lost; like a visitor to a strange world, unfamiliar even to myself.

The sky beyond our home had darkened with an unexpected collection of gray storm clouds. The dreary atmosphere made the warm glow of our home an even more welcome sight. One place, at least, had remained unchanged. The home which my father and I shared was still a sanctuary.

My father met me in the entryway, as if he had been waiting for my return. I wondered if he had been.

He questioned me briefly about my day, his posture tense, but he seemed relieved when I assured him all had gone well. He was particularly interested in hearing about my trip to town and took special note of Abel paying for my meal, but was otherwise reassured.

"I understand how it can be," he said. "I'm glad it went well."

"Me too."

Settling into bed that night, the dark night only intensified the blackness of the day. William's death had broken my heart. What had come next had shattered those pieces all the more. Never again could I be the Elise who existed before, not anymore. Having loved and lost William had changed me irreparably, and my life in Chapel Grove had to be rebuilt from the ground up. On my own, though, this time.

Rain pelted the roof with increasing intensity.

Well, not entirely alone, for my father remained unchanged. This knowledge soothed me. I was deeply grateful for my father and all he did to care for me. The violin, for instance, was a luxury he hardly needed to provide. The gift had shaken me from my inertia, reawakening me from my daze. He had sacrificed greatly to make that happen.

A flash of light seeped through the edges of the window coverings. A few seconds later, thunder rumbled in the distance. I sighed.

No, I was certainly not alone, yet it was difficult not to feel different. It wasn't as though Rodney or Abel or anyone else had been unkind. They meant well.

Another flash of lightning, followed by thunder—closer this time.

The trouble was, what once felt comfortable and familiar now felt alien. My interactions with townsfolk had been light and joyful before William's death. Now, they were awkward, stilted.

Would it ever improve? It had to.

But when? How?

A flash of lightning and clap of thunder happened almost simultaneously this time, the rain pelting with fury.

Over the coming weeks and months, things would hopefully settle into place. I comforted myself with this thought, but I had scarcely begun to settle when something jolted me awake. My vision was blurry at first, making it difficult to see what startled me, then I sat with a start. Silhouetted in the moonlight was a figure. Terror obliterated all calm.

But then, my eyes adjusted, and I took in the details of what I was seeing more clearly.

"William?"

But upon my acknowledgement of the apparition, it vanished.

I sat in my bed, stunned. Was this vision a trick of the light? My mind, simply unable to settle?

A sign?

The reality of the situation swept over me again. Although my time with William had been cherished, the temporary rise in mood only made the ensuing crash more pronounced. Once more, my pillow became drenched with tears. Once more, I found myself despondent, wondering how I would survive until morning. Once more, I wished I could have been taken with him.

I wept until no tears remained, then drifted into a blessedly deep sleep.

Grief did not follow a predictable path; it moved in fits and starts, ebbs and flows.

Chapter Seven

The next morning, the storm gave way to cool, pleasant weather. Sleep had refreshed me somewhat, softening the harsh edges of the previous night, and the dull ache of grief became slightly more manageable. In the light of day, the questions surrounding the apparition in my room receded to the back of my mind.

Determined to more solidly reestablish the routines of normal life, I readied myself for the day as usual, choosing a simple dress and arranging my hair into a neat braid before descending the stairs.

My father's absence suggested he was likely in his workshop again, but it was evident he had received a visitor, for a bow-topped wicker basket sat upon the table, overflowing with red and gold apples. From the Purcells, no doubt, the apple farmers on the other side of town.

A kind gesture, I thought, plucking one of the smaller golden apples from the basket. Although isolation had been preferable following William's death, I realized that many of the kind gestures in the days and weeks following had gone unnoticed by me because of it. A pang of guilt struck me. As hard as it was to reengage with the town, perhaps it was time I made a more concerted effort to do so.

My contemplations were interrupted when my father entered the kitchen from his workshop.

"Good morning," he greeted. Wood shavings from the morning's work clung to his beard. "You've seen the apples then?"

"I did," I said, holding up the apple in my hand.

"Casper brought them," he said. One of the Purcells, as expected. My father then grinned, his eyes twinkling with a mischievous gleam. "But he also brought news."

"What kind of news?"

"A show has arrived in town."

"A show?" My mind conjured visions of a grand circus, complete with elephants, a flying trapeze, perhaps even a lion tamer. Could Chapel Grove accommodate such a spectacle?

"From how he described it, it sounds like a traveling freak show of sorts, but with unusual objects and such."

"Indeed?"

"Yes, and I hoped you might accompany me to see it. This afternoon, perhaps?"

It was a timely suggestion, given my notions of rejoining the life of the town as I had before William's death. Still, the prospect of such an event was daunting. The exhibition would certainly draw a crowd, the thought of which brought me great anxiety. Being alone was far simpler and more comfortable.

Nevertheless, the hopefulness in my father's eyes, combined with his unmatched generosity in recent days, made the invitation one that could hardly be refused.

"I would love to."

Despite my many reservations about going into town that day, I could not resist thinking about what the exhibition might showcase. What might be on display? Whatever the case, the aspect I most anticipated was spending time with my father. Believing this to be a good opportunity to show my appreciation for my father's care, I retrieved some coins saved in my dresser drawer to cover the cost of the exhibition. I then met my father at the door before we stepped into the gorgeous Fall afternoon.

Upon reaching Main Street, the location of the exhibition was immediately apparent by the large crowd gathered at its far end. As we drew closer, we discovered the exhibit. It was housed within a large wagon, perhaps a repurposed gypsy caravan, with sides painted robin's egg blue and red trim around its windows and doorways. The windows had drapes that obscured the interior from view.

On the side of the wagon, above one of its large windows, was a dark-red wooden sign with white lettering that read:

MCCALMONT'S TRAVELING CURIOSITIES.

Below it, in smaller letters, was written: ENTRY 10 CENTS.

A large black draft horse stepped out from behind the wagon as we approached, its towering presence making the wagon seem smaller by comparison.

Despite the unassuming appearance of the wagon, the hushed conversations in the waiting crowd created an undeniable buzz of excitement. I glanced at my father, curious about his thoughts, when suddenly we heard a voice near the wagon.

"Welcome, welcome!"

A man emerged from the caravan, greeting the arriving guests: the Archers, Miriam cradling their newest baby. The man assisted Miriam up the steps, then turned his attention to the gathering crowd as the couple disappeared behind the curtain. "Prepare to be amazed at McCalmont's famous traveling curiosities!"

The man was, himself, a spectacle, so extravagant compared to those around him. Everything about him starkly contrasted with the typical Chapel Grove resident, making it obvious that he must be the McCalmont for whom the collection was named.

"Come and see mysterious artifacts from around the globe! Personally collected by yours truly."

His light hair, touched with gray, was parted precisely. Similarly, his facial hair was short and meticulously kept. His suit was of a fine material, possibly silk, its dark hue contrasting sharply with his white shirt and a shiny green bow tie.

His whole being captivated me, appearing to be from another world entirely.

Before long, I watched the Archers emerge from the door, wide-eyed and whispering to one another with unabashed delight. *What could they have seen to inspire such a reaction?* I wondered. My curiosity only grew more with each party who exited, bearing expressions of equal enchantment.

McCalmont periodically offered more promises to the crowd, eliciting gasps and exclamations of awe from all.

"The artifacts I have collected will astound and amaze."

"They are not for the faint of heart, I warn you now!"

"My collection will entice the imagination of the young and old alike!

So many promises made, I thought. But what could be so exciting in such a small space? Yet, his words seemed truthful, judging by the feedback from those who exited.

Upon reaching the front of the line, I retrieved the coins from my bag.

"My treat," I told my father. He moved to protest, but I turned to pay before he could object. McCalmont accepted the coins and slipped them into a satchel at his waist. When his eyes met mine, I found myself momentarily stunned. The eyes were a bright, otherworldly green. Jewel-like. My gaze fixed upon his.

"Thank you, miss," he said, awakening me from my hypnotic state.

I nodded wordlessly, returning to myself. McCalmont swept aside the red curtain over the wagon's entrance, allowing us to step into the caravan.

The curtain fell behind us, muffling the man's voice. A heavy perfume enveloped us, making the space feel a world apart from the outside commotion. As my eyes adjusted to the dim light of the oil lamp overhead, I saw that the space was indeed cramped, the center aisle so narrow that it couldn't accommodate two guests side by side. Every available space, however, was filled with artifacts.

The first to catch my eye was a large jar containing a large fleshy object, labeled FREAK PIG: 8 LEGS, 3 EYES, 2 TAILS, 2 NOSES, 2 EARS. LIVED FOR SEVERAL HOURS.

I then examined a collection of framed butterfly and beetle specimens high on the wall. There was a large reddish-brown spider encased in a clear dome, marked MEXICAN REDRUMP TARANTULA, whose companion was far preferable: an iridescent blue butterfly labeled BLUE MORPHO BUTTERFLY: SOUTH AMERICA.

Beyond these were what appeared to be the dark, shriveled heads of infants, but which turned out to be a collection of VARIOUS SHRUNKEN HEADS FROM HEADHUNTERS OF ECUADOR.

My father nudged me. "Look," he said, pointing.

Following his gaze, I saw the ALLURING TAHITIAN MERMAID, a shriveled three-foot-long creature whose face was nothing short of ghoulish.

"Strange," I remarked.

This was nothing compared to that which resided in a glass case near the back of the wagon. The sign before her said: MUM-MIFIED REMAINS: HER NAME IS ALICE. Her face, frozen in an everlasting scream, sent a shiver down my spine.

The other exhibits were equally bizarre, macabre and unseemly, with more objects than I could fully comprehend.

CEREMONIAL TIBETAN PHURBA: USED FOR RITUAL HUMAN SACRIFICE.

STONES FROM MAN PRESSED TO DEATH.

SUNDIAL OWNED BY JOHN PROCTOR, HANGED IN SALEM, WITH WIFE ELIZABETH FOR SUSPECTED WITCHCRAFT IN 1692.

WOLF GIRL OF INDONESIA.

TWO-HEADED SNAKE.

THREE-HEADED DUCKLING.

BLACKBEARD'S TREASURE MAPS.

Somewhere between the CYCLOPS BABY SHEEP and the AUTHENTIC GUILLOTINE BLADE, the collection began to overwhelm my senses. That is, until a peculiar instrument caught my eye, the label causing my heart to skip a beat.

THE RESURRECTIONIST'S FLUTE.

The flute was of curious workmanship, fashioned from a bone-white material with decorative engravings along its sides. Despite my limited knowledge of woodwinds, this instrument seemed anything but ordinary.

The flute's label was frustratingly brief, comprising only those three enigmatic words: THE RESURRECTIONIST'S FLUTE.

Though the entire exhibition had served as brief distraction, the flute's promise recalled the apparition from the night before.

Had it been a sign?

A more rational part of my mind quietly reminded me of the three days spent vigilantly watching over William's lifeless body. The miracle of resurrection had seemed so certain, yet it was not to be.

My experience the preceding night had surely been nothing more than a fluke; a restless and desperate imagining borne of longing.

The dead could hardly be resurrected.

Once gone, things remained that way.

How could I have thought otherwise?

Nothing here could possibly be real, only a silly sideshow. A product of smoke and mirrors.

My heart sank. I was finished.

Beside me, my father observed the sights in silence.

"Ready?" I asked.

He glanced at me. "Sure."

"I can leave you be, if you prefer," I offered, not wanting to rush him.

"No, no, I've had my fill."

We exited. The man, this McCalmont, now appeared entirely different to me—a hoaxer, a conman. Even his bright green eyes no longer held any charm for me. It was all an illusion, nothing more.

"You won't believe your eyes!" he exclaimed with a flourish to the crowd, taking money from the next patron—the next fool.

He was right, and I was ready to go home.

Visiting McCalmont's Curiosities brought an unwelcome change to my dreams. Night after night, the sequence replayed: a forest filled with wicked creatures from the exhibit, having regained their life force.

The two-headed snake, now larger than life, would pursue me relentlessly down a narrow path in the forest. The path would halt abruptly, leaving me face-to-face with the wolf girl, who had become more wolf than girl. She would glare at me, a low growl emanating from her.

Primordial dread would root me to the spot, and death would seem imminent.

Instead, the music of the flute would emanate from the forest, eliciting a hiss from the wolf girl. William would then emerge from the trees, and the monsters would flee in his presence.

We would embrace upon the monsters' defeat, but each time before our lips would meet, the dream ended, and I awoke frustrated.

Like the apparition I had experienced the night before the exhibition, this dream felt all too real. It was vivid, my heart still thumping with fear, my arms still weighted with the ghost of William's touch.

The dream recurred so faithfully that the anticipation disrupted my sleep. Despite my terror, I longed for William's embrace once more. Yet, my grief could no longer bridle me. Each morning, though my mind screamed in protest, I pulled myself into the world where chores awaited, violins needed repair, and neighbors sought help. Sundays were marked by worship with the congregation, where I battled against the impulse to isolate myself and instead took my place among them.

The days were largely free of rain, allowing me to spend time each day in the cemetery with William. Each visit soothed my soul, purging and healing my grief through the music of the violin. This reprieve softened the harsh pain of mourning, allowing me to entertain the notion that perhaps the future could still hold meaning for me.

McCalmont's Curiosities lingered in town far longer than I had anticipated. To my dismay, the wagon was visible from William's plot. Far fewer people surrounded it, suggesting that the macabre display might soon pack up and leave. I prayed it would, for perhaps then the persistent nightmare concerning those objects would cease to haunt me.

Chapter Eight

Mr. McCalmont, however, was not the sole source of my unease during this time. Abel Sinclair, whose presence had been sporadic in my life until then, began to appear frequently around Chapel Grove. Our encounters became near daily occurrences. Initially, I dismissed it as mere coincidence; yet this reasoning faltered when I noticed Abel watching me more than once. This habit was reasoned away without great concern at first. But as it persisted, I grew anxious that perhaps I had unintentionally attracted his interest. Unsure how best to handle the situation, I avoided him as best as possible.

One evening, this became more than a minor nuisance. Upon arriving home, my father stood in the entryway, a peculiar look on his face.

"Father? Is something the matter?" I inquired, trying to decipher if there had been an accident. He seemed more disturbed than alarmed, as far as I could discern.

"We have a visitor," he replied curtly, gesturing towards the parlor.

"Do we?" I was perplexed by his demeanor until I stepped into the parlor to find Abel himself.

"Elise, I hope you will pardon the interruption to your evening," he said, standing with flourish.

"It's - it's no trouble." I stammered, casting a glance at my father, whose face betrayed no emotion, before returning my gaze to Abel. "What brings you here today?"

My father spoke before Abel could respond. "Abel requested to wait for your return as he has something he wishes to discuss with both of us."

"That is correct," Abel confirmed.

"Regarding what?" I asked, though my stomach churned even before receiving an answer.

"Dear Elise, you have scarcely left my mind in these past days. Since our encounter in town, I have been captivated by your talent, your grace, your beauty—everything about you," he said, pausing to let his words linger in the air. "You have enchanted me."

I felt a growing sense of unease but stayed silent, unable to find the right words.

"I realize my timing is less than ideal," he continued. "You see, it seems as though fate has brought you to my attention."

He paused, seemingly expecting a response.

"What do you mean?" I asked.

"You have captured my heart, Elise, and I wish for you to become my wife."

"I—" My heart sank. "Oh, Abel, I—"

"The timing is not exactly auspicious," my father interjected, coming to my aid. My discomfort eased slightly at his intervention.

"Of course, I understand that." Abel replied, unfazed. "I know that you have only recently lost your intended, and I am truly sorry for your loss. Elise, I know I am not your William"—I winced at the mention of my beloved—"but I am a good man. I can offer you a good life."

"I…" I hesitated, shaking my head. "I don't…"

"You would want for nothing," he assured. "Neither of you, should you accept."

"I'm sorry?" I asked, puzzled as to how this might involve my father.

Abel turned to my father. "I understand you may not have accumulated a substantial fortune in your line of work. I mean no offense, of course," he added, "it's merely a fact. What would happen to dear Elise should something befall you?" He paused for effect. "We Sinclairs have abundant resources, which would be available to you and your daughter."

I glanced at my father, who remained silent. If I had needed an ally before, my need was greater now, yet he offered none. My lips felt parched.

"And you, Elise, you could devote your days to playing the violin, learning from the masters all around the world, performing in such places as France, Italy, and Munich. I could open doors for you that you can only dream of. But more importantly, Elise, I promise to make you happy, if only you would give me the chance."

My mind spun, wondering how Abel could think this an appropriate proposal. It seemed only yesterday William had passed.

"I realize this all is a surprise to you. Naturally, I do not expect an answer this evening," he said, a softness to his expression, "But I could not allow another day to pass without making my intentions to you clear. I wish to marry you, Elise, and I hope you might give me the chance to provide for you. I would consider it an honor."

I wished to protest, to let Abel know that marriage was out of the question, but my father spoke first.

"Please, we need time to consider this," he said. "I need time to speak to my daughter."

My father met my eyes with an expression I could not decipher. Understanding evaded me. Was it not sufficient to politely decline? Appropriate, even?

"I will be at your disposal whenever you wish to discuss this further," Abel said.

I wondered if he addressed my father or me. He left, escorted to the door by my father, while I stood in shock, staring at the floor.

I heard the front door close. My father returned to the parlor.

"Such audacity," I said quietly, shaking my head. "To come here at a time like this and make such a request."

My father did not join in my condemnation, but remained silent, avoiding my gaze.

"You are correct. The situation is less than ideal."

"To say *the least*," I prodded.

"Yes." He said nothing more, his expression unreadable.

We stood in silence for a moment. I stared at him, expecting him to elaborate, or at the very least offer some kind of explanation for his dispassionate response.

"And?" I pressed.

"And…" He sighed, finally meeting my eye. "Darling, well, perhaps dreams change."

"What do you mean by that?"

"Elise, darling, perhaps this is all for the best."

I stiffened. "Father—"

"I am concerned," he said softly. There was a gentle reluctance in his voice that extinguished my anger and transformed it into a quiet despair. "There's no denying I am getting older. I won't be here forever, my love. I need to know you will be taken care of, regardless of what happens."

"I can take care of myself," I asserted, yet even as I spoke, I knew it sounded hollow.

"You have never experienced true poverty, my darling, and I hope you never do. Despite my efforts, Abel is right in observing that violin making is scarcely profitable," he said as tears welled up in my eyes. "I have little to offer you in terms of inheritance or any long-term support."

I felt my defenses crumble as devastation washed over me. My father wished for me to consider Abel as my husband.

"I never intended to burden you with this, a worry I had hoped to bear alone; but I cannot let you reject this opportunity without being fully informed."

"This is overwhelming," I whispered, as it was all my constrained throat could manage.

"I understand," my father confessed. "But despite my attempts to educate you within the limits of my income, consider the opportunities that would arise if you were to marry a man like Abel. A whole world would open up for you, one in which you would thrive. My brilliant, beautiful, intelligent daughter."

"But I can't," I replied, my eyes beginning to mist.

"It is a challenging decision, darling, but you must think beyond your current anguish and consider the future."

"But how can you find this pertinent, so soon after William's passing?"

The accusation apparently stung, and he paused before responding. "Darling," he said tenderly, "I know how deeply you loved William."

"Father…" I said, tears beginning to fall down my face, unable to put into words my objections.

My father wrapped me in his arms, stroking my hair. "I know how much you loved him, but, my love, as the world continues to turn, so must we."

His words echoed hollowly in my mind. I recoiled from him in disbelief.

"How can you say such a thing? Has Mother's death faded so far into the past that you've forgotten?" Anger, momentarily subdued by grief, surged forth at his apparent hypocrisy.

"That was different," he replied softly.

"How? Explain!" I demanded. "After all, you have not remarried."

"It is a different matter entirely." His tone remained low, steady.

"It is *not*."

"Whether you like it or not, it *is*," he said with finality.

I glared at him. "Because I am a woman, you mean."

"Yes," he admitted tersely. "I wish it weren't an obstacle, but unfortunately, it is."

We stood still, sizing each other up as my stomach churned.

"I must leave. I need to clear my head."

I walked out the door once more, stepping into the elongated shadows cast by the early evening light. I needed solitude to process my thoughts. More than that, I needed to see him again.

My William.

Chapter Nine

The door slammed shut behind me.

Suited to becoming a Sinclair, Abel had said of me. So what? Good enough, then? Of fine enough quality? Suitable breeding stock? The notion only enraged me more as I made my way to the cemetery.

The insult was exacerbated by my father's betrayal. *Dreams change*, he had advised so simply, despite never marrying again after my mother's passing. He never attempted to offer me a proper maternal figure after my own mother died.

What did he know about any of it?

The autumn leaves, which had enchanted me earlier in the day, now brought no joy in my state of righteous indignation.

As I continued to walk, however, despair began to overshadow my anger. Although I hated to admit it, my father was correct regarding my future prospects. Without marriage, my future appeared uncertain. I possessed no profitable skills, save perhaps for playing the violin like a street corner busker.

What would become of me, should I refuse this opportunity? Even if another opportunity arose, it would undoubtedly pale in comparison to what Abel could offer.

I turned the corner toward the cemetery, yearning for William's presence like never before.

The fact that Abel was a good man scarcely mattered. Neither did his intelligence nor the opportunities his wealth could provide. The stark reality was, he wasn't William. Perhaps someday in the far-off future, I might consider such a proposal, but being thrust into this position so soon felt unbearably cruel. William's grave was so fresh, in fact, that greenery had barely begun to sprout.

Could I not be allowed more time to grieve?

Upon reaching William's grave, the enormity of the situation overwhelmed me, and I collapsed to my knees, weeping.

In such a state, I hardly expected company, yet as the worst of my tears subsided, I became aware of someone nearby. Turning to look, I was startled to find a figure standing behind me.

I gasped, stumbling over a loose stone as I stood.

"Don't be afraid," the figure spoke. As he stepped forward, his immaculate attire was unmistakable.

"Mr. McCalmont," I replied uneasily, "What are you doing here?"

"I heard someone crying, and felt it was only right to see if I could assist," he explained.

I quickly wiped the tears from my face, averting my gaze. "No, thank you."

"May I ask what has upset you so much this evening?"

Why? I wondered, but instead asked, with a nod toward his wagon, "Surely you have business to attend to?"

"It's no trouble," he replied simply.

While his concern might have been appreciated, his presence remained unwelcome due to the nightmares conjured by his wagon of horrors.

Yet he continued, "If you don't mind me asking, are you the violinist who has been playing out here recently?"

"I suppose that would be me," I admitted.

"You are truly talented."

"Thank you."

Mr. McCalmont then glanced at William's headstone. "Who was he to you?" he inquired. "A brother, perhaps?"

I shook my head. "No."

He looked at my left hand, which I self-consciously folded into my right.

"A husband?" He was not easily dissuaded.

"My fiancé," I answered, my lips tightening as I looked down at the ground near his feet.

"A pity, miss." He removed his hat—a fine black silk, like his suit, lined with a dark green.

Not wishing to extend the conversation, I merely lifted a shoulder, as though it mattered not.

"How tragic it would be if death were truly the end."

I glared at him, suspecting he wanted me to be taken in by his so-called resurrection flute—a ploy, perhaps, to garner more interest in his collection.

"Sir, my love is gone," I said. "I will grant that perhaps, in some more spiritual sense, this is not true. Nevertheless, as far as I am concerned, all that was once dear to me is dead and buried before me." My lip trembled, threatening more tears. Despite my efforts to contain them, they fell anew. I covered my face with my hands, striving to regain control of my emotions.

Once the tears had subsided, Mr. McCalmont, who had stood silently during my outburst, spoke softly, "You misunderstand me."

I wiped the tears from my face and looked at him again, frowning. If I had expected an apology and to be left in peace, I was mistaken.

"I am not suggesting some distant possible future for you and your William. I am implying that death does not have to be the end, as most perceive it."

After an evening filled with nonsense, I found I had no further tolerance for it.

"That is enough," I said. "Now, please. Let me be. You mock my grief."

He made no move to leave, his manner remaining placid. "I mean no mockery, miss." He spoke evenly, even as my tone grew sharper. "I mean what I say."

"And what is that, exactly?"

He paused, a gleam in his eye. "What if I told you there was a way to have your William back?"

I glowered. "I would have to say you were either insane or simply cruel."

At this, to my great surprise, he laughed. "Now, now—neither of those are true."

"You are mad, then. Simply insane." My accusations, far from offending him, seemed to energize him.

"The world, my dear, is more vast, more expansive, and full of more magic than you could possibly imagine. Look around you!" He lifted his arms, gesturing grandly. "This town. It's so small. So secluded. You have been raised here, I presume?"

"I have," I admitted.

"I, on the other hand, have traveled this great Earth, from the jungles of South America to the mystical temples of Asia, to the vast plains of Africa. I have seen things your young eyes can only dream of. Witch doctors, oceans, immense mysterious creatures. Had you seen the wonders I have witnessed, you would not dare question the veracity of my words."

I reflected on the artifacts from his travels that had been exhibited.

"I'm aware you've been to my exhibit. With your father, if memory serves me right—the violin maker?"

"Yes, we visited, but those items couldn't possibly be real." Initially, I thought of the mermaid, which seemed utterly ludicrous, but then my mind wandered to the dark forest of my nightmares. I longed for his collection to consist of clever deceptions.

"Miss, you do me a disservice," he said, with more amusement than offense. "What makes you consider them anything but authentic?"

"They simply cannot be. The mermaid, for example." I raised an eyebrow, silently questioning.

"The ocean is so vast, you can scarcely believe it. There exists a fish with a large horn on its nose, and yet you doubt the existence of a mermaid?"

He had a point, I supposed. I hadn't seen much of the world. But still, it couldn't be true.

"A resurrectionist's flute," I challenged. "Nothing can bring back the dead.

He fell silent for a moment, regarding me with an impish grin. He stroked his chin thoughtfully. When he spoke again, his voice was lower, almost conspiratorial.

"At last, we reach the crux of the matter. Being a musician yourself, you understand that music possesses a certain kind of magic, correct?"

"In what sense?"

""Of course, in the way it can communicate hope and devastation with precision beyond even the finest wordsmith, but it extends further than that."

"What do you mean?"

"My interest in this subject began several years ago. A man attended one of my performances. This was back when I was part of a larger traveling band, and there were seated audiences. This man, elderly and of feeble mind," he gestured to his temple, "was scarcely present mentally. His eyes glazed, he barely drooled in his own seat. More body than spirit, if you asked me. His family's reasons for bringing him were beyond me, perhaps a peculiar form of denial, but that isn't the main point. There was a performer, a dancer. She danced to a certain kind of music. Not my preferred style, really, but one popular in a bygone era, perhaps the very time in which the man was raised." His green eyes sparkled. "Do you know what happened?"

"What?"

"The man *came to life.*"

"What do you mean?"

"I mean to say that the state I described was temporarily suspended. During the song, at least, he appeared to find himself again. His eyes cleared. He tapped his toe in time with the music, engaged with those around him. It was a remarkable sight."

The violin my father had gifted me came to mind. Had it not sparked a rebirth of sorts?

"And all that, from one song." He held up a finger, lowering his voice to a whisper. "One song. The perfect music, played at the perfect time."

The tale held me enthralled, my mind caught between skepticism and belief.

"Regrettably, the man eventually returned to the state from which he came. I share this story with you for a specific reason. You, of all people, must grasp that music possesses a singular power. It can elevate a weary spirit in ways that words alone cannot. It can rekindle passions once believed to be extinguished. It can transport you through time, reigniting fires once thought cold. Music has a unique ability to touch the soul as nothing else can." He gazed skyward. "Yes, music is the perfect conduit."

"Conduit?"

"Don't you see?" he said, his intense whisper charged with excitement. "The soul, though intricate, is housed within a body that is comparatively simple. It is fueled by a certain amount of electricity that can be replicated with the right instruments—music being the foremost among them."

I raised an eyebrow, but Mr. McCalmont was undaunted.

"A soul, of course, cannot be duplicated," he clarified. "But if the body it inhabits is restored... well, what prevents that soul from returning to reclaim the body?"

No matter how outlandish it seemed, this concept, this idea, was not something I could readily dismiss—not given my troubled state of mind.

"You doubt me." It was a statement, not a question.

"I do," I admitted.

"Yet, I have seen these things happen. And I can prove it to you."

Proof of such ability seized my full attention. "Is that so?"

"Yes. But you must return later tonight." He glanced back at his wagon. I followed his gaze to see a small line had formed during our conversation. "It seems I have matters to attend to before then."

I hesitated, contemplating how I might slip away under the cover of darkness, wondering whether such actions would be wise.

What would my father say about such a thing?

Reflecting on this, my anger toward him rekindled. Perhaps I longed to make my own choices regarding this matter. Having lost so much, all I risked was a few wasted hours.

Sleep would be elusive, anyway.

Admittedly, I was also wildly intrigued by Mr. McCalmont's claims.

"When shall I meet you, Mr. McCalmont?" I asked.

He grinned. "Call me Cassius."

Chapter Ten

Mr. McCalmont—Cassius, as it were—instructed me to return after nightfall when the moon was high, minimizing the chance of disturbance. I gave him my word.

In hindsight, I should have been more prudent. Yet, I was young, driven by desperation, and burdened by grief, leaving little room for practicality. My curiosity about what Cassius could offer blinded me to the potential hazards.

Then again, I was intimately familiar with the transformative power of music. What else could turn grief into poetry or convert fleeting happiness into a tangible experience? The notion that music might resurrect the dead seemed far-fetched, and yet, my own experiences lent some credence to the idea.

When I first started playing the violin my father had given me, I emerged from a state of lifelessness, becoming someone who could once again engage with society; someone who had begun to heal. And though it was peculiar, hadn't William continued to exist in some ethereal form, appearing in my dreams, manifesting as a haunting presence in my room, or as a lingering scent on the breeze?

I have seen these things happen, and I can prove it, Cassius had said. The prospect of studying the evidence for myself was too tantalizing to refuse.

Arriving home, I found my father waiting by the door. "Elise, where have you been? It's late. I was worried."

"I just needed some fresh air," I replied.

"It's getting dark," he noted, and indeed it was. The sun had set completely, and the first stars were beginning to shine.

"I know." My response was terse, yet I felt there was little more to convey.

"Elise, I understand this is challenging," he sighed.

I shook my head. "I don't want to talk right now."

"Okay." He deflated slightly. "Is there anything I can do for you?"

"No, thank you. I think I'll settle in for the evening, if that's alright."

"I'll be here if you need me," he assured me, adding with a trace of vulnerability, "I love you."

My heart softened a bit. "I love you, too, Father."

We parted, and I climbed the stairs to my room, shutting the door behind me before sitting on my bed, facing the open window. As the remaining daylight vanished, more stars emerged, marking the passage of time until it was right to leave for the cemetery. The sounds of my father downstairs told me he was preparing for bed, ultimately retiring to his room. Hearing his door close, I waited a little longer. Rushing was unwise, as attracting his attention was a risk I could not afford.

When the moment arrived, I descended the stairs quietly, listening intently as I took each step. My father's reassuring snores allowed me to take the final steps unnoticed, and I slipped outside into the night, lighting my torch once I had reached the garden.

Though familiar with the path to the cemetery from frequent visits over recent weeks, I had never journeyed in such darkness. Carefully, I navigated the terrain, my torch guiding me. As I approached the cemetery, a figure stood by the entrance. It was Cassius, awaiting my arrival, and my heart raced with anticipation.

I made my way across the cemetery lawn toward him, mindful of the graves. At the sound of my footsteps, he turned his gaze from the sky to me.

"Elise, it's a pleasure to see you," he greeted me warmly. "What a beautiful night, isn't it?" He seemed unruffled, as if we were not in a graveyard at all.

"I suppose," I acquiesced, feeling far less comfortable than he appeared.

"In any case, I'm pleased you are here." He beckoned for me to follow him. "Let us not delay. Please, come with me."

He led me to the cemetery's far edge, near the woods. In a clearing beyond, a dark mass lay upon the ground. At first indistinguishable, as we neared, it commanded a visceral reaction.

"A common raven," Cassius said matter-of-factly.

"Yes," I said, covering my mouth. It was unmistakably dead, crumpled as it was on the earth. A fetid smell emanated from it, causing me to take an involuntary step away. Cassius apparently noticed, for his mouth twisted into a strange smile.

From the satchel on his shoulder, Cassius drew out the resurrectionist's flute, its bone-white material and intricate carvings distinguishable even in the torchlight's dim glow.

"Are you ready?" he asked.

I nodded. "I am."

Cassius lifted the flute to his lips and began to play a mournful melody. As he played, I fixed my gaze on the black bird. To my great astonishment, feathers along the bird's back twitched slightly.

Could it be?

Cassius gradually quickened the pace of the tune. The mournful melody shifted to a lively jig, and in response, the dark form pulsed in rhythm with the music.

My breath caught as fascination and fear flooded me equally, while the music played on and the bird rose from the ground. The raven's feet were briefly unsteady upon the earth, and it shook itself, as if shaking off the remnants of a deep sleep. Its feathers took form and, at that moment, it stood there: glossy, regal, with eyes shining with intelligence.

It was alive. *Raised from the dead.*

With my mouth agape, I glanced from the raven to Cassius, who observed the bird with immense satisfaction, and then back again. The creature extended its magnificent wings, flapping them a few times before eventually taking flight.

I watched, stunned, as it soared into the night sky. Moments later, the raven's unearthly croak echoed through the night, sending a shiver down my spine.

My head spun, scarcely daring to accept that what I had witnessed was anything other than an elaborate magic trick.

But how could this be?

I caught my breath and lowered my gaze from the raven to Cassius. Only then did I realize he had ceased playing and was watching me with anticipation.

"Do you believe me now?"

Chapter Eleven

The reanimation of the raven produced such a deluge of possibilities, questions, doubts, and desires that words were difficult to come by.

Upon finding my voice, I asked simply, "How?"

Cassius dismissed my query with a wave of his hand, as though it were inconsequential. "How is not important. What I need to know, however, is this. Tell me, Elise: forgetting everything you think you know, if your William could be brought back to you, what would that be like?"

The question required little reflection, for this was the very miracle I had fervently prayed for, yearning for relief from anguish so profound it manifested as physical pain. Countless times, my soul had cried out for solace from my suffering.

Yet my pleas had been met only with more hardship. Faced with the torment of being asked to marry another, I dared to envision what could be instead.

"It would be wonderful," I murmured.

"It can be so, Elise. Miracles can and do happen, as you, yourself, have now seen."

"But *how*?" How could something which stunk of death now breathe, fly—live—once more?

"You see, ever since you and your father came to my exhibition, I have been pondering just that."

This was hardly the anticipated response. "What do you mean?"

"Music, as we have discussed, is uniquely powerful."

He extended the flute, clearly intending for me to take it. I hesitated.

"Please," he urged, and I accepted it cautiously, reverently. "This flute, though powerful, is limited. A violin, on the other hand, may possess the qualities needed to be even more potent."

As I cradled the flute, the future I had imagined with William once again seemed attainable. My fingers traced the carvings along its side, trembling with the recognition of the force within. Yet, according to Cassius, it was inadequate.

"Why a violin?" I asked.

"As you are well aware, a violin is a temperamental instrument, each having something akin to its own personality. Where one may have a laissez-fair manner and be simple to care for, another may be mercurial and intolerably sensitive to change. Each violin must be treated with care, as an individual. Much as the practice of medicine must include consideration for the needs of the patient, violins require individualized care. In this way, violins are peculiarly *human* in nature."

His explanation evoked memories of my father meticulously adjusting the sound post of a particular instrument, striving for the optimal placement. Sometimes, a stubborn violin required choosing one wolf tone over another. Some were beautifully resonant, even with haphazard placement, offering numerous decent options. Some required different posts depending on the season to bring forth the desired sound, or so their owners insisted. And that was just the sound post, without even mentioning the myriad other components of the instrument.

Therefore, his explanation was entirely in keeping with my experience with violins.

"That is why I am interested in a violin of rare workmanship," Cassius said. "Something that I believe you can provide."

"What kind of violin?" I contemplated the violin my father had most recently finished. Though it was undoubtedly treasured, I would gladly sacrifice it—and more—in return for William.

"One crafted by you, of course."

I balked. "By *me*? I think you are mistaken, sir. I can play the violin, but I have never crafted one. My father is the luthier, not I."

"I am not interested in a violin from your father. I want his daughter's violin—an original Elise Knight violin." He said this with such nonchalance I feared he did not truly understand my position.

"But, sir, violin-making is not something learned on a whim," I protested, my voice catching with the thought that my chance to restore William might slip away with this condition. "It requires time. Practice."

He chuckled, seemingly indifferent to my protestation. "My dear, you worry too much. You must understand. The unique sensitivity of violins makes them suitable for this task. They are porous, in a sense, absorbing the characteristics of their makers, their players, and even the environments in which they reside."

Assuming this was true, I doubted he would benefit from a violin as flawed as one made by my inexperienced hands. My doubt must have been apparent, for he continued.

"The innate imperfections in a violin made by you, then, would retain qualities which only you could imbue. Your situation, unfortunate though it may be, makes you a, shall we say, intriguing candidate to craft this instrument."

"Oh?" I asked, but he merely shrugged as though such a statement were self-evident. My father had crafted countless violins in my lifetime, many of which I had observed taking shape. He had enlisted my help on occasion, yet crafting one myself seemed a dubious prospect.

"I worry that a violin crafted by my own hand might not even play correctly," I confessed.

"Worry not, dear Elise. I trust that your father will help guide you in this work—as close as you two are, I hardly believe he would leave it to you on your own. However, you must be sure the work is your own."

"What if I gave you a violin I had played on? One that is important to me?" I asked. Whether the one my father had most recently given me or the one which had been mine for several years before, surely they carried parts of my essence.

He shook his head. "It wouldn't be the same, love, and that is what I intended to expound upon. For this violin to possess a power akin to this flute"—he gestured—"it must embody your unique character, your unsullied hand, your manner enmeshed within its innermost being. Those, regardless of workmanship, are the inexpressible qualities which will make it so valuable." He looked at me seriously. "I believe the more of yourself you invest in the instrument, the more powerful it will become. That is why you, and you alone, must craft it. Do you understand?"

Perhaps I did, and yet one question remained. "How can I be certain you can achieve this?"

He pointed skyward, where the raven had soared away. "It has been accomplished before," he assured me, "though on a much smaller scale. As I mentioned, I have witnessed many wondrous things during my travels that would astonish you."

Indeed, it appeared there was more beyond the confines of Chapel Grove than I could ever have imagined.

My William, restored for such a small price? It seemed impossible, and yet...

Images of my beloved's face in those first three days flooded my mind. His complexion had been warm with life, his features vibrant, making me believe he might rise once more. Was it truly beyond belief, especially after seeing the raven's resurrection?

"Do I have your interest?" Cassius interrupted my thoughts.

In my mind's eye, all doubt evaporated, replaced by the vision of William standing at the altar—not swathed in burial shrouds, but attired in his finest ensemble, chosen specifically for our wedding.

Standing.

Smiling.

Full of promise.

Alive.

Awaiting me, if only I dared take the chance.

"Of course," I said breathlessly.

Chapter Twelve

Though my mind raced upon the route home, sleep nonetheless took me quickly that night. When the early morning sun shone through the window, my mind resumed the pace once more. Could I have really been party to such a miracle?

Upon my bedside table lay the feather from the raven, which Cassius had given me as a reminder of what had taken place. I took it in my hands, more closely examining its glossy surface. No, surely, the events of the previous evening had actually happened. A raven which had been dead upon the ground had been brought back to life by the power of Cassius's flute.

Having already agreed to make a violin for Cassius, all that remained was to enlist my father's assistance. This was a tricky proposition, for the project would require more than just his expertise, but also his fine maple and ebony. How to convince him to sacrifice such precious material to what he would see as a passing fancy, I knew not, but was determined to do so, whatever it cost.

After preparing myself for the day, I entered the kitchen to be greeted by what appeared to be a peace offering: a place at the table laid with a selection of bread and jams. A glance through the window told me my father had already retreated to his workshop for the day. I considered the plate momentarily, but decided to speak with him first. Breakfast could wait and would taste better on a less-nervous stomach.

My father's concentration was so intently focused on his work that he didn't notice my entrance into the workshop.

"What are you working on?" I asked.

His hand jumped in surprise.

"I'm sorry, I didn't mean to startle you."

"No, no," he said, setting the violin down on his workbench. He dusted off his hands and turned toward me. "I'm glad to see you."

"What are you working on?" I repeated.

He gestured to the violin. "This crack here. I'm determining whether it can be repaired."

"Oh." I shifted my gaze to my feet, uncertainty swirling within me. So much needed to be discussed after the previous night's events.

Thankfully, my father spoke first. "Elise, I apologize for last night."

"You need not," I insisted, shaking my head. "I understand."

"Nevertheless, I am sorry. I know it was imprudent."

"Father, I know you want what is best for me." It was as good a time as ever to make my request. "And—well, that is why I wondered if you would entertain… an idea I had, I suppose."

"Oh?"

"Yes." I leaned against the workbench. "I thought, perhaps, I might learn to make violins, like you."

He stared at me for a long moment before speaking again. "Lissie…" He removed his glasses, absently cleaning them with his shirt. "I don't know."

"Father, I understand it's not as easy as you make it seem," I said, observing a small smile at the compliment. "But I thought—hoped—that by doing so, I might secure my own future. Without Abel."

"Darling…"

"Father, please," I insisted. "Who knows? Maybe it could… I don't know, maybe it could give me a life back." *In more ways than one.*

He replaced his glasses and looked at me. "Violin-making is challenging, darling. It demands patience. It is not something that can be learned overnight. It's certainly not something you've ever shown interest in before, I might add."

"I know that. Perhaps I never had the motivation that I do now." Seeing his mind work, I pressed once more. "Might I have a chance, at least?"

He leaned on his elbow against the bench. "The materials aren't exactly cheap, love."

"I know." As rejection seemed imminent, my heart constricted. Yet a glimmer of hope appeared as he looked at me with gentle eyes.

"You know I want you to be happy," he said.

"I know."

"I also must know you will be taken care of."

I nodded. "I understand."

"If I should agree to this, then, it is under one condition."

"Anything, Father," I said.

"If, upon the completion of this project, we should find that you are not fit for the work, in the interest of securing your future, you will agree to marry Abel."

It was a terrible idea, one that made my stomach churn, yet it also seemed to be the best solution for everyone to get what they wanted—at least for now.

I looked away momentarily, gathering the strength to say what needed to be said, and then turned back to him with a serious expression.

"I will, Father."

"If that's the case… then I will agree."

My heart leaped with joy. "Thank you. Oh, Father, thank you! When can we begin?"

He contemplated for a moment, glanced toward the spot where he stored his extra wood, appeared to weigh his options, and then motioned to the space beside him.

"Take a seat."

Chapter Thirteen

By the time my father insisted we break for lunch, any trepidation I had felt about creating this violin had transformed into eager anticipation. He had shown me the mold upon which the violin would be formed, reassuring me that almost any mistake could be rectified and that, provided the work was done carefully, a functional instrument was well within my reach. I had begun cutting the end blocks, which would be ready to be glued and clamped by tomorrow—or perhaps later this afternoon, since there was no time to waste.

Ideally, this would be the case, for, much to my chagrin, my father explained that creating this violin would take at least six weeks. This timeline was longer than I preferred, but little could be done to alter it.

After lunch, I made my way to town, eager to inform Cassius that the work had begun. My stiff limbs stretched pleasantly as I walked.

Two geese swam lazily in the creek as I passed, floating among the dangling branches of the willows. In just a few weeks, they would be gone, leaving Chapel Grove's cold winter for warmer weather down south.

Shortly thereafter, life could be so different.

My heart warmed at the thought. Life would indeed change, as long as the work was done correctly—work that was to be carried out on two fronts: the functional and the spiritual.

The functional aspects of the violin were of relatively minimal concern, given that my father would guide me in its construction. As for the spiritual work, Cassius had merely advised that the more of myself I put into the violin, the more powerful it would become.

Most of the violin would be assembled as prescribed, with no reasonable variations to be made. It was pointless to consider the symbolic significance of different types of wood for creating the violin, as the wood used would depend on what my father had on hand and was willing to spare for what he saw as a casual dalliance.

My first thought, then, was of decoration, perhaps adding details to the violin that were personal to William and myself. Anything added to the violin would need to be carefully balanced against its functionality. A violin is dependent on the flexion of its body to produce sound, so much so that even its necessary protective varnish can inhibit its resonance. Any addition, then, needed to impinge as little as possible on the flexion of its body.

The cemetery lay before me. I turned toward town, thinking within this confine.

Ink could be used, perhaps, as it would penetrate the wood without stiffening it, and could be applied in discrete locations, minimizing questions from my father. The idea settled my mind for the moment, just in time to pass the cemetery.

My pace slowed, then stopped before the gates of the cemetery as I gazed upon the rows of headstones. My heart ached at the sight, yearning for William's presence beside me on this chilly afternoon. *Six weeks, maybe seven or eight at the most.* By All Hallows' Eve, surely, a vague thought which solidified into my personal deadline. Not long at all, given what lay ahead. I vowed to do everything possible to make that a reality, then continued on my way to the main road.

The excitement surrounding McCalmont's Curiosities had diminished considerably, judging by the absence of patrons, though this could be explained by the time of day. Still, it troubled me that Cassius may have to leave Chapel Grove prior to the completion of the violin. I desired no complications and delays in my pursuit of William.

The wooden step before the door of the wagon creaked with my weight. I rapped upon the door, then stepped down out of the way. A soft padding of footsteps within was followed by the opening of the door.

"Miss Knight!" Cassius's green eyes were even more striking in the bright daylight. "What brings you here this morning? Good news, I hope?"

"It is," I replied, speaking with a degree of timidity. "We have begun work."

"Have you really?" He smiled. "Splendid, splendid." A far-off look came over his face before he spoke again. "Now, do you happen to know how long this will take?"

"Around six weeks. That is acceptable to you?"

"Oh, yes. Perfectly acceptable."

"Will you be staying that long?" The question sounded childish as I spoke it. It was implausible for a traveling showman to linger so long in a town where his novelty had worn off.

"I understand that this is important to you, but you must understand that it is to me, as well."

"But your business—"

"Please believe that I would not offer if I did not mean it," Cassius interrupted. "I have a small nest egg and can return to touring when it suits me. Until that time, I mean to make myself available to you, should a need arise." A shadow crossed his face.

"Sometimes, when meddling with fate like this, unforeseen barriers can arise."

I frowned. "Like what?"

"It varies." His tone invited no further questions. "And, should the need arise, I wish to help you overcome any such obstacles."

What these obstacles might be, I knew not. As I contemplated this, I gazed at the wagon, which prompted another question, perhaps less important, yet it begged to be asked. "Do you sleep in there?"

"I do, indeed," he replied, a mischievous smile playing on his lips. "Why?"

I shook my head. "Simple curiosity. It hardly seems big enough."

"Big enough for my purposes."

"It doesn't frighten you?"

"Why should it? They are merely things. Well," he corrected himself, "they are *more than* things. They are the wonders I have collected on my many travels. It is soothing, being surrounded by my life's work."

"Even Alice?" The question slipped out before I had sufficiently considered its propriety, yet rather than taking offense, Cassius laughed heartily.

"Especially my sweet Alice."

The thought of sleeping next to her, her face in that silent scream, made me shudder. Certainly, anyone who slept next to such a creature would be doomed to hear that scream for themselves.

What a strange man. Yet, naturally, only a strange man would display such things in the first place.

"Well," he continued, gesturing toward his wagon, "unless you have any more questions, I have work to attend to, as it seems you do as well."

"Of course," I said, pardoning myself. "Thank you, Mr.—Cassius."

He inclined his head in acknowledgment. "I'll be seeing you soon, love."

Chapter Fourteen

Upon returning home, the demands of everyday chores took precedence over continued violin-making. Though it was disappointing, I reasoned that a hearty meal and a good night's rest would only improve the quality of my work.

The next morning's task was to glue the corner and end blocks to the mold. I had just clamped the final block into place when a voice called from outside the workshop.

My father and I exchanged looks.

The voice called again, more insistent this time. "Hello?"

"Are you expecting a visitor?" my father asked.

"No, I'm not." Perhaps it was Cassius, on his way out of town? That seemed unlikely, not to mention less-than-ideal. Perhaps it was simply someone in dire need of violin repair.

"Hello?" the voice called again, closer this time.

"Continue working," my father said, rising to head to the door. "I'll take care of it."

"Okay."

My father's footsteps grew faint as I adjusted the clamps, ensuring the piece was securely fastened. The click of the lock and the door creaked open: slowly at first, and then all at once.

Distantly, my father's voice revealed our visitor. "Abel, I apologize. How good to see you."

My shoulders slumped. Cassius would have been preferable.

"I hope I am not interrupting," spoke Abel's muffled voice.

"No, not at all."

"I simply wondered if Elise might be available to speak?"

I set down the work in front of me, knowing it may be a moment before I could return to it in peace.

"Of course," said my father, then called for me. "Elise?"

"Coming." I sighed, bracing myself for the encounter. My father mumbled a vague excuse and slipped back into his workshop, shutting the door behind him. Abel stood there in a crisp, spotless white shirt and dark slacks, his glossy dark hair neatly parted and combed. In one hand, he held a bouquet of lush, plum-colored dahlias, their stems wrapped in coordinating purple silk secured with a pearl-headed pin.

"Elise, so lovely to see you." He extended the dahlias, which I accepted.

"Thank you. They're beautiful."

"My mother will be glad to hear it," he replied, explained. "They are her cultivation."

"They're lovely. Thank you."

"Not as lovely as it is to see you," he added.

"Thank you," I mumbled, fingering the silk along the stems.

A silence fell, during which my gaze remained fixed upon the curled petals of the blooms.

"Amusing yourself in your father's workshop, then?" Abel asked, peering over my shoulder.

"Making a violin, actually."

Abel's eyebrows rose. "Is that so? I was unaware you shared his talent for violin-making."

"It will be my first," I admitted.

"An ambitious endeavor. My mother always said it was good for a woman to have her own pursuits."

"Thank you," I said, shifting uneasily, caring little for his mother's words of wisdom, nor for how he seemed only more intrigued. If only he would come to the point he wished to make.

For better or worse, he did.

"If you are busy, I do not wish to keep you," he said, "but I wondered if you had given any more thought to my proposal?"

My pulse quickened. "I—I mean, a bit," Indeed, I had, though not in the context he would likely have preferred.

"And have you arrived at any conclusions?"

"Not—well, not yet. I have been so busy, you see."

"Of course." Abel nodded. "I simply do not want the offer to linger too long." His eyes met mine, so dark gray they appeared almost black. "I am not particularly used to waiting."

"Of course," I said understandingly, though his demeanor unsettled me. His reaction was that of a screaming infant whose desired object was just out of reach, but judging this to be an uncharitable thought, I cast it away.

"If you will not think me overly forward," he continued, "perhaps I can offer something to tip the odds in my favor?"

"Oh, I don't…" Perhaps if I explained that another six weeks of mourning were requisite before I could possibly decide—

But Abel went on, stopping my thoughts short, "France is lovely this time of year."

"I'm sorry?"

"Perhaps a honeymoon in Paris could be arranged, should we marry this fall."

"I—*oh*." Was he, in fact, anticipating a decision so soon?

"Alas, I understand. It is a big decision, one which I have had far more time to consider."

I tucked my hair behind my ear, still studying the dahlias in my hand.

"If, however, there is anything more I can do to speed the process along, you will be sure to let me know?"

"Yes, of course," I said. Perhaps he believed my decision was inevitable, a troubling thought I quickly pushed aside. "Thank you."

"Please, if that changes, allow me to do what I can. Whatever you or your father may need."

"I will be sure to do so."

With that, Abel extended his hand, clearly seeking mine. I hesitated but acquiesced, and he placed a gentle kiss upon it.

"Farewell," he said, releasing my hand, allowing it to fall back to my side. "I hope to see you soon, Elise."

"Farewell."

He turned and walked away, and as I closed the door behind him, my stomach twisted in knots. Leaning against the door, I let out a sigh, clutching the bouquet of dahlias against my chest. Abel's investment in our engagement was far greater than I had anticipated.

However, I scarcely had the opportunity to dwell on this predicament before my father reappeared, having observed Abel's departure.

"Those are lovely," he said, gesturing toward the flowers in my hand.

"Abel's mother grew them," I replied.

"I believe we have a vase inside. Would you like me to care for them?"

"Sure. Then shall we continue?" I suggested, motioning toward the workshop, trying to project an air of casualness to deter any questions he might have, at least until I had better gathered my thoughts. Perhaps he would believe that I was simply so engrossed in the art of crafting violins that any distraction was unwelcome.

My father wavered for a moment, then seemed to understand. "Yes, we shall."

The remainder of my time in the workshop unfolded methodically. While I had to wait for the glue on the corner and end blocks to set, I continued working on other sections of the violin that could be secured independently. Despite the meticulous nature of this task, Abel's visit instilled a renewed determination to complete the violin as quickly as possible. Six weeks was already an excruciating wait.

That night, I experienced an uneasy but, fortunately, dreamless sleep. My nightly excursions into the forest seemed to have finally ceased.

The morning consisted of finishing the corner and end blocks, after which my father suggested taking a break. During this interlude, I managed to do some laundry and prepare a meal for later that evening. When he arose and saw what had been accomplished, he readily agreed to my request to continue working and at least begin crafting the ribs. With his guidance, I was able to finish planing the wood for the ribs of the center, upper, and lower bouts. His admiration of my work greatly encouraged me.

The following days proceeded in similar rhythm—shaping the ribs, installing the linings, and removing the mold. Throughout the process, I remembered the admonition to imbue the violin with traces of myself. Rote as the current work was, there was little more I could do but pray over the pieces. I also hummed tunes that reminded me of William, like the song I played for him during his recovery from a broken arm two years prior.

Memories of our shared past flooded my mind, painting vivid scenes of our childhood, where we played in the creek and caught frogs and grasshoppers together. Joyous visions appeared of our future children, delighting in the same simple pleasures. I offered silent prayers in my heart, and when I was certain my father was out of earshot, aloud, hoping fervently that such a future would come to fruition.

My concentration faltered when I imagined William's fingers running through my hair, the thrill when his hands brushed against my waist. Such thoughts were best reserved for times when I wasn't engaged in shaping the wood, distracting as these alluring fantasies could be. Perhaps due to the frequency of my thoughts about William, I could have sworn he was near during the quiet hours of the night—a tangible presence within my room, complete with form and fragrance.

The next stage in the violin-making process involved cutting and then beginning to thin the back plate. Difficult work, to be sure, but with my confidence growing day by day, this task, along with the remaining work, seemed entirely feasible. Everything was going according to plan, and a lightness filled my heart.

That is, until my father became ill.

Chapter Fifteen

My father's illness took hold far more quickly than anyone could have imagined. Indeed, by the time the bouquet of dahlias had browned and wilted, dark circles had already blossomed beneath my father's eyes.

"Just a bit under the weather," he would say when asked about his sleep habits—an explanation I accepted too readily as I returned to work on the violin's back plate. My father had supplied a fine piece of quarter-cut maple for the endeavor, a precious resource which only strengthened my resolve to do the work correctly.

When the moment arrived to cut the piece, my father, who stood behind me, was suddenly seized by a fit of coughing. Concerned by its unusual persistence, I turned and gently placed a hand on his back.

As the coughing subsided, I asked, "Are you all right?"

"It's just the wood dust," he explained, dabbing at his mouth with a handkerchief from his pocket.

Of course, I nodded, accepting his words. *Mere irritation of the lungs, nothing more.* Such was an unsurprising consequence of the task at hand. It mattered little that this kind of thing had not happened before, nor that I was unaffected. In my dogged pursuit of crafting the violin, any notion that my father's symptoms were in any way unusual was roundly dismissed.

My only defense for this neglect is how quickly the disease caught hold of my father's body.

Later that same week, Rebecca visited once more, and our conversation soon turned to the preparations for her upcoming wedding. I marveled at the calmness with which we discussed the event, my previous jealousy replaced by warmth. These feelings, however, were abruptly extinguished by a question prompted by my father's passing through the room.

Rebecca frowned and, lowering her voice, asked, "Is your father all right?"

"I suppose," I said, responding all too quickly, in a tone far more certain than I felt.

After Rebecca's departure, I rejoined my father in the workshop. With his reddened eyes and pallid face, his condition could hardly be denied.

"Lissie," he said quietly. "Would you mind terribly if I lay down for a bit?"

"Not at all." With my growing unease around his condition, it seemed proper to do something, anything to help. "Can I prepare you some tea before you do?"

"No, no, just some rest will do." he said, his eyes crinkling into a weak smile. "But if you need anything, please let me know."

"I will," I said. I shut the door gingerly behind him, a storm brewing in my mind despite my efforts to push it aside.

The following days were a delicate dance between my father and me, tension simmering in the air as we deliberately buried ourselves in our respective projects. He occasionally ventured out, claiming he needed fresh air, only to return more somber than before.

The more we attempted to ignore the signs before us, the more stubbornly pronounced they became: my father's weight loss and the resulting gauntness in his usually round, boyish face, for one. There was also the day, possibly during the process of gluing the back plate to its ribs, when I noticed the red spatter on his handkerchief. Our eyes met, and he hurriedly tucked it away before returning to his work. Despite the dread this sight inspired, I respected his unspoken request not to mention it.

The matter was hardly far from my mind, but my concerns were pushed away, lest they distract me from my work. For the same reason, I made no visits to Cassius during this time, choosing instead to dedicate every available moment to the violin.

I have often wondered whether the events that followed might have been different had I recognized the cough earlier. The idea of summoning Dr. Bell had crossed my mind, but I dismissed it, assuming my father would do so if he deemed it necessary.

Perhaps all would have been as it was, but this question nonetheless still haunts me on sleepless nights.

At any rate, it was only a matter of time before the issue could no longer be ignored.

The day began like any other. My mind was preoccupied by the task which lay ahead, which would most immediately consist of finishing the violin's linings. Once completed, I could then begin the belly plate. Such progress buoyed my spirit, and it was with this optimism that I made my way down the stairs.

Upon entering the kitchen, it became evident that this morning would differ. My father sat at the table, his fingers interlaced, with two plates of untouched food before him. His eyes, usually a bright blue, now appeared a dull gray.

"Elise, we must speak."

At once, the façade we had so carefully maintained crumbled. Pretending otherwise was a waste of time.

"I know," I said.

A long pause ensued as we looked at each other, settling into the new reality in which we acknowledged that my father was very, very sick.

What more was there to say? He buried his face in his hands for a moment. When he lifted his head, his eyes brimmed with tears. All at once, he seemed woefully mortal, and any words of comfort I might have offered faded away in the shadow of fear. "What shall I do?"

He did not answer immediately, a silence which was unbearable.

"I am afraid."

"I know you are, love." He rose and embraced me, and I buried my face in his chest, sobbing. Despite the guilt of allowing him to comfort me at such a time, I couldn't stop myself.

"It will be okay," he murmured, softly stroking my hair. "I love you, Lissie."

My sobs turned to hiccups, and eventually the tears ceased.

My father then spoke again. "That is why I must ask you something."

"Anything." Perhaps he needed medication that could be procured with a journey of a few days, or perhaps he could travel to a place where he might be healed. These hopes, however, were in vain, and my disappointment was not unexpected.

"I cannot leave you, my darling," he said. "Not without knowing of a surety you will be taken care of."

I understood at once he was speaking of Abel. "Is there not more we could do?"

He shook his head. "Darling, I have been seeing Dr. Bell. I did not wish to worry you, but this malady remains something of a mystery to him." Another bout of coughing interrupted him. "He said there are, perhaps, a few more treatments to be tried, but nothing so far as been effective, as you well see. Anything else could, at best, buy a bit of time."

"Perhaps a bit of time would be enough," I said, caught with sudden hope. Was it not all that was needed?

His brow furrowed. "We both know how this will end," he said quietly. "Delaying it may allow for better preparation, but it will hardly change anything."

"Father…"

"Elise," he started, another coughing spell postponing his next words. "I'm sorry, love."

"Surely I can find a way to make sure I have what I need," I insisted softly.

"Darling, there already is a way. Abel will be able to provide for your needs—and then some. You will have opportunities I could never have provided for you."

This might have been the moment to tell him of my arrangement with Cassius, but something within me hesitated. If my father didn't believe me, his involvement might only worsen things. His illness might worsen more quickly if strained by the idea that his daughter had lost her mind.

There must be another deceased creature around Chapel Grove with which Cassius could prove himself.

This thought vanished again as I observed my father's frailty. Where would I even begin?

The weight of everything was too much to bear. The impending loss of my father. The possibility of marrying a man for whom

I felt no love, while anxiously awaiting the return of the one I had promised to marry. My plans were coming apart at the seams.

"Father, I do not believe I can do it," I whispered, succumbing to fresh tears.

My father held me close as I wept once more. "I know this is not what you wanted, darling," he said softly.

"No," I emphasized.

"I know." He sighed. "Darling, I see no other way to be sure of your well-being after I pass."

"I do not wish to be simply cared for, as a horse by a stable boy. I wish to marry for love. I want…" The rest was unnecessary—who I wanted was clear. Even in these circumstances, even believing with all my heart he would return, I could hardly say his name. I bit my lip to stifle further tears.

"I know you do, my love." He paused, weighing his next words carefully "That opportunity, regrettably, has escaped you. You have mourned, and you may continue to mourn, but my spirit cannot rest in peace if I am wondering what will become of you when I die."

"Father," I said, unsure how to complete my thought. What was there to say? How could he understand that all I needed was time for everything to be set right?

"Forgive me, Lissie," my father spoke into the silence. "I do not have the luxury of sparing your feelings any longer. My time on this earth is rapidly coming to an end. I cannot spend my last days wondering if you will starve. I cannot rest, wondering if you will sleep on the streets."

"I won't—"

"Elise, you underestimate the situation in which you find yourself." His tone suggested finality, something which was intolerable under the circumstances.

"Why does it matter so greatly to you that I marry him?" My voice rose, but my father took no apparent offense. On the contrary, a look of great peace came over him.

"It matters to me because nineteen years ago, I promised your mother I would care for you. That vow is as binding today as it was on the day of your birth."

I closed my eyes, pained.

"You cannot understand how deeply I love you, how much I desire for you. I would move heaven and earth to provide the things I believe you deserve. I cannot leave you to your fate, to whatever may come of you after my death. I must know, for my sake and for yours, that you will be safe. Fed. Loved. Cared for. And right now, your best chance - a great opportunity, if you will not mind me saying so - is with Abel Sinclair."

I shook my head stubbornly. "I cannot," I said, despair overtaking me nonetheless.

"I implore you to be sensible." He said this with such resolution I could only stand silently, absorbing the magnitude of the situation. "Think of the places you could go, the things you could do, by allying yourself with the Sinclair family. You could develop the skills to play in places like Vienna. Paris. To see the birthplace of violins in Cremona. You could do so many things, so much more than would be possible in Chapel Grove."

I could envision these things, of course, and knew that under the circumstances, as my father understood them, there was no question that he was right. What could I possibly say to disabuse him of this notion? Any counterargument would be feeble, at best, and at worst, he might think the stress had driven me to madness, only diminishing his trust in my judgment.

There was nothing to be said. My shoulders slumped under the weight of failure. I looked at the floor, then back to my father.

"Father, please—please, leave me to my thoughts. I need time alone to think." This was all I could request under the circumstances.

"I understand. Please know I only want what is best for you, my darling."

My lip trembled once more. "I know, Father."

I opened the door of the workshop with my heart thumping, knowing exactly where to go next.

Chapter Sixteen

The secluded path beside the creek beckoned. Cassius had suggested this course may come with unexpected barriers. Perhaps this was exactly the kind of situation about which he had warned me. If so, perhaps he had a solution for my father's affliction.

As if in response to my thoughts, a croak echoed from the trees above. I glanced upward to discover the raven perched among the branches. The large black bird rested in one of the taller trees beside the creek, gazing down at me intently. It ruffled its feathers and croaked once again.

Surely, Cassius could help.

It must be acknowledged that my father could hardly be blamed for his position. From his perspective, I was being reckless, rejecting Abel's proposal due to transient state of grief. Abel was, after all, a man whom many young women in town adored. The benefits afforded to the woman he wed would be unparalleled.

If it were merely a matter of my foolishness, if William truly were lost forever and no revival was possible, then perhaps I could count myself fortunate. I might even enjoy the attention of such a suitor. However, settling for anything less than William was inconceivable, for I had faith that Cassius would bring him back to life. With such a promise in mind, nothing else could compare.

During our childhood, William had been a mischievous little boy who helped me catch frogs in the creek when he had a moment to spare from his numerous farm chores and many siblings.

I smiled, thinking of a slightly older William, during the days when the twinkle in his eyes had lit a spark within me, the goofy grin on his face becoming older, one of a man rather than a boy. Over time, that smile caused an unfamiliar lurch in my abdomen, something difficult to understand at first, but which became coherent the first time we kissed, unbidden by our former childhood innocence.

If William's life could be restored, there was hardly another option but to pursue it.

The town of Chapel Grove was just awakening, and Main Street was alive with the bustle of early morning business. I kept my head down on my way to the wagon, not wishing to draw unnecessary attention. There, Cassius was crouched, paintbrush in hand, evidently touching up its turquoise paint. His head turned at the sound of my approaching footsteps, and he set the brush down and stood, his face brightening. As I drew nearer, his smile faded, replaced by a look of concern.

"Elise, what has happened?"

Though I intended to reply, emotion overwhelmed me once more.

"Come, come, let us have some privacy," he suggested, guiding me behind his wagon where his horse was the only witness, its large brown eyes peering at me beneath his forelocks. The horse trotted in our direction.

"Not now, Osiris," said Cassius firmly. Affronted, the horse reluctantly stepped back beneath the shade of a nearby tree.

Upon reaching the relative solitude, I spoke. "I needed to see you."

"What has happened?"

"My father. He is sick."

"I was afraid of this," said Cassius softly. "How sick is he?"

"Very." His grim face suggested he understood without further explanation. "I simply do not know what to do."

"How awful," he said, the passivity of this statement inducing my realization that he did not fully understand the strain this placed on our plans.

I glanced toward town. Despite the absence of passersby, I lowered my voice. "He wishes for me to marry. To be sure that I am taken care of."

"Of course," he said. "And yet you have other plans."

"Yes," I said. "Plans that are rather difficult to relay to him."

"Hmm." He leaned against the wagon, lost in contemplation. Anxieties began to creep back into my mind. What if he couldn't help me? What if I couldn't find a suitable reason not to marry Abel—at least one strong enough? Could I flee, escape my destiny, and still reclaim my William? No, surely not; the tools needed for the violin were here with my father in his workshop. My heart raced with these worries.

Finally, Cassius returned his gaze to mine. "How is the violin progressing?"

"It is coming along," I replied. "But several weeks of work remain."

"Hmm."

"And, well, my father may not have that long left."

Cassius stood, his mind far away as he traced his jawline absently with his fingers. His expression was unreadable as he considered the matter. "Could the wedding not be agreed upon, but simply delayed?"

The suggestion struck a sharp pang in my stomach. I shook my head. "No."

"Not to go through with it, of course," he clarified, "Not while you await the return of your William. But agreed to, set in motion, in order to appease everyone involved." He shrugged. "Perhaps the idea of a solid agreement would put your father's mind at ease, with a date set suitably far into the future to ease your own."

"Not a chance," I said firmly.

"One might argue, though, that finishing the violin with your father would be a suitable memento of him, a last joy-filled experience before losing him forever. Surely any a suitor, no matter how ambitious, would find it within themselves to empathize with that desire."

As greatly as I disliked it, this reasoning made its own kind of sense.

"Perhaps," I admitted reluctantly.

"Your father may also see the opportunity to complete of the violin as an act of mercy to you, under the circumstances."

Although I still disliked the plan, it was rational. I could tell my father that I wished to complete this final project with him, and perhaps he would find it agreeable if I committed to Abel.

Abel. Could I agree to such a thing under false pretenses? It seemed unfair to entangle him in this mess, unknowing as he was of my intentions.

Still, upon William's return, my engagement to Abel would be nullified. Even if disappointment followed, surely everyone would understand. Such an occurrence could hardly be blamed on me, as there was no reason to suspect my involvement. Only a madman would.

The idea eased some of the tension from my shoulders. My father wanted me to be cared for. I wouldn't disappoint him; I was ensuring it would happen, one way or another.

But what if the violin failed? What then?

I considered Cassius for a moment, reflecting on all he had shown me. The raven's miraculous return had provided enough evidence, in my mind, to trust his abilities.

However, if all else failed, I could concede to marriage with Abel. Though far from my first choice, it promised a decent enough future; one that would allow my father's spirit to rest in peace, one way or the other. The thought was unpleasant, the likelihood appearing so distant that I dismissed it.

Yet there remained one unresolved dilemma, one neither Cassius nor I had addressed.

"I cannot do the rest of the work alone. I need my father's assistance. If he dies..."

Cassius paused, his arms crossed, a finger resting thoughtfully on his lips.

I continued, "His illness seems to be progressing quickly. I worry he will not survive long enough to finish the violin. Even if I convince him..." I couldn't bring myself to finish the thought.

Cassius looked pensive for a moment before a look of revelation came over him. "You know, I may have something that will help."

My eyes widened with hope. "Really? What is it?"

He had been leaning against the wagon, but now he stood upright. "As you know, I am a collector. I possess something that I believe could hold value for your father."

"Really?" My heart leaped.

"I think so," he replied, then added in a more cautious tone, "Now, Elise, I do not believe your father will be cured. Death is still sure, but if I am not mistaken, I believe what I have will almost certainly prolong his life sufficiently to see the completion of the violin."

And the return of William, I hoped desperately. "That would be wonderful."

"Splendid. Now, I do not have it ready right now, but I should be able to find it once I finish." He gestured to the wagon. "If you will return tomorrow, I should have something ready for you by"— he paused, seemingly contemplating something—"mid-afternoon. Would that be acceptable?"

"Yes," I responded cheerfully. "Thank you. Oh, thank you."

"I'm pleased to be of assistance, though sorry for all the trouble you have faced."

"I appreciate that, but you need not be. You will be the solution to much of the trouble, should all go as planned."

He grinned. "Indeed."

Chapter Seventeen

The promised treatment for my father buoyed my soul as I made my way home through the rising hum of business on Main Street. With the miracle of the raven as evidence, whatever treatment Cassius had was certain to help my father's illness.

With that concern momentarily set aside, my attention shifted to the more pressing matter at hand: convincing my father to persist in working on the violin. Time had now become more valuable than ever, and none could be squandered if I was to complete the violin by All Hallows' Eve.

Regrettably, the treatment would not be available until the next day, and its effectiveness remained uncertain. Since I couldn't reveal the treatment to my father without disclosing my involvement with Cassius, he couldn't share in my current relief at the prospect of more time. I needed to find another way to persuade him to continue our work.

The songbirds which had chirruped in the trees along the creek had quieted for the day, and the raven was nowhere to be seen.

Words were assembled and rearranged as I walked home, interrupted by my heart's yearning for a simpler time: the time when I could spend time with my father free of such pressing concerns; before William died, before my path forward became a murky web of lies and half-truths. I recalled that time with great sadness, but there was little benefit to wallowing.

When I reached home, I found my father by the fire, engrossed in a book while seated in his chair. Despite my finding the room stifling, a heavy winter quilt lay across his lap—a troubling sign, yet the promise of treatment offered a small measure of comfort.

Upon my entrance, my father looked up, inserted a bookmark into his book, and set it aside.

"Forgive me, Father, for my insolence," I began, my voice steady.

He looked at me sadly, removing his glasses and setting them atop the book. "Elise…"

"I understand you only want what is best for me," I continued, determined to speak my mind before doubt could take hold. "I trust you, Father. I do. And so"—I forced out the words, unwilling to linger on their bitterness—"I will agree to marry Abel." My stomach twisted in protest.

"You will?" My father frowned, likely perplexed by my sudden change of heart.

"However," I added quickly, to prevent any premature relief on his part, "I have one condition."

He hesitated. "And what is that?"

I knelt before him, as if in prayer, making a heartfelt appeal. "Please help me finish the violin." His brow creased in confusion. "I realize this request may seem strange," I acknowledged. "But I have cherished our time together and wish for it to continue, even if only this once. As a token of remembrance."

The conversation was disrupted by a fit of coughing. I placed my hand on his shuddering form, realizing the bones in his back were palpable. When had he become so thin? Worry nettled me that the additional work would compromise his present condition even more.

"Do you need some tea?" I asked.

He shook his head in response.

Cassius, I reminded myself, *the treatment*. If my father had witnessed the raven's revival as I had, if he truly grasped the potential, he would certainly agree. I had to persevere and suppress my emotions in pursuit of that hopeful outcome.

Once his coughing subsided, he appeared even more fatigued, his eyes darkened within his reddened face. He seemed smaller in his chair than before. "My darling, I do not know if the decision is up to me."

"What do you mean?"

"I mean that I cannot promise I have the time left to help you." A profound sadness shadowed his features.

"Let us make the time," I insisted. He began to object, but I interrupted, "Please hear me, Father. You need not lift a finger. I will do the work myself, at your direction, leaving you free to rest. I can carve the wood beside the bed when you are tired, or outdoors so you can get more fresh air." I knelt next to his chair and placed my other hand over his. "Please."

I watched as he pondered, wishing I could convey how much this endeavor meant to me. The joy—our joy—would be immense should we complete this task.

However, a full explanation was impossible, and without it, uncertainty clouded his expression. I pressed on. "Father, I recognize the unlikelihood of my future as a luthier. I can, however, manage the household while you assist me. You need not lift a finger. I will take care of you, and all else."

He scrutinized me, possibly wondering why I was so insistent. I averted my gaze, worried I might reveal my own deception, when he finally spoke again.

"I confess I have enjoyed working on the violin with you. I have enjoyed our time together. I also recognize that, though I believe this to be the best option for you, there is no doubt this time should have been reserved for mourning."

I smiled with gratitude.

"However," There was a distinct tremor in his voice, "I worry I will not live to see you married."

"I know," I replied, biting my lip. Despite my efforts, I could not completely alleviate his fears, much to my regret. "I will work diligently. I will work quickly. And if—" I continued hesitantly, understanding that without his conviction, this was all for naught. "If your condition should severely worsen, we may move the wedding forward."

He looked at me carefully. "You give me your word?"

"I do."

"I mean it, Lissie. Do you promise that, should I assist you with this violin, you will agree to the marriage?"

I nodded.

"If that is the case, then I will agree. I will help you make the violin."

My heart swelled, relief flooding my soul. "Thank you, Father. I will not disappoint you."

"I appreciate that," he said, massaging his temples. "I suppose that means you wish to begin immediately?"

Indeed, this was my hope during my walk home. If I could work tirelessly, I would have done so. However, my father was clearly exhausted. With the treatment from Cassius impending, there was little to gain from further compromising his health. He needed to remain well if this plan was to succeed.

"Now, why don't you get some rest? I'll make a nice stew for dinner. Something hearty."

My father eased back into his chair. "I will not object to that."

"We can resume our work tomorrow." I rose from my spot by the hearth and kissed his clammy forehead.

"You are so good to me, Lissie," he said softly.

I placed a hand over his. "You were first."

The remainder of my day was spent busily preparing the stew, tending to the laundry, mending clothes, tidying the garden, and engaging in some light cleaning around the house. I then ventured into town to purchase bread and butter to accompany our dinner. Although I longed to continue working on the violin, completing these tasks would only further encourage my father to rest.

If Cassius's treatment proved as effective as promised, there was no reason to fear my father's passing before William's return. I envisioned his joy when he realized he had been too hasty in trying to marry me off to Abel.

Thus, I completed each task with immense satisfaction. I delighted in being able to support my father's health and well-being, even before the treatment commenced. After dinner, my father appeared noticeably less wan, and the knowledge that Cassius had something even more potent filled me with peace.

After helping my father settle into bed, I banked the coals for the night and retired to my own bed. The next day's endeavors would demand my full energy, and I lay down, enveloped in tranquility.

Chapter Eighteen

Hope, however, can be a woefully fickle thing.

The following morning, I rose early, determined to maintain the momentum of the previous day. The sky was overcast, casting a dull light throughout the house and creating a humid atmosphere.

The kitchen was quiet and serene, and I busied myself preparing a hearty breakfast, planning to tackle the morning chores afterwards. I imagined the satisfaction etched on his face upon witnessing the progress I had made.

However, the peacefulness shattered like a fragile soap bubble when I saw the condition of my father. Despite a hearty dinner and a restful night's sleep, he appeared even paler and weaker than the previous evening. His coughing was now accompanied by more vivid red stains on his handkerchiefs. The relief I had felt at the prospect of the promised treatment was replaced by a silent plea, a dread of what might transpire should it fail.

"Good morning, Father," I greeted him. "I've prepared you breakfast."

He glanced at the fried eggs and toast on the table with bloodshot eyes and responded wearily, "Thank you. It might be a while before I regain much appetite, my dear."

"You must keep your strength up, Father."

He reluctantly consumed a few bites of dry toast, and I persuaded him to drink some tea, hoping it would offer him some relief, however slight. A heaviness settled over my own heart.

I looked longingly through the workshop window. The unfinished violin beckoned to me, but I told my father, "It's a bitter morning. You need to rest. You'll feel better tomorrow, and we'll continue then." I fervently hoped this would hold true.

"Perhaps we can work on the violin this afternoon," he suggested.

I hesitated, not wanting to exert him unnecessarily. Yet, my hands itched to resume their work. "Perhaps. In the meantime, you must rest. Would some fresh air be beneficial?" I gestured towards the porch.

"Thank you, Lissie. I am actually feeling rather chilly. Some more tea might be nice, if it's not too much trouble?"

"Of course," I replied. I helped him settle in his chair, tended to the fire, and brewed more tea.

The best course of action was to keep my father's mind and body unencumbered, allowing his energy to fight off this dreadful illness. I prayed that such time would be well spent.

I returned to his side, placing the mug on the table beside him.

"Thank you, darling."

"Of course."

While my father savored his tea, I spent the rest of the morning tidying the house until afternoon, hoping that Cassius would be ready with the treatment. Time seemed to linger, but staying busy helped allay my impatience.

Though Cassius had given me no firm hour to meet him, I did not wish to arrive before he was ready. When the hour seemed appropriate, I returned to my father. His pallid face chilled my heart.

This treatment, whatever it was, had to work. It simply had to.

"Father, I could use a bit of fresh air."

He closed the book around his thumb to mark the page. "Of course. You need your rest, too." He gestured around the room, perhaps suggesting I had been overly industrious.

"It was nothing," I insisted. "Do you need anything from town?"

"No, dear. Enjoy your time." He gave me a sleepy smile which suggested he may spend much of that time asleep. *All the better*, I thought. He needed the rest.

Cassius was leaning against the side of a freshly painted wagon as I approached. He was munching on an apple recognizable as one from the Purcell family, marked by its dappled red and gold hues. He wore a dark blue suit with a matching hat, a debonair ensemble far more formal than typically seen around town. Osiris's sleek black coat was partially visible behind the wagon.

"The wagon looks nice," I commented.

"Thank you, Elise," he replied, nodding towards the ominous clouds in the sky. "It's fortunate I finished yesterday."

"It is," I responded, my interest waning.

"At times, one simply gets lucky with timing. Alas, enough small talk then." He took one last bite of his apple. "Here," he said, tossing the core to Osiris. Cassius retrieved a handkerchief from his pocket, wiped his hands, and replaced it before reaching inside his jacket. "I suppose you're here for this?"

My heart soared. A small, largely unacknowledged part of me had been concerned that Cassius would tell me he had been tragically unable to locate the treatment; that my father was simply out of luck and so was I.

The size of the vial between his fingers, however, gave me pause. I took the small object from his outstretched hand with great care. "What is it?" I asked, examining it between my fingers.

"The answer to your current problem," he said simply.

The vial was so minuscule as to be underwhelming. It was only about as wide as my little finger, and only about half as tall. A cork at the top kept the liquid inside; a clear, unremarkable substance.

I glanced from the vial back to Cassius, filled with skepticism. Shouldn't so powerful a thing appear more impressive somehow?

His expression was unreadable, and though I didn't wish to be impolite, my doubts overcame my discretion.

"It looks like water," I observed.

Unperturbed, he replied, "Do not be deceived by appearances. It is far more powerful than it appears."

I examined it again. "You are sure it will work?"

"My dear, I am positive." With a hint of amused impatience, he elaborated, "I acquired it several years ago during my travels. This elixir is from a village tucked in the remote jungles of southern America. In that village, it is almost entirely reserved for its high chiefs, to preserve their lives as long as possible, and thus maintain the integrity of leadership. It is, naturally, heavily guarded due to its importance, and I was very fortunate to find someone willing to trade me for it."

"What did you trade for it?" I asked.

"That is of no great concern," he responded dismissively with a wave of his hand.

His statement only fueled more questions in my mind. If the substance held such value and potency as he professed, what could possibly equate in trade? "But—if this is so precious, surely it must have been costly."

How could it be deemed worthy of giving to me for my own purposes?

He looked at me with patient understanding. "Have I not explained, Elise? My fascination with extending life and resurrecting the deceased drives me. As such, I've gathered numerous artifacts pursuing those goals."

"But then, how are you so willing to part with it now?" If such was his aim, the life of my father would pale in comparison.

"What you hold in your hand is not the entirety of what I traded for, of course. I have used other parts of it for experimentation, but I believe I have come as far as I can with it. Thus"—he gestured to the vial in my hands—"you have what remains."

Feeling slightly reassured, I nodded. "And you are certain it will work?"

He nodded earnestly. "I have seen it do incredible things, love."

Cradling the diminutive vial, I recognized its immense value—irreplaceable, even. Concerned about losing or damaging it, I carefully tucked it within my dress, nestled securely close to me, allowing me to frequently verify its presence.

"Thank you," I said.

"It is my pleasure. As precious as that substance is to me, I believe you will give me something yet more valuable."

I still pondered how a violin crafted by my untrained hands might equate in value to such a notable substance—one that individuals might commit heinous acts to possess, something desired by rulers far and wide.

"Only made more powerful, in fact, by all this turmoil, I believe," he added, which redirected my attention.

"What do you mean?" I asked with furrowed brow.

He remained poised. "You have become more invested in the making of the violin, have you not?" he said. "As I have told you before, the more of yourself you put into the violin, the more likely it is to work. This tragic situation will likely drive you to put more of yourself into it than you already have, I'm sure."

My pain in exchange for power. I brushed the thought away. Though troubled, I lacked the luxury of time to dwell on it before Cassius interrupted my contemplation.

"What you must understand," he advised, "and concentrate on is the manner in which to employ it. Simply administer a small quantity of the liquid to your father each day, perhaps in his evening tea if that suits his preference."

"I believe that should suffice." It promised to be an easily maintained routine, one that, even if the elixir failed, would offer comfort to my father.

Cassius raised a hand, bringing his thumb and forefinger close together. "A minute amount will be sufficient, so be sure to use it sparingly. I believe the contents of that vial will last until the completion of the violin."

"Of course," I agreed, although the vial was so small that I struggled to believe it could be enough, but there was little point debating it. What other options did I have? "Thank you," I said.

"My pleasure. Now hurry home, and you will see that this will solve your current problem."

"I will." I fervently hoped it would. "Thank you, Mr. McCalmont."

I turned to leave, but Cassius spoke again. "Please, you must remember to be careful," he cautioned as I turned back to face him, "for as I have implied, I would not be able to replace the elixir, should something happen to it."

"Of course." A thing jealously guarded in the depths of exotic jungles would no doubt be difficult to replace. "I will take care of it."

As I walked home, a sense of relief returned to me, now confident that the elixir would work as Cassius claimed. Beyond considerations for the violin, I recognized the additional time with my father as a gift in itself, and I could hardly wait to tell him about it.

Yet, I was struck by the realization that I couldn't tell him about it. What would I say? Any conversation with Dr. Bell would quickly unveil the story as a fabrication. No, it was better for him to simply get better without knowing why.

These thoughts were interrupted by a sudden unease halfway down the path home. I halted, sensing that I was being watched, although I saw no one.

Even when I looked around, the feeling persisted, rooting me to the spot. The dim light seemed to darken, the rustling branches startled me, evoking nervous imaginings that I tried to dismiss. My hand rested on the vial, still nestled safely. Precious as the elixir was, could someone seek its power for themselves?

With cautious steps, I trudged forward. When no harm befell me, I reasoned the experience away as being overly protective of this precious substance.

Still, my peace had been disturbed. I hastened home at an increased pace, frequently checking that the vial was secure and glancing over my shoulder, wondering if whoever had watched me would reveal themselves. The first droplets of the day's rainstorm began to dot the ground.

Relief washed over me as I entered our home and shut the door behind me. No one could observe me here. I leaned my back against the door, my protective barrier from the outside world. Here, my father and I were safe.

Yet, he hadn't greeted me upon my return, which was unusual. In his current state, he was unlikely to be in the workshop.

"Hello?" Silence greeted me. I padded into the sitting room, where I found my father, his eyes closed, head resting on his chest. After a moment, the steady rise and fall of his chest was visible. He had merely dozed off.

His sleeping form was noticeably thinner than usual. Even in repose, he appeared so frail. Despite his recent exhaustion, it was still unusual for him to nap in the middle of the day, especially while sitting upright. This was not an encouraging sign.

His peacefulness provided a momentary reprieve, as no coughing shook his form, which usually occurred throughout the day.

My fingers brushed against the vial, my only hope.

Chapter Nineteen

That evening, the gloom outside developed into a heavy rainstorm, with noisy droplets pattering incessantly on the roof. The leftover stew from the previous day seemed even more appropriate for the dreary day and made dinner preparations far simpler.

Before starting the meal, I carefully placed the vial towards the back of a cabinet where it would remain safe. Although I was eager to administer the treatment to my father, I was acutely aware of the risks involved in adding it to his soup, especially given his recent lack of appetite. When he ambled into the kitchen while the soup was being reheated, my decision was validated; it would indeed be more challenging to do so without his notice.

"I apologize," he said, "I did not mean to fall asleep."

"Perhaps it is a side effect of the weather," I said. "A good meal will help."

My decision to reserve the elixir for my father's evening tea was justified by how little soup he ate. Despite Cassius instructing that only a small amount was needed, my father would likely be better off receiving the full dose.

Shortly after dinner, my father settled into the sitting room with a book in his hand. I laid a blanket over his lap.

"May I bring you some tea?" I asked.

"That would be lovely." His sunken cheeks and colorless complexion inspired only more impatience to administer the dose.

It must work, it simply must. Despite Cassius's past successes, the sight of my father appearing so unwell filled me with apprehension.

In the kitchen, I began warming the kettle, then checked that my father was still comfortably seated before retrieving the vial. It was remarkably small and unassuming, its contents entirely colorless.

Was it odorless as well? Upon removing the small cork and holding the vial to my nose, it seemed so. It was likely flavorless too, but none could be spared to verify.

I replaced the cork, set the vial aside, added tea leaves to the strainer, and placed it in the cup. As the kettle began to whistle, I promptly poured the water into the cup, careful not to scald myself in my impatience.

While the tea leaves imparted their essence into the water, I looked over the vial again. It held such a miniscule amount. How could it possibly last? If the substance indeed helped my father, I would need enough to sustain his health until the violin was complete.

No, more than that. My father needed to stay well through to the return of my love. Nothing else would suffice.

With trembling fingers, I tipped the vial over the cup. In my nervousness, more than the intended amount vanished beneath the liquid's surface.

Cassius had said a tiny amount would suffice. Perhaps I could use less next time? But after securing the cork and tucking the vial into the back corner of the dish cupboard, I determined that question would wait for another day. My mind was already burdened for the evening. By this time tomorrow, the elixir would have shown its efficacy—or not.

While stirring the tea, I silently prayed for its success, then took it to my father.

The loose floorboard just inside the sitting room creaked beneath my feet, causing my father's eyes to drift open at the sound. Once again, he had dozed off—a grim sign, as I had been gone mere minutes.

"Hello," I said, momentarily setting aside my worries.

He hmphed sleepily in return, which prompted another bout of coughing and a corresponding knot of concern in my stomach.

"I've brought your tea," I announced.

His eyes fluttered open briefly before closing again.

"*Father.*"

He yawned, the action further irritating his lungs.

"Thank you," he said upon recovering, reaching for the mug.

"Careful," I warned, then watched intently as he lifted the tea to his lips.

My hands were clasped tightly. *Will it taste peculiar? Will he notice?*

He set the mug down. "Thank you."

"You are welcome," I replied simply, as though what I had just watched was trivial. He took another sip, and I felt the tension ease from my shoulders. It must have tasted normal, or at least ordinary enough.

He looked at me, and I realized how rude my staring must be.

Snapping out of my trance, I sat down in the chair opposite him and sipped my own tea, observing until he finished his before assisting him to bed.

"Do you need anything more?" I asked.

He shook his head. "No, darling. Thank you."

"Of course," I replied. "Good night."

I then retired to bed, wondering whether I could expect to awaken and find my father well. Perhaps it was wiser to moderate my expectations and hope for a less-sick father, one whose cough was less severe, whose appetite improved, and whose complexion held a bit more color.

Whatever the outcome, I was thrilled by the prospect of further proof of Cassius's ability to restore William. I reveled in the thought as I drifted to sleep.

The next morning, I awoke with a mix of excitement and anxiety. Cassius had promised improvement, and now was the time to see if his words held true.

As I reached the downstairs living area, I turned the corner and was greeted by my father. Following a familiar childhood routine, he sat quietly eating while engrossed in a book. His cheeks were a vibrant, almost impossibly healthy pink, and he radiated vitality.

"Good morning, darling."

"How are you?" I asked, too distracted by his transformation to offer a proper greeting in return. Even the skin around his eyes looked like that of a younger man, as if he had shed at least a decade.

He shook his head in disbelief. "I can hardly comprehend it, but I feel... well, I feel wonderful."

"Really?" Cassius had assured me things would improve, but I could never have imagined to what extent. Better was, indeed, a gross understatement. "You look wonderful,"

"I hope you will forgive me for eating without you this morning," he said. "I was simply ravenous."

I slid into the chair across from him. "All is forgiven." My mind spun with the implications of the fact that the elixir had worked.

"Today feels like a good day to work on the violin, don't you think?" he mused, nudging the last crumbs on his plate with a fork, then glancing at me expectantly.

A smile spread across my face. Whatever the future held, there was immense joy in knowing my father was well again. We would share more time together, perhaps enough for him to witness William's return.

Beyond all else, my father's miraculous recovery confirmed this: Cassius could indeed be trusted to fulfill his promises. It hinted at more good news to come.

"I think so, too," I said.

I could hardly wait.

Chapter Twenty

The remainder of that day was dedicated to working on the violin's belly plate, an intimidating task which was approached with optimism in light of my father's health. He had rosy cheeks, sparkling eyes, and the ease with which he moved had improved markedly.

It had been foolish, however, to suppose that my father's sudden return to health would lead him to abandon the topic of Abel. The very next day, not long after we resumed working on the belly plate, the subject arose once more.

There was an aura of abnormal quiet about my father before he spoke, unassumingly enough. "We have been invited to dinner this evening, you and I."

I raised an eyebrow, puzzled as to why dinner plans made him so uneasy. "Have we?"

"Yes." He hesitated. "We have been invited to dine with the Sinclairs."

My heart sank with sudden understanding. I set down the gouge and belly plate and turned in my chair. "When did this invitation arrive?"

"A servant of theirs came this morning when you were still in bed," he admitted sheepishly.

"Oh."

"I have already told them we could come."

I slumped in my seat, much like a petulant child. "I really do not want to," The violin demanded all my attention. I had no time to entertain a soon-to-be brokenhearted suitor.

"I know," he sighed.

"I don't think I can," I said, more softly this time.

"Lissie—"

"Could we not claim you are too ill to come?" I already knew what the answer would be.

"That would be dishonest," he admonished.

The double-edged sword of his health. I had not foreseen this drawback.

"Elise, darling…" His tone had shifted, less sympathetic and more troubled.

"What is it?" I asked.

He folded his arms, gazing down at the floor as if gathering his thoughts before speaking again. My stomach flipped as I waited, dreading what was to come.

"I know that I seem to have healed. I cannot say why, but it is undeniable. I also understand that Abel is not who you envisioned. I acknowledge your concerns. Truly, I do." His expression softened. "You loved William. Yet, what I advised before remains true; despite my apparent recovery, who can say for how long this will last, or if it is merely a temporary reprieve?"

I longed to confide in my father about the treatment, but how could I? He would surely inquire about its source, and despite the compelling nature of the treatment, I knew he would be skeptical of raising the dead. I could not afford any additional complications to the plan.

How could I begin to explain that my love for William continued to burn, and would forevermore, that the path which we both believed was buried in the Chapel Grove cemetery would be restored?

I shook my head, overwhelmed by the impossibility of my situation.

"You promised," he said gently, without rebuke, yet rendering my arguments powerless.

Indeed, I *had* promised. The wood before me, that which would form the violins belly, had been provided on this condition.

"I did."

"And I have upheld my end of the bargain."

Indeed, my father had kept his word. What more could be said?

"Okay," I relented, "I will go."

We concluded our work early that afternoon to prepare for dinner. I daydreamed about feigning illness, even knowing that it wasn't a real option. Declining a dinner invitation from the Sinclairs would be improper under any circumstances, especially with the engagement on the horizon.

Still, one could dream.

My stomach was in knots as I dressed. Even my willingness to attend the dinner felt like a betrayal to William, let alone the agreement which must be made.

Understanding there was no alternative did little to improve my mood.

I continued pinning my hair into place. The only way I could maintain my composure was to stay focused on the ultimate goal.

It was all for William. All of this—every unpleasantness, every sacrifice, every lie—was in order that he may return. When that happened, all this could fade to a distant memory. Whatever it required, I would endure, believing it would someday be justified.

Without this belief, our dinner plans would be unbearable.

In the early evening, a carriage arrived to transport us to the Sinclair residence. A kindly footman assisted us in boarding, and we settled into our seats. The sky was dusky and pleasant, yet perhaps due to my already morose state of mind, as we passed the woods, I was reminded of the legend of Humming Hattie.

For generations, the children of Chapel Grove had whispered this tale among themselves since the time my father was young. Its authenticity was bolstered by parents who used it as a cautionary tale to keep their children safe from wild animals. However, the legend of Humming Hattie was rooted in truth.

Hattie Price had been born into a respectable family and was generally regarded as a quiet and esteemed woman in town. Upon the discovery that her husband planned to leave her for someone else, she was shattered. Enraged by this betrayal, she decided to punish her unfaithful husband in the harshest possible way. Humming their favorite tunes and acting as if they were going on a picnic, she led her three children to a shallow pond in the woods and drowned them one by one, humming all the while. Once the horrific task had been completed, she slit her wrists and lay beside their bodies to die.

Though the details of the story varied with the storyteller—with some controversy over the method by which the children perished—the outcome remained unchanged. Humming Hattie's spirit was said to wander the woods outside Chapel Grove, eternally humming the haunting melodies her children heard as they met their end.

"Don't go in the woods, or Humming Hattie might drown you, too," parents would warn. Meanwhile, children had a tradition of hiding behind trees, softly humming songs before leaping out to scare their playmates.

With a pang, I remembered the time William and I stumbled upon the mischievous Alexander brothers tormenting poor little Oliver Hendrix with a particularly cruel prank involving the legend. Oliver was several years younger than us, perhaps only four or five at the time.

Despite the fearsome reputation of the Alexander brothers, William did not hesitate to defend Oliver. We had encountered the scene while returning from running errands for William's mother in town. Oliver was encircled by Rupert, Bernard, and Silas, his face blotchy and red with tears streaming down his cheeks as he stood immobilized by humiliation. The crotch of his pants was dark with urine.

"Thought Hattie got you, huh?" taunted Rupert, the eldest, who had towered over his victim.

"It's not funny," Oliver had said, his voice quiet and trembling.

At this, the boys had roared with laughter.

"Did you see his *face?*" Bernard had howled to his brother Silas, who wore an old dress shirt and whose hands were coated in something red—likely tomato sauce.

Judging by the sauce on his clothing, it was evident that Oliver had been lured into the woods and ambushed by Silas, dressed as a bloodstained Hattie, resulting in the accident.

William had placed himself between the two parties. "Leave him alone," he said.

Noting the tremendous size differences between the brothers and William, I watched with concern. The brothers exchanged disdainful glances.

"Why should we?" Rupert had scoffed, rounding on William.

Though I was tempted to encourage William to leave the situation, the sight of Oliver with his puffy eyes cast down, arms folded, and thoroughly soaked pants quelled any argument.

"He's half your size," William had argued. "Leave him alone."

Bernard sneered. "Get back to the farm. We will handle this dullard as we see fit."

Shaking his head, William had glanced back at Oliver. "Go with Elise."

I glanced from the brothers to William, reluctant to leave him alone. "Are you sure?"

"Yes. Bring him to my house, and my mother will help."

The protective ferocity in his expression silenced any argument I might have made.

""Be careful," I urged, guiding the humiliated boy back to William's home, where, as promised, Mrs. Whittaker cleaned him up, provided some of William's old clothes, and ensured he had a good meal before sending him home.

"Tell your mother I will return your clothes in a few days," Mrs. Whittaker had told him, "And just stay away from those boys - *and those woods.*"

"I will," Oliver replied. By the time he was escorted home by William's brother, his eyes were still puffy from crying, but he had carried with him the glow of charity.

William returned home shortly after, a black eye blooming and scrapes on his arms and legs, yet a sparkle in his eye signaled that he would have done it all again, given the chance.

Recalling William's noble and kind nature tugged at my soul, further darkening my mood for the evening ahead.

Chapter Twenty-One

The grandeur of the Sinclair estate exceeded my expectations. With its flickering torchlights, exquisite brickwork, lush gardens, and imposing size, it seemed more like something from a fairy tale than the modest Chapel Grove.

Perhaps it was just a matter of comparing it to the homes I was accustomed to seeing, but I had to admit that I was momentarily lifted from my gloom by sheer fascination. It was the kind of home where one might expect to dine with royalty.

We were helped from the carriage by the same kind coachman from before, and we expressed our gratitude. He then guided us up that grand staircase to the extended front porch, where we were greeted by another Sinclair servant—a young woman with reddish hair peeking out from beneath her bonnet.

"This way, please," she instructed, leading us into the truly magnificent foyer. I was sure our entire house could have fit within its walls.

The young woman showed us into the sitting room, where Abel and his parents rose to meet us. I offered the servant a smile, though she kept her gaze lowered as she stepped aside to make way for us. Abel's father was a heavyset, jolly-faced man.

"So good to see you, dear," said Abel's father, grasping my hand warmly with his wide fingers.

"You as well, Mayor Sinclair." I withdrew my hand and turned to Mrs. Sinclair, a fair-haired woman with gray eyes like her son, whose smile was tight upon her face.

"Elise. So lovely to have you here, and your father," Mrs. Sinclair greeted.

"Thank you," I replied. Mr. Sinclair and my father then proceeded to fall into the standard introductory small talk as I turned my attention to Abel.

"I am honored you joined us," Abel said, extending his hand graciously. It was only polite to take his hand, but the kiss he placed upon it sent an unpleasant tingling sensation through me, prompting me to withdraw my hand as soon as was decent, and fold my arms around myself.

"Please, have a seat," he said, gesturing towards a set of sofas near the entrance. Their frames were crafted of rich, dark mahogany, and their teal brocade fabric was reminiscent of peacock feathers. "You must be freezing. Can Isabel get you something to drink?"

"Oh, really, I'm fine."

"No, no," he insisted, calling out, "Isabel!"

The red-haired servant hurried in from the next room. "Yes, sir?"

"Fetch a nice sherry from the cellar for our guests," he directed with a flick of his wrist.

"Yes, sir," she replied, and departed.

Abel's eyes sparkled with an unspoken question: *Are you impressed? All of this could be yours.* Rather than respond, I averted my gaze, taking in the room's details. Elegant furniture surrounded us, much of it intricately carved mahogany, adorned with a variety of brass vases and sculptures. A grand piano stood in the room's corner, near an impressive fireplace mantel with an elaborate wrought iron screen.

"Abel," Mayor Sinclair said, "I wanted to show Elise's father the piano. We'll be back shortly." He winked and led the other parents away, leaving Abel and me to navigate the discomfort.

I examined my nails, realizing my left hand could use a trim before I played the violin again.

"How was the ride over?" Abel asked.

"Fine. Quite pleasant. Thank you," I replied.

"It was no matter."

After this brief exchange, an uneasy silence descended upon us. Yet I would soon long for that awkwardness, given what happened next.

Abel began to recount his family's trip last spring, during which his parents had purchased the new piano that his father was now showing mine. I listened without much interest until Isabel returned with two glasses of sherry. A misstep on the rug sent the poor girl tumbling, the drinks spilling into my lap. I gasped at the sudden cold, momentarily stunned, but also concerned for the girl who had fallen.

Abel rose from his seat beside me, an action which was interpreted as a rush to his servant's aid. Instead, he looked down upon her and growled, "*Foolish* girl."

His face contorted with rage as he glared at Isabel, who was cowering on the floor, her complexion ghostly pale.

"Do you not know how important this guest is?" he demanded.

"Abel, really…" I interjected, trying to defend poor Isabel, my earlier unease momentarily forgotten. He paid me no mind.

"And this sofa. *Ruined!*" He grabbed the servant's wrist, dragging her to her feet, prompting a cry of pain.

"I apologize! Sir, I truly apologize," Isabel gasped, her voice trembling.

Abel scoffed. "My *God*, woman. If you are unable to do something so damned *simple* as to serve a drink properly, you must seek employment elsewhere."

Her eyes welled with tears, her lips pressed firmly together.

His face was mere inches from hers as he continued, "After everything we have done for you," he spat.

"Really, it will wash out." I said, attempting to reassure both Abel and Isabel. "It was a simple mistake. Please, let her go."

Abel slowly peeled his eyes away from his poor servant and turned his attention to me. A chill formed within me as I noticed his formerly gray eyes had darkened to black.

Seizing the brief distraction, Isabel pulled her hand free from his grasp and quickly added, "I will make more, sir. Please, sir."

He glanced back at her, seemingly caught off guard. "This will not happen again."

Isabel nodded and exited the room without another word.

Abel's reaction, so abrupt and severe, occurred with such little acknowledgment it might have been as insignificant as swatting a fly. His eyes returned to their original gray hue.

"As I was saying, Paris in the Spring is really only so-so. If you really want somewhere enjoyable, I would highly advise Venice," he continued, as though nothing unusual had transpired.

I was left speechless by Abel's swift transformation, rendered all the more jarring by his nonchalance. Unsure what to say, I murmured, "Of course."

He prattled on while I barely listened, nodding occasionally as though riveted by his analysis of the virtues and weaknesses of Paris and Venice.

Isabel returned with the drinks. "Here you are," she said softly. "Again, sir—miss—I apologize. I will address the stain this evening, Mr. Sinclair. You'll never know it was there."

"I should hope not," Abel replied tersely.

"Thank you," I told Isabel. Her tear-streaked eyes reminded me of tormented young Oliver Hendrix. I leaned forward, wanting to speak up for her, to express my sympathy, but the words failed to leave my mouth, and she walked away.

Later, I rationalized that expressing sympathy might have further provoked Abel, that this fear prevented me from speaking out. It remains one of many things I have lived to regret.

Not long after this incident, the elder Sinclairs and my father returned from their exploration of the adjacent room, my father commenting on the fine wood carving on the piano's lid.

"Oh, what happened?" he inquired upon noticing the stain on my dress.

"It is nothing, it will wash out," I mumbled.

"Isabel," Abel told his mother. They exchanged a look of mutual disdain.

I looked at my father, uncertain what to say. Conveying my anxiety about the situation in present company was challenging.

At that moment, another servant entered the room, this one an older woman with dark hair.

"Dinner is served," she announced, rescuing me from further discussion of the unpleasant topic.

I was seated beside Abel at one of five finely arranged place settings. Mayor Sinclair presided at the head, opposite his wife, with my father positioned directly across from me. The table was draped with an exquisite white tablecloth, and atop it lay delicate china edged with blue flowers, surrounded by a variety of utensils.

The dinner was a sumptuous affair, beginning with an array of fresh salad greens lightly dressed in vinaigrette. This was followed by French onion soup, accompanied by slices of crusty bread, and concluded with roast beef served alongside a medley of fall root vegetables. Dessert was a light, lemony sponge cake adorned with a sugary glaze.

I tasted little of any of it, however, preoccupied as I was by the earlier scene in the sitting room.

My father had once told me that a man could be measured by his treatment of those beneath him. If this was indeed the case, the conclusion was grim, made only worse by my recalling William's strong sense of justice during the carriage ride over. Abel had always presented himself as the epitome of a gentleman, but clearly, this behavior was reserved for those he deemed worthy.

I observed Isabel as she efficiently cleared away the dessert plates, disappearing into the kitchen.

The thought struck me: if Isabel could provoke such ire in Abel, what of me? He had showered me with gifts over the preceding weeks—a gesture I had regarded with mild irritation at most—but perhaps there was something more ominous at play. Abel now seemed more like a predator, ready to strike with venomous intent if provoked.

And then I recalled the blackness which had clouded his eyes.

Abel's father interrupted my thoughts, unpleasantly reminding the table why it had been gathered. "Elise, we understand that you have been in mourning with the passing of your previous suitor. We are all deeply moved by your difficult circumstances."

"Thank you," I replied, shifting uneasily in my chair and glancing at my father.

"As they say, however, the world must go on."

I swallowed hard, my eyes drifting to the table before me. My father seemed blissful and satisfied, completely unaware of Abel's recent display.

Mr. Sinclair continued. "My son, Abel, you understand, has reached an age where it is only appropriate for him to marry and start a family. He had been thus far *resistant*," he said, a note of bitterness underlying his even tone. "That is, until his recent enchantment with you, and your talent for the violin."

Enchanted. Like a siren, perhaps, though an unwitting one.

"My dear Elise," Abel began, picking up where his father had left off. "I recognize that the circumstances under which I ask this are not the best, but, well, whenever does life go as we plan? " He smiled, an expression which he may have believed endearing, but which instead had an oily, unpleasant sheen. " I know you miss William. However, if you will allow it, I can, and will, give you a wonderful life. I desire to hear your sweet music each day. In return, I will give you everything you could ever desire."

I felt a flush rise to my cheeks as I focused intently on my hands, as though they held great interest. Despite Abel's poor treatment of Isabel, I had made a promise to my father. Breaking it now—based solely on Abel's behavior that I alone had witnessed— would jeopardize everything. If I raised objections to marrying Abel again, my father might perceive it as another excuse, albeit a more cunning one this time.

In any case, I had no intention of seeing this engagement through, did I? At least now, I could now proceed without guilt, prepared to break it when the time came.

Abel then produced a small box from his pocket, placing it before me.

"What is this?" I asked.

"Open it."

Inside, I found a gold ring set with a large, deep green emerald, flanked by two smaller diamonds. "It's beautiful," I acknowledged, for indeed, it was.

Abel's mother spoke next: "It was mine." If I had expected a pleased expression on her face, I was mistaken. She instead wore the expression of one tolerating an offensive odor.

"It's yours, if you choose to accept it," Abel added.

"I can only consent on one condition," I began, seeking my father's support. He looked at me solemnly as the room filled with silence. "My father has been ill recently." Though this objection seemed somewhat weak with my father looking so well across from me, I pressed on. "Therefore, I will agree to your proposal. However, I must insist our marriage is delayed until the completion of a project which my father and I have started."

The three Sinclairs exchanged glances, perplexed, perhaps thinking that after showcasing their wealth, I would surely grovel at Abel's feet. They did not understand the far better prospect awaiting me.

"What kind of project?" The eldest Sinclair's skepticism was undisguised.

"A violin. I have begun crafting a violin with my father."

There was a moment of silence following my statement, during which Abel's parents exchanged glances, engaging in a wordless debate. I observed them closely, trying to understand what was being communicated.

"*Victoria* would never have made such demands," his mother interjected.

"*Mother,*" Abel warned, glaring at his mother with a shadow reminiscent of the way he had regarded Isabel. My heart thudded into my throat.

Unfazed by this tension, Abel's father chortled, "Now, now, Ida, that subject is neither here nor there. If this is really what Abel wants, it is hardly worth the fight."

Regaining his composure, Abel redirected his focus from his mother to me, his expression softening into one of kindness and courtesy. "If that would bring you happiness, Elise," he said, "then I am willing to wait as long as necessary."

"That will indeed make me happy," I replied.

"Then it's settled," Abel's father declared, clapping his hands with the satisfaction of a concluded agreement. "Upon the completion of this violin, you and Abel will be wed."

And so, the decision was made.

Most of those around the table rejoiced at the resolution, my father included, albeit discreetly, perhaps mindful not to gloat. Within the celebratory atmosphere, I fulfilled my role, smiling as any recently engaged woman ought, even donning the ring that, despite its beauty, felt cumbersome and unwelcome upon my hand. Even the frosty demeanor of Abel's mother thawed as she bid me farewell, if only slightly.

Despite my cordial behavior, however, a sense of filthiness reigned within, inciting a desire for a good cleansing. This sensation persisted for the duration of the carriage ride and through preparation of my father's tea, gradually diminishing only once the emerald ring was safely placed within my dresser drawer.

I yearned for the day it could be returned to Abel.

Chapter Twenty-Two

The following morning was a moody Sabbath day, which meant that, despite my longing to continue work on the violin, it was not to be. With the engagement now officially agreed upon, the delay was even more unwelcome. The dreary, rainy day visible outside my window only deepened my melancholy.

As I walked to church, I clutched my shawl tightly around my shoulders, yearning for the comforts of home. But my worries only grew when, upon arriving, I was met with a ripple of excited whispers. Was my shirt stained? Had I neglected an important occasion? A nagging suspicion whispered the truth.

It was confirmed when the overly exuberant Mrs. Stanway approached, enveloping me in a heavily scented embrace. "Elise, dear! Oh, how wonderful, I've just heard the news."

My cheeks burned with embarrassment, surely glowing a scarlet hue. How could word have spread so quickly?

"What a lucky young woman you are," Mrs. Stanway continued with a knowing wink. "*Abel Sinclair*! I could never have imagined. Oh, we are all just so pleased to hear it. We have worried about you, you know, since William. You simply haven't been the same."

I offered a half-hearted shrug, unsure how to respond. Just then, Rebecca and her fiancé, Frederick, arrived, and Mrs. Stanway departed to spread her freshly confirmed gossip.

"Elise, such wonderful news," Rebecca exclaimed, her sincerity making it hard for me to correct her.

"Thank you," I replied, watching with envy as Frederick wrapped an arm around her slim waist, their happiness seemingly effortless.

Rebecca's pale eyes lit up, and she exclaimed, "Oh, Elise, he's here!"

No, he can't possibly be.

Yet, there he was—Abel, at my side, acknowledging well-wishers with a relish I couldn't muster. My forced smile grew increasingly more tiresome, as I pondered his unexpected presence.

The Sinclair family was not known for attending services at Chapel Grove. I presumed they worshiped elsewhere, though I hadn't given it much thought until now.

Whatever the case may be, there we were, Abel by my side acting like any proud groom-to-be, while I fantasized about escaping to my home and hiding in bed. Was it too late to feign illness before the service began?

Regrettably, such was not to be, and shortly thereafter, I found myself sitting on a pew in the chapel between Abel and my father, my hands folded tightly in my lap while the choir sand "Crown Him With Many Crowns". *The service will not be long*, I attempted to comfort myself. Then, my father and I could return home, prepare a simple meal, and indulge in light chores before continuing to work on the violin.

Reverend Willard commenced his address once the choir concluded.

"We know that our Father giveth and taketh away. We also know that when one door is closed to us, another will undoubtedly open. Though we have been saddened by the loss of our own William Whittaker, we know that the pairing of Abel Sinclair and dear Elise Knight will be fruitful and blessed." Reverend Willard's gaze met mine, his eyes twinkling. "Our Father, truly, works in mysterious ways."

My stomach churned. *Would there be no solace on this day?*

I caught the steely gaze of one of William's sisters, her look piercing. I imagined the thoughts racing through the minds of William's family, still heavy with grief. If only they understood that he wasn't forgotten. If only I could explain...

But many secrets had to remain unspoken, so I shrank into my seat as Reverend Willard's sermon began.

It would be incorrect, however, to assume this to be the end of my worries that day. Even as the Reverend began his sermon in earnest and the congregation fell into a kind of somnolence. The feeling of being watched persisted. *No one is watching, and if they are, it has to do with Abel.* Despite my attempts to ignore the feeling or reason it away, it continued to nettle me.

When it persisted, I looked about to discern the source. This did not take long, for I soon found its source to be a woman sitting several rows beyond. If I had thought the glare from William's sister venomous, it was nothing compared to this woman's.

Could she be a distant relation of Wiliam's?

The peculiarity of it scared me, as did the fact that nobody else seemed aware of the tension. Was she merely a figment of my imagination?

As she passed the collection plate, a momentary softening of her glare only deepened the mystery.

I recalled Abel's uneasy dinner with his family the night before. Victoria, his mother, had been mentioned. Yet this woman seemed closer to my father's age, too old to be a romantic rival. Her tightly pulled hair accentuated a stern, weathered visage.

The question remained: Who was she, and why did her presence so disturb me?

"Elise?" Abel had evidently noticed my attention diverted from the sermon.

"Do you know her?" I inquired, nodding toward the woman whose gaze had now centered on the front of the church.

"Who?" Abel glanced casually in her direction. "No, I don't believe I do." He then promptly returned his attention to the pastor. Vexed by his lack of interest, I was unconvinced he had actually seen the woman.

By the time I looked again, the woman had vanished. Her disappearance, rather than offering relief, only deepened my need for answers.

Who could she be?

This question occupied my mind throughout the rest of the service. When it concluded, Abel invited me for a carriage ride that afternoon.

"I apologize. I wish I could join you, but I fear I am not feeling well."

"Nothing a carriage ride in the fresh air couldn't fix, I am sure?"

I waffled for a moment, searching for the right words. An idea struck, and I whispered conspiratorially, "Womanly troubles, I confess."

"Be on your way, then."

There was no further argument.

As my father and I walked home, the rain eased to a light drizzle, mirroring the tumult inside my mind. The dreary weather, far from unwelcome, felt oddly comforting.

Once home, I retired to my room, shedding my church attire, hoping to discard my sour mood as well. My thoughts, although disturbed by the enigmatic woman from the sermon, were more consumed by the situation with Abel.

I sat on my bed in my underclothes, listening to the rain resume its drumming on the window, pondering what the rest of the day might bring.

My routine of playing for William at the cemetery had given way to my violin-making endeavors. The Sabbath might have been the perfect occasion otherwise, but the rain posed too great a risk for the instrument.

Yet, a far greater issue loomed: I was now formally and publicly engaged to Abel Sinclair.

I rested my elbows on my knees, cradling my head in my hands.

No, serenading my lost love would likely seem improper at best, and at worst, attract unwanted attention to my plans for the violin.

The thought doused me in a desperate kind of sadness, regretting the missed opportunities to do so before. Another small joy had been unceremoniously stripped away, with no opportunity to bid it farewell.

I hoped fervently that this pain, all of it, would be worth it in the end.

Chapter Twenty-Three

The morning air still carried whispers of the previous day's storm, a misty gray fog obscuring the sun as it crept over the horizon. Its rays touched me gently, awakening a clearheaded determination to continue my work.

My father was still asleep when I arrived downstairs. However, thanks to the guidance he had given me before, I was able to press on with crafting the belly plate. With him still asleep, none would chide me for skipping breakfast in favor of hastening the work. Thus, I headed straight to the workshop.

Aside from the soft rattle of the doorknob and the creak of the old wooden door, the workshop was serenely quiet in the morning stillness. Cobwebs adorned the corners, their strands glimmering with the first light of day, lending the place an enchanting quality. As a child, I had imagined my father aided by elves or fairies, much like the cobbler in old fairy tales. That morning, the workshop's ambiance stirred those impressions anew.

The workbench awaited just as I had left it—the spruce belly plate centered on its surface, a portion already hollowed from its heart, tools resting beside it. I placed my hand lightly on the inner surface, reacquainting myself with the piece. My fingers traced its thickness, assessing where to begin this morning's work.

The first few carvings with the knife felt unfamiliar, awkward to my hand, but soon the rhythm returned, freeing my mind to wander.

Not long ago, my father had explained that no violin could ever be identical to another. Even if crafted by the same artisan from the same tree, each would have its own unique character. Cassius shared similar beliefs, asserting that violins had temperaments and preferences. He sought not the work of an expert luthier, but a creation by—well, me.

Both men had suggested an intrinsic connection between a violin and its maker, a bond that was growing clearer as I progressed, becoming more attuned to the wood's needs, more emotionally intertwined with the violin's creation.

What struck me more intensely, however, was the way in which both my father and Cassius spoke of a violin as one might about a living organism, sensitive to its environment.

If this was an apt comparison, then perhaps the vibration of my fingers, adjoined as they were to someone in mourning, someone suffering, changed the wood in imperceptible, but important, ways.

Perhaps the violin could be swayed one way or another, nurtured or neglected, with every good and evil thought that crossed my mind affecting it in some intrinsic manner.

If this were indeed true, I pondered what relationship I might have with the violin. It would be mine, down to its very core. A piece of myself would, in the end, be intertwined with every fiber of its being.

Like a mother raising a child, perhaps.

Like God knitting together one of His children.

I paused to examine the thought, then cast the blasphemous thing aside as one would a dirty piece of laundry before continuing. However, my quiet meditations had rendered me unaware of my father's entrance into the room, and I was startled when a voice close behind me spoke.

"It looks nice so far." My father was just behind me, and his expression took on a note of apology. "I didn't mean to startle you, darling."

"Quite all right. I suppose I was just focused," I replied.

"Naturally," he conceded with a small pause as we both appraised the plate on my workbench. "Have you eaten?"

"No, not yet." My heart settled into its usual rhythm.

"You should."

"I will in a bit." I then registered his uncharacteristically meek manner, the way in which he shifted in his stance, and realized he wished for my company.

"Actually, I am rather hungry, now that I think of it." I set the unfinished belly plate and tools down on the bench.

My assumption proved correct, as scarcely into our breakfast, my father spoke softly, "I recognize yesterday must have been painful for you."

I busied myself with spreading butter on my bread. "It was."

He remained silent for a long while, sitting with his hands clasped before his still-empty plate, even as I cleaned the knife of butter and picked up the jar of raspberry preserves. "I am sorry."

"It's not your fault," I mumbled.

"I know I have pushed you into this."

His wringing hands and averted gaze inspired sympathy. I cleaned the knife and closed the jar of preserves, then set both within my father's reach.

"You did it for my good," I said, though not entirely convincingly, wishing to ease his conscience. It was true, after all.

"All the same. What with this illness seeming to have abated, I worry now that I have been too hasty."

"You could hardly have known. Nobody could have foreseen your recovery."

Except me, and Cassius. If my father had known the cause of his mysterious healing, perhaps we could have rejoiced together. The extra time given to us could have been enjoyed more thoroughly.

"You have done nothing wrong," I insisted, hoping he would take my word for it. Hoping once more that the violin would be worth all I had done in its pursuit.

"I hope you will not hold my decision against me," he said.

I replied, quite truthfully, "I would never."

Though the mood had lightened with my father having unburdened his conscience, guilt still hindered my appetite. Nevertheless, I finished what I could before helping my father clean up and accompanying him back to the workshop.

In the quiet therein, my mind was absorbed with thoughts of when I might finally complete the violin. By my best estimate, it would take at least four more weeks, the majority of which would be spent waiting for its lacquer to cure. Perhaps in warmer weather, this process might quicken, but that was not the current situation. Its completion would be largely at the mercy of the elements.

This thought dampened my spirits, but they were later revived when my father peeked over my shoulder.

"Would it trouble you if I took a closer look?" he asked.

"Not at all."

He picked up the belly piece, caressing its surface before measuring its thickness with a caliper. "It really does look nice, especially for a first violin." He continued measuring, then used a pencil to mark several points with an X. "Thin these a bit more, then you can move on to sanding the surface. Maybe this evening, you can even begin carving the f-holes."

"Is that so?" I basked in the warmth of his encouragement. Upon returning to work, I admired the piece myself. It was not as smooth as my father's, of course, but it would be sufficient for my needs.

When that moment arrived, I would receive something valuable beyond imagining.

Chapter Twenty-Four

Over the following days, the violin gradually took form. The completion of the belly plate, which included the creation and fastening of the bass bar, was a significant milestone. Before attaching the bass bar, I quietly slipped into my father's workshop after he had retired for the night and inscribed the words of 1 Corinthians 13. Although the message would eventually be hidden beneath the finished piece, its presence satisfied Cassius's request for a personalized instrument.

Once the glue had set, it was time to carve the f-holes into the belly plate. Departing from tradition, I added three notches instead of the customary single notch on each side of the swirl's center, as if to subtly convey "I – love – you" with each one.

It was nearly time to assemble the body when Abel showed up for another visit.

A sense of precognition accompanied his knock upon the door, such that I suspected exactly who had come without looking. I looked at my father as if to plea for a reprieve, but that same inner wisdom knew that it was no use. Reluctantly setting my work aside, I walked over to the door.

"Elise, a lovely morning," Abel greeted me.

"Indeed," I replied.

"I presume you have received the confections I sent?"

"Oh, yes," I answered, recalling the elaborately wrapped box of chocolates he'd sent earlier that week. "Thank you very much."

"I aim to please," he said with a touch of arrogance, which only heightened my desire to return to the violin, but it seemed I had no such luck. "I was thinking today would be a lovely day for a carriage ride together."

"Oh," I said tentatively, glancing back toward my work bench, then at my father, who had made himself scarce and was of no help. "I don't know…"

"Please, I insist," he urged.

Taking one last wistful look at my workstation, I reasoned that this brief interruption might secure me some uninterrupted work time later. "Okay," I agreed.

"I assure you, your violin will still be here when you return."

And so, we set off in our carriage, along much of the same route my father and I had taken the night of our dinner.

Along this route, Cassius's wagon was visible, something I had not noticed before.

"Did you visit his exhibition?" asked Abel.

My heart palpated, but I replied, "I did, yes."

"Rather pedestrian, if you ask me," Abel said dismissively. "Though I cannot for the life of me determine why he is still here."

I wondered if he would feel the same, had he seen the full extent of Cassius's talents.

"It seems he is fixing up his wagon," I suggested.

"Seems like he would be better off doing so in the city. Maybe make a bit more money while he does so, yes?"

"Perhaps," I responded, then glanced toward the woods once more. Our conversation dwindled, leaving me to ponder the tale of Humming Hattie once more. I contemplated how consumed one could become with grief.

"What is on your mind?" Abel asked.

I wavered for a moment before answering. "Nothing, really. Silly, really, but Humming Hattie."

"I beg your pardon?"

"Surely you have heard the story?"

He showed no sign of recognition.

"The ghost story about these woods, about the woman who drowned her children here."

"How very macabre," he remarked, and then we sat in silence again, until he gestured to my left hand. "Where is the ring? I've noticed you're not wearing it."

I swallowed. "Such a beautiful ring seemed unsuitable for the workshop."

He looked at me, something stirring behind his gray eyes which was difficult to read. "I am not as foolish as you think I am," said Abel softly.

"What do you mean?"

He tilted his chin upward, his mouth flattening into a thin line. "I suspect that, though you have formally agreed to my proposal, your heart is not entirely in it."

I wavered, but, now caught, determined I had no choice. "Yes, that is the case."

He nodded. "Perhaps it would help to divulge the full circumstances under which I have sought your hand."

"What circumstances would those be?" I asked, having already been made privy to the apparently hypnotic effect my violin playing had upon him.

"In recent months, Mother has been fussing after me incessantly," he said with a touch of amusement, then poorly mimicked her voice. *"A man your age, unmarried? People will think there's something wrong with you."* He then resumed his usual tone. "Her solution to the problem was Victoria Astor."

Victoria Astor, the daughter of the foundry owner John Astor, was a beautiful, vivacious green-eyed blonde girl about my age. She was not a common sight in Chapel Grove, preferring instead to spend her time abroad.

Given these facts, Abel's objection was unclear.

"She is very beautiful," I pointed out.

"As is a statue, or a painting. Tori also happens to be remarkably dull, and I very much wonder whether she has had an original thought in her life. But my mother—well, she sees what she wants to see. That is, the connections to be made through such an alliance between the Sinclairs and the Astors." He shook his head irritably. "Not exactly a match made in Heaven, if I may say so myself."

"Is that why your mother seemed so cold at dinner?"

"Yes, it is. Alas, I feel something stronger than my mother's social ambitions has brought you into my focus."

"And what is that?"

"Providence."

I looked upon him, quite taken aback. "What do you mean?"

"One day, when I had had my fill of Mother's harping about Victoria and her father's connections to the railroad and the foundry and the mines throughout the states, I left, insistent on solitude, allowing no servants to join me. I needed to clear my head. It was on that day that I heard something positively enchanting."

I remained silent at this reminiscence.

"Perhaps I am a silly romantic at heart, but I wish for a marriage filled with more than status or convenience."

"Like what?"

"Excitement. Intrigue. Someone who might surprise and delight me. My mother cares little for my happiness, focused as she is on how good such a marriage between Tori and myself would make her look, as if she reigns as queen and I as nothing but a pawn. But this is not a game. This is my life, of which I am the master. Her incessant nagging and her committed ignorance of my desires drove me out into the wilderness, and in that frustration, I heard something calling out to me, like a siren to a lonely sailor at sea."

I fiddled with my nails nervously, reminded of how I had made the same comparison myself. Did he remember the fate of sailors who answered such temptation?

"When I saw you playing your violin that day, a seed was planted in my heart, an idea that perhaps could solve both our woes. I know that the loss of William, so young and apparently healthy, was a tremendously unforeseen tragedy. That is why I thought, why not escape Chapel Grove together and create our own destiny?"

Creating my own destiny. That is precisely what I was trying to do by making the violin.

"Although I may not be your first choice, Elise, I see in you someone with more potential than Chapel Grove can offer. You were not schooled in any private institutions, yet your father has taught you so much. You are bright and talented. Think of the opportunities a place like France or Italy would afford you. That is something you could do once we are married. You would have freedom beyond your imagination."

Briefly, only briefly, I confess to envisioning such a future. There was a particular brightness of hope about the scene. With my father free of his mortal pains and afflictions, could I accept such a thing?

The flattering words he spoke were hard to dismiss outright, as was the thought of experiencing a world beyond all I had imagined.

Abel continued to speak, however, and the reality of my situation was once again made clear.

"It could all be yours, should you see this engagement through."

If thou therefore wilt worship me, all shall be thine. Like a striking lightning bolt, my mind forcefully recalled the passage of scripture wherein Satan tempts the Savior, offering Him all the kingdoms of the world in exchange for His worship.

I then recalled the scene from dinner the other evening, the way Abel had transformed before my eyes, enraged by a simple mistake, despite the poor girl's penitence.

No, there was far more to Abel than the gentlemanly façade before me. An ugliness lay within, obscured by an attractive exterior. Attaching myself to Abel would be like chaining myself to a lion thought to be tame but instead lay in wait for the opportunity to strike.

My mouth went dry at the sudden discernment. Abel turned his gaze toward the front of the carriage, his jaw clenched in apparent displeasure at my speechlessness. I hardly knew what to say under the circumstances, but when he looked at me again, I uttered, "I must finish the violin."

"And then the marriage shall proceed?" His honeyed tone was replaced with one of formality.

I thought about this statement, and, lying by omission, nonetheless said, "Yes. Yes, it will."

Abel settled comfortably against the back of his seat. "Tell me more about this violin, then."

———————————————————

We chatted along the way home as best as I could manage, but I was still glad when we returned to my home, where Abel assisted me instead of the coachman.

"Farewell, dear Elise," he uttered, placing a gentle kiss on my hand. "I vow, I shall win your heart yet."

Chapter Twenty-Five

Now and then, there are days in one's life which appear shrouded in an aura of gold. The day following the carriage ride with Abel, turned out to be one of those mysteriously lovely days, the first I could recall since before William passed away.

The day began unassumingly enough. The sun barely peeked over the cloudless horizon, promising a gorgeous farewell to September. Though it was earlier than I usually preferred to wake, I felt remarkably refreshed this morning. It seemed like the perfect day to venture into town before my father rose for the day.

The walk into town was lovely. I reveled in the dewdrops clinging to the grass, the crisp morning air, and the early birds serenading along the creek road.

Though few others were about at that hour, I cheerfully greeted everyone I encountered on my way to the general store. There, I purchased a package of bacon—nice and thick as my father liked it—along with apples from Purcell's orchard and freshly roasted coffee beans.

Afterward, I stopped by Yancy's bakery to buy fresh, flaky pastries filled with blackberries. Gerald Yancy himself kindly gifted them to me.

"You really don't have to," I protested, offering him money to show that I was perfectly able to pay for the pastries.

"It's just wonderful to see you happy," he replied. "That is enough payment for me."

I thought for a moment about refusing again but realized it would be futile. "Thank you, Mr. Yancy."

"You're most welcome, Ms. Knight."

As I left, the bell above the door chimed as it swung shut, and I stepped onto Main Street, which had come to life. The lively activity was pleasing once again, invigorating after my long period of withdrawal.

An unexpected reunion with Rebecca was a delightful surprise, and I felt no jealousy as we discussed her visit to Mrs. Miller for wedding dress alterations in preparation for her upcoming marriage to Frederick.

"I am so happy for you," I said, embracing her warmly.

"Thank you. So, you'll be there?" she asked hopefully, having just informed me that the wedding had been postponed until the end of November.

My heart raced at the realization that, by that time, my William would be home from his premature foray into death. We could attend Rebecca and Frederick's wedding together.

"We will," I assured her.

Looking back, I realized she had no idea who exactly I was referring to when I mentioned "we," as I was lost in the pleasant imaginings of the days to come.

"Before then, of course, we have the Harvest Festival to look forward to, don't we?" Rebecca remarked.

The Harvest Festival was approaching, and I had nearly forgotten about it. "I nearly forgot all about it," I remarked. This annual event in Chapel Grove was scheduled for the evening of All Hallows' Eve.

Perhaps William would be back for the occasion, provided I could complete the violin swiftly.

Could such a thing be dreamed of?

Rebecca went on her way, and I caught sight of Cassius's wagon. It had been further upgraded and repaired, judging by the bolder red paint upon the sign advertising MCCALMONT'S CURIOSITIES. Beneath these words, tantalizing previews had been added of the things within:

REAL PRESERVED MERMAID

PERUVIAN SHRUNKEN HEADS

AUTHENTIC EGYPTIAN MUMMY

A good way to advertise, to be sure, though none of those exhibitions held any of the wonder of the resurrection flute. I couldn't help but wonder why he wasn't more eager to display such a wondrous artifact.

After briefly pondering this, I made my way back home. The creek road was more enchanting than I remembered since my childhood days. With all these delightful developments, I returned in high spirits, humming melodiously. As expected, my father was still not awake, so I began preparing breakfast.

Just as the first batch of bacon was set to cool, my father entered the kitchen.

"Someone has been busy," he noted, taking in the pleasant aroma. "It smells wonderful. And pastries?"

"Yes," I replied, a hint of coyness in my voice. "Blackberry."

"What have I done to deserve this? Something good, I hope?"

"It is simply…" I said, thinking how to phrase it. "A nice day. The kind of day which was deserving of such a treat."

My father regarded me intently. "Indeed," he agreed, then served a pastry onto each of our plates.

As we began eating, my father cleared his throat, signaling a forthcoming conversation.

"Elise, I've been thinking," he started, a smile playing on his lips. "Your work on the violin has truly inspired me, and I was considering—well, I hardly dare get ahead of myself, but..." He paused to wipe his face with a napkin. "Perhaps I might begin crafting another one myself."

"You are feeling that well?" I asked incredulously.

"It seems unwise to say so, but yes, I am," he confirmed.

"I am glad to hear it," I said, far understating my joy. My father, who was once so ill, now felt well enough, optimistic enough, to consider such a project.

His remarkable turnaround made me wonder whether Cassius might have been mistaken, a thought that lingered as my father and I went to the workshop. Although Cassius had cautioned that the elixir would not cure my father, he was indeed *better* than before. Healthier. Perhaps Cassius had been cautious not to overpromise, or maybe my father had not been as ill as we had feared.

Regardless, when my father set about selecting the wood for his violin, I dared to dream that he might live far beyond William's return.

Might he live long enough to become a grandfather?

As I worked on the neck of my own violin, I watched my father trace the body mold onto the wood—a process he had once taught me. He caught me observing him, his blue eyes vibrant with health and vigor.

Was my hope so unfounded? How could I doubt his full recovery when he seemed so restored, no longer the man who had once been so gravely ill?

In fact, he had even regained weight, despite our rather modest meals.

My thoughts danced upon the flowers which had bloomed upon the developments of the morning, waltzing from whether William and I might have a little boy or girl first, pirouetting around the idea of more than one child, finishing in a grand jeté to the idea that, perhaps my father's next violin might be a gift for my own child, who might learn to play as I did.

The rest of the day unfolded as beautifully as it had begun, filled with the best of emotions. As I lay my head upon my pillow, it was clear that I must never share these hopes with Cassius, for fear he might shatter them with his skepticism.

Perhaps foolishly, I chose to trust what I saw and drifted into a restful sleep, filled with immense hope for the future and pleasant dreams of what it could hold.

Chapter Twenty-Six

I should never have expected such transcendence to last.

Some of the glimmer remained as the sun rose the next morning, a bit of fairy dust in the air as I contemplated all that had occurred. My father, feeling well enough to start crafting a violin of his own! Perhaps he truly was on the mend.

Upon entering the workshop, my father completed the task of resetting the sound post on another violin before turning his attention to his personal project to work on his own. The joy radiating from him was infectious, inspiring hope as I embarked on carving the scroll for my violin. I traced the spiral onto the blank, my father guiding me through the initial steps of carving. Meanwhile, he began the process of thinning the back of his new instrument. He spoke of potential artistic modifications, inspired by the enhancements I'd incorporated into mine—at least, those he was aware of.

By midday, I had completed some of the initial carving on the scroll. Motivated as I was to work with haste, the growing strain in my back was impossible to deny. My aching muscles cried out for relief. I then realized that my eyes had been fixated so intently on the piece that, when I finally gazed into the distance, my vision blurred.

I attempted to resist the obvious need for rest, but a slip resulted in a sizable cut on my finger, courtesy of the chisel. The sudden, sharp pain elicited a gasp. I placed the piece on the workbench, noticing blood already staining its surface.

"Are you all right, Lissie?" my father asked.

"All is well, it is just a cut." I applied pressure with my other hand to stem the bleeding.

"Are you sure?" He set aside his work and approached, noting the blood on the wood.

"The varnish should cover that," I remarked, recalling an earlier suggestion to leave traces of myself on the violin. This realization dulled the pain considerably.

He nodded, though his brow remained furrowed. "Do you need help cleaning up?"

"No, I can manage." He cast a momentary glance backward at his own work area. Brief, but enough that I noticed it. Far from being offended by it, his investment in the work brought me great joy.

"Shall I fetch you a bandage?" he offered.

"No, really. I will go in and take care of it. It is not such a major injury, and I believe I could use a break anyway." I gestured toward his work bench. "Please, return to your work."

He hesitated a moment, then acquiesced. "If you are certain."

As my father eagerly resumed his work, I felt a compulsion— and acted on it—to discreetly wipe a bit more blood from my finger onto the block. For William.

Rising from my seat, my muscles protested vehemently, much tighter than I had realized. Despite my reluctance to pause, taking a break was the wisest choice. Pushing myself further could lead to more serious mistakes, not as easily overlooked.

While tending to my injured finger and wrapping it in cloth, I thought perhaps a short walk would be an ideal break for both body and mind. Outside, a gentle breeze rustled the leaves, and the beautiful autumn weather beckoned.

Bandaged and refreshed, I returned to the workshop.

"Heading out for a walk," I said, and my father turned to me from his work. "Can I fetch you anything before I go?"

"No, dear, go and enjoy yourself." He returned to his task, and I set off.

Choosing to walk was immediately validated by the peacefulness it instilled. The air along the creek road carried the smoky aroma of wood smoke, and fallen leaves crunched underfoot. This respite would surely leave me rejuvenated and ready to resume my work.

However, midway down the creek road, my plans were altered when an unexpected presence emerged from the forest ahead.

Humming Hattie, my anxious mind supplied, but rationality quickly dismissed this thought. No ghost was coming from the woods to harm me.

Yet, who could it be? It was unusual to encounter anyone along this path.

The woman wore a brown dress which fell to her feet. Her gray hair, though pinned back, was unruly in places, defying any attempt to tame it. As she approached, recognition rooted me in place.

She was the unknown woman from church the previous Sunday, the one who had stared at me with such hatred in her eyes.

I stood frozen, casting a backward glance toward home. Should I run, I wondered? Would my father hear me if I screamed?

And yet, a kind of intuition calmed my spirit as she drew closer.

"What do you want?" I asked.

Contrary to what I expected, she did not seem angry. Instead, a quiet distress lingered on her face, a storm brewing in her eyes. However, her next words disturbed me once again.

"I do not mean you harm," she began. "But I know what you are doing with Mr. McCalmont. It must stop at once."

Chapter Twenty-Seven

Exposed, I found myself standing there, uncertain about how to proceed. Should I confess to everything or feign ignorance?

"I know that your intended has passed away," the woman continued.

I stood in silence, neither affirming nor denying the statement.

"I also know you are working on a violin."

Such was hardly a secret, I reassured myself. "Yes, with my father," I replied.

"I also know what it is intended to do."

My mouth fell open, and I shook my head slightly in disbelief. How could she possibly know?

"Do you know Mr. McCalmont?"

"I do," she confirmed, her face tense, "and I am aware that you do not comprehend the forces with which you are meddling. If you did, you would cease immediately."

"I do not understand what you mean." My words caught in my throat, emerging with a slight quiver.

"I mean that I have seen Mr. McCalmont's work before."

"What do you mean? Who are you?"

"It matters not who I am, but who Mr. McCalmont really is." She opened her bag and pulled something from within. "This is Louella. Louella Bennett."

The woman handed me a photograph of a sad-looking girl with dark hair. She appeared to be only a few years younger than myself, her round cheeks betraying her youth. She held a sleeping child in her arms—a younger sister, perhaps—barely more than a baby. The child wore a light-colored lace dress and a matching cap, under which tiny, coiled tendrils peeked out.

"She was my friend," she began, pausing to draw a handkerchief from her bag and dab at her eyes. "She was so lovely. So young. Younger than yourself, in fact, when she had baby Sophia."

Realization dawned upon me; the girl and the child were mother and daughter. The woman's use of the past tense did not escape my notice.

"She was the most pleasant child, cherished by all who knew her, despite the circumstances of her birth."

"What do you mean?" I asked.

"Louella was hardly more than a girl herself when Sophia was, regrettably, born out of wedlock. As such, Louella suffered great losses—to her status, her reputation—when she fell pregnant, and especially after Sophia's birth. She had been, in a way, marked." She shook her head. "I loved Louella all the same, but I was the exception. Most of the town, even her friends, turned away from her. They were, perhaps, worried for their own reputations. But whatever the reason, she needed someone. They needed someone, and my late husband and I opened our home to them both."

"That was kind of you," I said gently, but the woman shook her head in disagreement.

"It is more a testament to the goodness of Louella than any remark on my own character, I believe. Even if I had cared for my own reputation, I could not leave her unaided. But despite the scandal, Louella was so happy with the birth of her daughter. Just a wonderful mother." She paused for a moment, seeming lost in her reminiscence.

"What happened to them?" I asked tentatively, uncertain whether I wanted to delve deeper into this painful memory.

The woman's eyes misted. She squeezed them shut and brought a hand up to shield her tears. "I loved her—loved them both," she said, a tremor in her voice. "I was heartbroken when... When she awoke one morning to find little Sophia still, cold, and blue in her crib."

"How awful," I replied, aghast.

She nodded, wiping her eyes. "Louella was devastated. She blamed herself," she said, then added with notable bitterness, "as did everyone else."

I looked at her questioningly, prompting her to elaborate.

"They believed it was her fault for having an illegitimate child. God's punishment," she said, shaking her head. "But I didn't believe any such thing. Louella may have been spared these accusations, however, for in the days following Sophia's death, she could hardly lift herself from bed. I recall her agony upon becoming full with milk which her baby would no longer nurse. Never have I witnessed such thorough devastation, for Louella had sacrificed everything for Sophia. The little girl was the only blood family she had left. She had done every possible thing to care for her, and then, she was gone."

An image of a tiny casket and tiny swaddling clothes flashed before my eyes.

"But then one day, Louella changed. It was like a switch had flipped inside her."

"What happened?" I asked.

"I inquired after the change several times before she finally told me. It was only after confronting her about a conversation I witnessed between her and a strange man in the garden that she told me," she sniffed. "The man was Mr. McCalmont, of course." She paused, holding my gaze intently, her anger resurfacing. "He made a deal with her, too."

Apprehension settled over me. "What sort of deal?"

"I was the only one she confided in. If only I had done more," she said, gazing upwards.

"What kind of deal did she make?" I prodded gently.

"A flute," she revealed, "Her baby back in exchange for a flute. That was the deal that Cassius presented to her."

A flute, I thought.

A flute.

My stomach dropped. My God.

"You see, Louella was highly skilled in whittling flutes. They were highly sought after. But this flute was different. She became obsessed. As one would if promised such a thing, I supposed."

The resurrection flute, the one which had brought the raven back to life. It must be.

So it was true.

I stood still, trying to comprehend it all, uncertain if I wanted to know more, but the woman was undeterred. "I begged her not to trust him, told her the whole notion was utter madness, for nothing can resurrect the dead. Yet, she was convinced, utterly certain that this man could fulfill his promise."

"What happened?" I asked quietly.

"You must understand that though Mr. McCalmont promises the world, he will only leave everything dear to you burned to the ground," the woman said, pursing her lips and closing her eyes tightly, as if bracing herself to divulge the young woman's dreadful fate. When she spoke again, her voice was softer and lower than before. "The last time I saw Louella, she was out of her mind. Screaming. Crying. Several men required to restrain her, to keep her from scratching at herself. She had already drawn blood from her arms."

My blood ran cold at the mental image.

"I hardly recognized her," said the woman.

"But what happened?" I implored.

"She came to me one day and showed me the flute. She told me it was finished, that she was set to meet with Mr. McCalmont and make the trade. Oh, I wish I had known then what I know now. Truthfully, I do not know the specifics of what happened. Only that when she had been gone for several hours, I ventured out to seek after her, wondering what had come of her. It was then that I saw her being taken away." She paused intensely. "To Kirkham."

"Kirkham?" I asked, scarcely able to believe it. "You cannot mean Kirkham, the asylum?"

"The very same," she said grimly.

"No," I said, not wishing to believe this. Kirkham's dark, forbidding building was visible on the route to the nearby city. Even passing the road beside the facility inspired dread. It was hard to imagine the young woman in the photograph so disturbed as to be dragged there, resisting and screaming. "How long ago was this?"

"Many years ago," she said. "Her parents have since moved, not wanting to be reminded of the whole sordid affair. The town was never the same, though they quietly tried to forget and move on."

"What do you think happened to her?" I asked.

"Something awful, to be sure," she said, her face paling. "Nothing I wish to imagine." She steadied herself. "Nonetheless, while she was torn from her life, Mr. McCalmont and his abominations quietly left town before I had the chance to give him a piece of my mind. Regularly did I think about avenging my poor friend, but I determined that vengeance is of the Lord. It would not do to darken my soul after what I saw happen to my poor friend. I eventually healed, as much as one does from a thing like that." She pulled out her handkerchief again, appearing in need of a moment to compose herself. "The last I heard, Louella was still in the asylum. She is living as a shell of her former self after the staff felt a lobotomy appropriate treatment for her situation."

An icy shudder coursed through my body. "How awful," I said, knowing the words were inadequate to convey the ruinous events.

"It is all well and done now, as far as Louella is concerned. None of that can be undone. What matters now is what we do moving forward."

I remained silent.

"You see, I tried my utmost to forget the entire sordid affair. I believed it was all over. Yet, in recent days, I've been tormented by dreams of Louella and baby Sophia—ghastly, sinister dreams. I saw Louella as she once was and as she is now, reduced to her helpless state. Other dreams featured sweet baby Sophia, but not as she was, instead as some kind of monster. Her laughter was not the warm, sweet laughter of an infant but something cold, menacing—evil." She placed a trembling hand to her forehead at the memory, then proceeded, despite the evident effort it took. "I awoke from these dreams many times, drenched in a cold sweat. It reached a point where I could not close my eyes without being besieged by these distorted visions. Initially, I could not comprehend them; I only longed desperately for relief. I resolved to find Mr. McCalmont, to discover what his current actions were. Upon finding him with you and learning of your situation, I realized it was happening once more."

I sat quietly, absorbing everything I had learned.

"You must understand that whatever this man has promised you is not to be trusted," she said bluntly, interrupting my thoughts.

"Mr. McCalmont has been good to me," I replied softly.

Beyond the promise of William's resurrection, had not Cassius provided the gift of more time with my father? The day my father and I spent working on violins together was a joy we would not have otherwise had. None of that would have been possible, had Cassius not provided the means for it.

She shook her head firmly. "I must insist—he cannot be trusted."

"You have not even told me your name," I said, shaking my head and taking a cautious step back. "Why shall I trust you?"

"My name is Vada," she stated dismissively. "But that scarcely matters, for can't you see? You may not know me, but if he has struck a bargain similar to the one he made with my poor Louella, he's only destined to bring more destruction and misery." Her voice rose in desperation, only to fall in her next statement. "I know you loved your William." Her tone was suddenly tender, a softness she had not previously shown.

"I do," I whispered, unwilling to echo her past tense, a detail she didn't overlook.

"Of course. There is no doubt that his loss has been devastating to you. But, my dear, he is gone. He is dead. You must remember that man cannot bring back the dead. Only God can do that, and if he has seen fit to allow your love to die, then that is all there is to be said." Her words rang similarly to all those who said it was for the best, and it rankled me. "My friend dabbled in the dark arts at the behest of this man, this demon, and received only devastation in exchange for her trouble. Meanwhile, he has evidently continued living his life without inhibition. But please, please, turn away from him. Cast him away from you, no matter what you think you might gain. *He is not to be trusted.*"

Vada assessed me critically as I nervously chewed a fingernail. "I can tell you do not fully believe me. Perhaps you have no reason to. I know that I am a stranger to you. I know that this Cassius must have done things for you, incredible things. I know it was true of Louella. Though I loved her so dearly, I could not save her. I failed her and cannot allow it to happen again."

"I will consider it," I mumbled.

"I wish you would not," she retorted. "I wish you would simply take me at my word, as only misery awaits down this road," she continued despite my silence. "I know that as sure as anything. I shudder to think who else he has done this to, but if Louella had been his only victim, she would be more than enough. Please know I am far more concerned about your welfare than Mr. McCalmont could ever be. He seeks only what he can extract from you and will then discard you and move on."

I studied her, deep in thought. She glanced skyward and made the sign of the cross on her chest.

"I know I may have overwhelmed you, but please, I beg you, heed my warning." She gazed at the photograph she held of Louella and the baby, caressing it gently. "And please, keep this as a reminder of my warning." She handed it to me. "It is the only picture Louella had taken with baby Sophia."

A thought occurred to me. I pointed at the photograph, uncertain how to ask, but needing to know. "Is she..." She cut me off, preempting the question.

"Yes, the baby in the picture has passed on. Louella wanted something to remember her by before her burial. It was left behind when she went to the asylum. Her parents, when they came to retrieve her personal effects, found it too painful to look at and so, I took it."

"This must mean a lot to you," I remarked, touched by the gesture.

"It does. It means more than you know," she murmured, sniffling. "Please, I will leave you in peace. But I beg you, heed my warning."

At this, she left me alone to my tortuous thoughts.

Chapter Twenty-Eight

What had Cassius done to Louella?

My gaze fell upon the photograph of her with baby Sophia. The little girl, with her delicate white dress and cap, looked perfectly suited for the waters of baptism, but was instead destined for the soil of eternal rest. Perhaps because the circumstances of this photograph were now known to me, Louella's suffering appeared to radiate well beyond the confines of the portrait.

I recalled my discovery of William's body, lifeless in his fields, and the emptiness which followed his death. How desperate Louella must have felt, having given everything for this child. Losing this beautiful baby, cheeks full, arms sweetly dimpled, who looked healthy in every way, must have been heart-rending.

A raven—perhaps the same raven—called out from somewhere beyond the trees, mocking me in my pursuit of answers. I cradled my head in my hands. Had Cassius broken his promise to Louella, absconding with the flute before resurrecting her daughter? That seemed unlikely. Perhaps such a betrayal might sadden Louella, even rightfully enrage her, but her madness told a different story.

I reminisced on the night of the raven's resurrection. The stink, the flies, the pathetic haphazardness with which it lay on the ground had all suggested the bird had been deceased. Upon Cassius playing the flute, the bird had been pumped full of life once more as if with a bellows, then flown away as if nothing had happened.

The flute appeared to, indeed, have the power to revive the dead.

Perhaps it only worked halfway, a sinister voice goaded.

A half-dead monster of a thing shaped roughly like the little girl in the photograph flashed before my eyes.

Scarcely after shaking this thought away, my mind's eye then conjured up a vision of Louella as Vada had described last seeing her: a wounded animal, cornered. She was a mother bear who had lost the battle to protect her cub, held held down by asylum workers who desperately tried to control her lest she injure herself further.

Blood dripped down her arms.

Her expression was wild and frenzied as she thrashed, trying to break free.

Then she was carted off to Kirkham, where she was lobotomized. Her mind, tampered with. I had heard of such procedures, used for those deemed incurable, knowing they could render a person little more than a walking shell.

A croak from the trees revealed the raven was still nearby.

Could it have been a tragic accident? My heart fixated on an image of a creature akin to the one Sophia might have become, only fashioned from William's remains.

The thought was unfathomable. I placed the photograph carefully in my bag, unable to endure Louella's accusatory gaze.

If such a fate were possible, I deserved to know. Perhaps the risks of this deal needed to be better understood.

Cassius needed to provide answers, and I was determined to get them.

I made my way to his wagon, my steps purposeful and eyes downcast, not wishing to greet anyone who might be out at that time of day.

Cassius was nowhere to be seen, but I knocked on the side of his wagon, hoping he was inside.

He opened the door.

"Hello, Elise," he greeted me politely, but surely, after noticing the fire in my eyes, he asked, "What is it?"

"I need to know about Louella."

One might hope that catching someone off guard like this would reveal guilt, recognition, or even anger, but his face remained indifferent. "Louella?"

"Louella Bennett," I repeated insistently. Vada had known too much about Cassius for me to dismiss her as merely mistaken.

"What about her?"

"What happened to her?" I pressed.

Cassius sat heavily on the step leading up to his wagon. "A tragic story, really. So young, so haunted. The poor dear." He spoke as though it was a matter of happenstance, an old story, something he had merely heard of, but had no part in.

This casualness infuriated me. "What did you do to her?"

A venomous flash of green shone in his eyes. "What are you implying?"

"A woman came to see me, Vada. She told me of the flute, how Louella made the flute for you after her daughter died, and how Louella now resides in Kirkham."

After a prolonged look at me, Cassius shook his head. "Elise, you must understand, these truths exist, yes, but they are not interconnected. The coincidence of two events doesn't always imply they influenced each other."

"But then, what happened to her?"

"Grief is an enormous burden, as you're well aware. Vada herself was so troubled following the loss of the child and her friend, it seems only natural she was desperate for an explanation. She pinned the loss—both losses, as I recall—on me." He sighed regretfully. "Perhaps she is hardly to blame. It is only natural for one to search for meaning in loss, to wish for revenge even when there is none to be had."

"But what could have possibly happened to drive Louella to such madness?"

Cassius rubbed his temples. "I do not wish to discuss this," he responded quietly.

"I do," I insisted. "I must. What happened? What happened to Louella?"

Cassius looked up at me, his hands resting in his lap, his expression somber. "Nothing will happen to you."

"What happened?" I demanded, my voice almost rising to a shout.

A vein throbbed at his temple, but I remained steadfast. The more evasive he was, the more essential the answers seemed.

I kneeled before him. "I need to know, Cassius," I urged, gently placing my hand on his, hoping the unexpected gesture might persuade him. He regarded me with sadness.

"Do you remember the night on which I resurrected the raven?"

"Of course."

"Do you recall what I said, about how much more powerful the violin would be?"

"I do."

"The flute is indeed powerful. I believed it to be sufficient for resurrecting a small being—a child." He swallowed hard, and I felt a flicker of regret for disturbing such an evidently painful memory, although it felt necessary. "I was mistaken." He ran a hand through his hair, disheveling it. "It failed. The failure was too much for Louella to bear."

"But *why*?"

"As I said, grief is a heavy burden to bear. In Louella's situation, I believe it was simply more than she could take to be so thoroughly, devastatingly disappointed by the outcome."

I tiptoed around the subject, pondering how much further I could push without halting the flow of information. "But...what exactly was the outcome?"

"Is it not obvious? *Death*!" Cassius exclaimed. "The child could not be revived, and nothing more could be done. As for Vada, she blamed me for Louella's inability to cope."

"That is all?" I asked. "The child simply... did not come back?"

His eyebrows lifted. "Is such misery not enough for you?"

"No, that is not what I meant," I began to explain. "Can you blame me for wondering, after hearing of such a thing..."

"You think I harmed her? As though I am a devil who intended evil toward someone I sought only to help?"

"Cassius, I—I apologize. I had no idea,"

"If you think me so evil, perhaps it is best you do not complete the violin," he said quietly.

"No." Even after all I had discovered, the thought horrified me.

"Your father is better, I noticed," he remarked acidly, inciting a twist of guilt in my side.

"He is, and I know—*I know*—it is all thanks to the treatment you gave me."

"If you think so little of me, perhaps I should take it back."

"No," I pleaded. "No, please."

"Do you have any idea of the lengths I went to obtain the elixir? I nearly died pursuing it, and the last of it…"

I barely heard the rest of his sentence; my mind was a blur. I processed his words. "I thought you traded for it."

He met my gaze steadily, his face revealing nothing. "In a manner of speaking, I did."

"Did you trade for it, or did you not?"

"What does it matter?" he deflected. "Has it not granted you more time with your father? Why does the cost matter?"

"It matters," I retorted, my voice trembling with quiet rage. "Just as much as Louella and her daughter mattered."

"Fine. If you must know, I stole it. I befriended the village elders, who spoke of a substance that could extend life, perhaps even grant immortality, and I became obsessed. I had to have it, but I knew they'd never part with it willingly. I sneaked in under cover of darkness, seized the bottle, and left, never to return."

"You did this to your friends? Stole something sacred to them?"

"With all due respect, you know little of what you speak, Elise. These people—if you can call them that—were savages. The elixir was saved *only* for their elites, their *chosen ones*." He shook his head. "The commoners of the village were nothing—*nothing!*—to them, fit only to do their unpleasant work at best, or at worst, be sacrificed to their gods, killed in front of their poor families who would be reassured that their slaughter was done for the good of the village."

A strange ringing filled my ears as this revelation settled in my mind.

Cassius lowered his voice, drawing closer. "Elise, understand me. I never wished ill for that poor girl. She deserved better, but I did what I could."

"What if it happens again?" I asked, unable to hide the tremor in my voice. "With William?"

"It will not," he assured me. "Please do not think of me as a monster. I sought to help Louella, as I stole the elixir with the best of intentions. As I have told you, meddling with these matters can be tricky business. I can only assume that she chose not to follow my instructions, to her great detriment."

I stared into the distance, my thoughts spiraling.

"As I said, the more of yourself you put into the violin, the more powerful it shall be. Did I not?"

"You did."

"So—if you must take anything from Louella's tragic story, please, take that. Follow my direction. Sacrifice all you can to the pursuit of creating this violin, and ensure you take no half-measures."

I looked upon the ground, twisting a strand of hair between my fingers, before meeting his eyes once again. "Are you certain you can bring William back?"

"Yes," he replied without hesitation.

"But how can you be so sure?"

"In the same way I was sure that I could bring the raven back. In the same way that I was sure the elixir would help your father. And it has, has it not?"

"Yes, it has," I acknowledged. "Better, even, than I expected."

"Then please—trust me. I know how much more powerful the violin will be than the flute could have ever been. You saw it work for yourself. The raven represents the power the flute holds. I know our friend has been nearby in the past few weeks, and I am sure you have seen it, too."

"I have."

"The flute is merely constrained by its own nature in ways the violin will not be," he reassured me.

"I am afraid," I confessed softly.

"Be not afraid," he said. "Only believe... And please, do not doubt or disparage me again Follow my instructions with exactness, and your results will be vastly different. As I have said, this can be a tricky matter. We must tread carefully. Now, if you will excuse me, the hour is getting late, and I confess, I am quite fatigued. Please return home and ensure your father receives today's provision of elixir."

"I will," I promised.

He shut the door, leaving me to return home filled with more questions than had been answered.

Chapter Twenty-Nine

During my return trip home, I began to contemplate what had previously been unthinkable: that is, allowing William to rest in peace.

This notion, though still unwelcome, was catalyzed by my discomfort with Louella's story. It became clear to me that her relentless pursuit and curiosity had caused more harm than if she had been left to mourn her memories of Sophia as they were.

Whatever had happened in the interim, whether she faced other horrors which broke her fragile mind, I knew not; but it hardly mattered in the end. It was during the creation of the flute that her mind finally broke.

Not ready to confront my father, I stayed out of sight, leaning against the brick wall of the workshop. I gazed at the half-bare trees lining the creek road.

It was among those trees that William first kissed me, I recalled suddenly.

The trees were fuller then—late spring—offering more seclusion. We had simply been sitting by the creek, chatting about something or other, when he placed his hand on mine. I had harbored romantic feelings for him for a while, but this was my first realization that they were mutual.

That touch had stirred something within my soul, as if I had been building up to that moment all my life, as if it were a waypoint on the path my God had lain out for me.

Pressing my hand to my heart, I remembered the way it thudded then and later when he leaned forward to place a soft kiss on my cheek. But it wasn't enough. In a boldness I can scarcely recall since, I placed my hand on his chest, entwined my fingers in his flannel shirt, and pulled him toward me.

The memory brought tears to my eyes, and I wept, recalling the warmth of his soft lips, the thrilling yet familiar feeling of them against mine. I cupped my face in my hands, anguished by all I had lost, wondering how things could worsen.

Could they indeed get worse?

Had Louella thought the same?

Though my deadline loomed, I was in no state to work on the violin. One afternoon was unlikely to set me back too greatly. More than that, with so much more at stake than previously realized, it was a necessary interruption.

Not wanting my father to see me in such a state, I dried my tears and went inside the house, where there was plenty to do: clothes and linens to wash, socks and stockings that needed mending long past respectability, dust to clear, beds to make, and dinner to prepare.

My troubled mind found solace in the simplicity of these tasks, a welcome respite from my myriad concerns and unanswered questions. By the time my father returned from the workshop, laundry was soaking in a washtub, including the curtains, a pot of French onion soup was simmering on the stove, and I sat doing a bit of mending.

"I wondered where you'd disappeared to," my father remarked.

"Just needed a break," I replied, hoping any traces of my earlier tears had vanished.

"Very well," he said, gesturing toward the kitchen. "French onion? Lovely. One of my favorites, you know."

I nodded. "I know."

He studied me again, perhaps sensing the terseness in my tone. "How long have you been here?"

I shrugged uncertainly. "Not long."

"Seems a while?" He nodded toward the piles of mending beside me, some done, some not.

I paused, hedging my response. "Just needed a break," I repeated.

He seemed to consider saying more but decided against it. "Perhaps I could use a break too, then. Could you use some help?"

Sensing a certain reluctance in his tone, I offered, "Not urgently, not if you'd like to continue working on your violin?"

His cheeks flushed.

"Go," I urged, expressing no discontent. On the contrary, his joy was balm to my despair.

"If you insist," he said. "Thank you, Lissie."

"Of course."

As he walked away, it was once more evident how much healthier he looked. Even the slight stoop of his back had straightened.

My mind tentatively revisited the topic I had been avoiding since arriving home. Cassius's dubious elixir had helped my father; there was no denying that. This miracle served as further evidence that Cassius could deliver as promised.

Then again, the potential risk had been so minimal. If the elixir had failed, my father would have continued to worsen, then perhaps die from his affliction.

The experiment with the elixir represented a classic case of nothing ventured, nothing gained, but undoing William's death was an entirely different matter.

Was I stranded in the wilderness on a fool's errand, thinking he could be revived? If miracles existed, surely they occurred only for those with the faith to seek them.

And yet, if it were to fail...

I shifted in my chair, considering the alternative: abandoning this experiment. Distasteful as this proposition was, it was worth contemplation.

Perhaps such was the working of fate, given how bizarrely such a thing could work at times. My father, for instance, had said he had become a luthier entirely by chance. At that moment, he was in his workshop, the place where he was truly at ease, truly comfortable, engaged in the very purpose for which he had been created.

Perhaps it was more than just fate, but providence: the word Abel had used when describing how my violin playing had stirred his soul.

Abel is not so bad, really, I could tell my father. I could accept Abel's proposal, run away with him, and live happily, traveling and enjoying the finest luxuries money could afford.

Still, a bitter taste grew in my throat at the idea of this future, contemplating Mrs. Sinclair as my mother-in-law: a bitter, unpleasant woman, far removed from the likes of Mrs. Whittaker.

But, should we leave Chapel Grove, this would be of little consequence, aside from the occasional holiday visit.

Upon joining an orchestra abroad and becoming a famous violinist in my own right, my memories of William could fade to the pages of a biography which may someday be written about me, the tragic personal history of one Elise Knight.

Elise *Sinclair*, rather.

Such a future did not seem entirely correct, but the path that had been disastrous for Louella was hardly simpler.

Did little Sophia have a casket, or was there only enough money for a burial cloth? Had she even been buried? I presumed she must have been, as several weeks had passed.

If so, was her body unearthed by Louella herself? I imagined the little girl in her grave, overgrown with moss, decaying, the scent reminiscent of the raven, with worms weaving through her skin as my needle through fabric...

I shuddered, banishing the thought.

Could such a sight drive one to madness?

Louella and Sophia, neatly posed in their first and last photograph together, the mother left with nothing but memories of her cherished child.

Next came the image of Louella—stripped of her humanity at Kirkham in the most final way imaginable. Final, except for death, I supposed.

Her eyes would no longer have the intelligent gleam in them, evident in her photograph even under the circumstances. Instead of being cared for in her time of need, she had been mutilated, left to rot.

Like her daughter.

I set my mending down and pressed my hands against my face, wishing to erase the story from my memory.

I wished I had never met Vada.

In my lap lay an especially hole-ridden sock belonging to my father. I stared at this sock for a long while before resuming my mending, deliberately fixing my mind on the steady in and out of the needle to distract from my troubled thoughts.

Chapter Thirty

That evening, my father exuded happiness, which softened a bit of my own gloom. Still, my own mind resembled a steady tightrope walk, trying to contemplate my troubles without prompting more macabre imaginings.

After tidying up post-dinner, I announced, "I'm quite tired." This was an understatement of the highest order, and I almost headed to bed when, with a start, I remembered the evening's crucial task. "Shall I prepare us some tea?"

"That sounds wonderful," my father responded.

"Go, sit, relax," I instructed. "I will bring it when it's ready."

The kettle was taking entirely too long to warm, I thought, for silence was a dangerous place for my troubled mind. I yearned for the peace that sleep would bring, yet waiting until morning was not an option. The ritual of making the tea, infused with its secret ingredient, was the sole reason my father felt well, the only reason he had joyfully chattered at dinner about the violin he was creating.

I carefully poured boiling water over the tea leaves, vigilant not to splash and scald myself, then returned the kettle to the stove. While the tea steeped, I retrieved the vial from the back of the cupboard.

Following my customary process, I dipped a toothpick into the elixir and stirred it into my father's tea, setting the vial on the counter. Despite my diligent efforts, my mind wandered—distracted, preoccupied.

Oh, if only I had replaced the cork and put the thing away properly!

For shortly thereafter, my father entered the room, unbeknownst to me. What he said in that moment escapes me now, perhaps irrelevant in light of what followed.

Startled, I spun around, my hand inadvertently striking the spoon, setting off a slow-motion cascade of events.

The spoon toppled the teacup over on its side.

The cup rolled, the handle stopping it, as liquid mercilessly spilled and trickled down the counter's edge.

I gasped in horror, my hand instinctively reaching out to salvage the situation, yet my misery did not end there. In my futile attempt to recover, my clumsy hand struck the vial, sending it tumbling down until it shattered on the floor, glass scattering everywhere.

"No," I shouted. "No, no, no!"

Despite my protests, it was too late.

The cup, the vial, and the precious life-saving elixir all lay ruined on the ground.

Ruined.

I stood frozen to the spot, repeating, "No. Oh, no," as if such a plea could reverse the damage.

"Oh, darling, it's just tea," my father consoled.

He didn't understand.

He would never understand.

As I surveyed the disaster before me, my breathing grew labored. The elixir, that miraculous, life-sustaining potion, was gone.

"Can I help you clean it?" my father offered.

"No!" I shouted, then noticed the hurt look on his face at my harsh response. "I apologize, but no," I amended, softening my tone. "Please, rest. I will handle this."

Realizing I needed space, my father nodded and left me to grapple with my predicament.

The borrowed time Cassius had afforded me had just run out, broken across the floor.

I looked around, searching for any remedy. Perhaps a bit of the elixir could be salvaged for tonight's tea, but not much more.

If my father became ill once more, how could violin-making continue at its present pace? No, such was not accurate. Instead, the pace must be redoubled, for none could tell how quickly my father's condition would deteriorate.

None besides Cassius, perhaps...

But this was not to be. Had he not, only earlier that day, threatened to take the elixir away when I had offended him? Moreover, he had warned me that no more elixir remained.

Perhaps it had been my own fault for entertaining the idea of a future without William.

Too numb to cry, I leaned over the spilled tea and elixir, blotting with a cloth and wringing it into the teacup, hoping to preserve as much as I could before decanting it into a canning jar. The discolored liquid looked unfit to serve anyone, much less my father. With any luck, despite its diluted state, the elixir might still offer some benefit.

Perhaps it could at least buy me sufficient time, my father sufficient energy, to finish the violin before...

I could hardly bear to finish the thought.

Heartbroken, I prepared a new cup of tea for my father using some of the rescued elixir. Though worried about dirt sullying the drink, it was a risk worth taking to stave off death, even for just a little longer.

The canning jar now occupied the spot where the vial had been, its brownish hue leaving me to ponder the balance of tea and elixir remaining. Despite my numerous uncertainties, I brought the tea to my father, handing it to him with an internal blaze of shame.

"Thank you," he said.

"Sure," I mumbled.

He raised the cup to his lips, and I watched with bated breath as he took a slow sip, swallowed, and then placed the cup on his lap. "Did you manage to clean up everything in there?"

"Yes, I did," I replied, adding, "and I apologize for being so rude. You were only trying to help."

"No apology needed," he responded calmly.

While we drank our tea, I watched my father for signs of distress. His manner was entirely normal, all things considered. When the last of the tea had been drained, I stood and collected the cups.

"Father, I am exhausted. May I bring you anything else before bed?"

"No, you have done quite enough, Elise." He took my hand, then patted it. "You are so good to me."

The words massaged remorse only deeper into my conscience.

Chapter Thirty-One

The next morning, my father's condition was of foremost concern. It had taken only a small amount of the elixir each day for him to regain his health, yet I was certain that the spill had rendered it powerless.

I had safely tucked the photograph of Louella and Sophia into my bag. If needed, I would return it to Vada. Her concern was justified, her desire to caution me commendable, but there was no question about whether to complete the violin. I needed to be certain if I could save William—regardless of the risk.

William was mine, and I was his.

My father had likely already risen for the day, perhaps having prepared himself some breakfast. Although I had done much to maintain the household, my father's miraculous recovery had fostered complacency. This could not continue, despite the need to hasten the completion of the violin.

Dinner that evening should be something hearty and restorative, like chicken soup. As I descended the stairs, I reasoned that a bit of preventive care could help prevent my father's illness from returning.

A persistent cough from the kitchen halted my descent halfway down the stairs. Was my father already worsening?

The cough was not so aggressive as it once was, but since it had almost disappeared with the first dose of the elixir, this was a significant setback. Bracing myself for what lay ahead, I entered the kitchen.

My father was seated at the table, eating a piece of toast. The rosiness of his cheeks and the brightness in his eyes had notably faded.

"How are you feeling?" I asked.

"A bit tired, I suppose. I had trouble sleeping last night due to the cough. Nothing to worry about, though, I'm sure." He cleared his throat once more.

"Of course," I replied, though my heart sank. It had only been one night.

With a heavy heart, I buttered some bread and added preserves, trying my best to engage in a conversation about the upcoming work on the violin. There was more to do, and faster than he could possibly understand. My heart felt as if it had sunk to my stomach.

"Are you feeling any better this morning?" he asked gently.

"A bit. I apologize again for my abruptness."

"No need, Lissie. Perhaps we are both a bit under the weather."

"Perhaps," I agreed.

My father then nudged his plate. "Would you mind terribly if I got started without you?"

"Not at all," I replied. It would allow me time to think. He moved to grab his plate. "Leave it, Father. I'll clean up." Under the circumstances, it was the very least I could do.

After tidying up, I joined my father in his workshop and resumed work on the violin's scroll. When I had previously envisioned this part, it was as a beautifully carved piece of art, worthy of exchanging for William; but circumstances had changed. It only needed to be functional, imbued with as much personal touch as possible.

My father might notice, but what of it? Any added details would be perceived as the result of his daughter's artistry and nothing more. He could never have imagined my plans, even in his wildest dreams.

But once William was back, all would return to normal, and everything else would be forgotten.

While I aspired to craft a violin worthy of pride, my main objective was to complete it, created with great love despite its imperfections. Comfort and playability were secondary to its ability to resurrect the dead.

Thus, while carving the scroll, I prayed over the violin like a mantra.

Please, allow William to return as he was. Let our paths be united once more. Let our story continue.

I could add etchings to the violin in discreet places as well. I planned to revisit the story of Lazarus and the resurrection of Christ and perhaps search through my Bible, as there must be other instances of miraculous resurrection. I would note them and perhaps inscribe a few verses on the surface of the violin, drawing strength from the faith they inspired.

"I think I could use a break." My father's voice brought me back to the surroundings of the workshop.

"Of course," I replied, glancing at him. Dark circles hung beneath his eyes. "Can I help with anything?"

"As I say, I'm just a bit tired." He looked upon the work before him with a measure of sadness.

"Please do. Go rest, and I will prepare supper shortly."

"Wonderful. Thank you, love."

By the time it was necessary to stop and cook our meal, I had completed the first half of the scroll. The muscles in my upper body protested after being hunched for so long, but the discomfort mattered little—for, after supper, once I had seen my father to bed, I would return to the workshop. Sleep could wait.

Sitting at the dining table only deepened my despair, for my father had deteriorated significantly. His face was pale and wan, and it seemed he had lost all the weight he had recently regained in just a few short hours. On top of that, his cough had resumed with a vengeance.

"This must be quite an unpleasant illness," I observed once we had finished our dinner. "Shall I prepare your tea a bit earlier this evening?" It was a comforting tradition, unlikely to exacerbate my father's condition.

My father looked wistfully toward his workshop but conceded. "Yes, that might be wise."

I prepared his usual evening tea, adding a small amount of the diluted treatment. Although it previously appeared unremarkable, its likeness to pond water was dispiriting.

I brought it to him in the sitting room, as usual.

"Thank you," he said, being none the wiser to my internal struggle.

"You're welcome," I said, refusing the temptation to sink into my own chair, knowing much work awaited me this evening.

After assisting my father to bed, I returned to the now-darkened workshop, a lantern in hand. My mind was distracted as I worked, troubled by how swiftly my father had drifted into sleep. The sound of his deep, slow breathing reached me even before I left his room. Such a development seemed ominous.

I carved until the early morning hours, completing one side of the scroll's snail-like whorl and beginning the next.

Despite my determination to press on, the sleepless night had already begun to exact its toll by the time the sun breached the horizon. My body ached, and my heavy eyelids threatened to fall over my blurred vision. I needed something. Coffee, perhaps, would be a start, though it might prove insufficient if this pace continued.

An idea flickered in my mind, suggesting that such endurance might not be necessary. I leaned back in my seat, contemplating.

When my father and I first discussed his illness, he mentioned private conversations with Dr. Bell, who had been confounded. My father claimed there were no solutions.

Yet, had they truly explored all possibilities?

I glanced back toward the house. Speaking with Dr. Bell may produce nothing of value, but there remained enough hope for revelation to warrant action.

Rising from my seat, I brushed the wood shavings from my clothes and departed for Dr. Bell's residence.

The sun had almost entirely cleared the horizon upon my arrival to the doctor's home. Though I disliked troubling him so early, he would surely understand my impatience.

After a polite tap at the door, it opened a crack, through which I could see the bespectacled Mrs. Bell. Her graying hair was still pinned into curls. "Yes?"

I had failed to consider who else the visit would awaken, but persisted. "I'm so sorry to trouble you this morning. I was hoping to speak with Dr. Bell, please. It's urgent."

"Of course, dear. Come in and take a seat."

"Thank you," I said, stepping inside. The house was adorned with crocheted doilies on every surface, needlepoints on every wall. Several chairs occupied the sitting room; one held a skein of yarn and a crochet hook tucked into a project underway. I chose a different seat before pointing to a needlepoint featuring a cardinal on a snow-covered branch. "This is lovely," I noted.

"Thank you, dear." Mrs. Bell beamed, then walked to a door beside the sitting room which led to another part of the house, serving as Dr. Bell's office for consultations and treatments. She knocked on the door, then opened it and spoke softly. "Dear, Elise Knight is here to see you. She says it's urgent."

Dr. Bell soon emerged from the office, his expression tense. "Has something happened to your father?"

"No, he is—not fine, exactly." Alive at least. How could I explain this? "Dr. Bell, I know my father consulted you about his illness. He showed improvement for a time—surely he informed you?" When he hesitated, I continued. "We believed he had been cured, but now his condition is worse than ever. He mentioned you'd suggested treatments that might extend his time, perhaps…" I stopped, noting his familiar look, reminiscent of when William died.

"Elise…" Dr. Bell exchanged a glance with his wife. "Why don't you step into my office?"

"Okay." My voice faltered, but I followed Dr. Bell into his office. Here, too, his wife's needlework was displayed, most notably an art piece depicting a single serpent coiled around a staff.

Dr. Bell closed the door, then offered me a chair before taking his own. He cleared his throat before speaking. "Elise, first, I wish to apologize for not expressing my concerns about your father sooner. He requested my discretion, and I respected that."

"I understand that, Dr. Bell. Please believe I am not upset by it. You have always had our greatest respect."

"I am relieved to hear that, Elise." He interlaced his fingers in his lap. "I wish I had better news to offer you."

He had made up his mind, but I had not. "Please, isn't there anything which could be done? Even a few more weeks…"

Dr. Bell shook his head gravely. "What your father is suffering from is unlike anything I've ever encountered."

"In what way?" I asked, my voice wavering with concern.

"At first, it appeared to be pneumonia, given the coughing and chest pain. According to what your father shared, these symptoms developed rather swiftly, a typical indication of pneumonia. However, the absence of both fever and sputum was puzzling. I initially thought it might resolve on its own," Dr. Bell explained as both of us shifted uneasily in our seats. "When it did not, I considered the possibility of a rare form of tuberculosis presenting without fever, yet this seemed unlikely without shortness of breath, especially when you remained healthy. Then, as your father began losing weight rapidly despite regular meals, it became clear he was afflicted by something unfamiliar, something quite sinister. I advised him to rest as much as possible and to maintain a nutritious diet, which he assured me he tried his best to do with your assistance." A hint of warmth touched his eyes as he added, "Tilda, my wife, concocted a syrup made from coltsfoot leaves for him to soothe his lungs, but unfortunately, it had no discernible effect."

The lengths my father had gone to in seeking care without burdening me brought tears to my eyes. He must have been terrified, yet he chose to shield me from his suffering. I hadn't realized his pain until now, though the memory of him rubbing his chest should have been a telling sign.

"I regret to inform you, Elise, that I don't believe your father has much time left."

I nodded, tears cascading down my cheeks. "I fear you are right."

"You have endured a terrible ordeal, and I am truly sorry for that. Are the Sinclairs at least treating you well?"

I remained silent for a moment, then replied, "Yes, I suppose they are."

"Did you come here hoping for a miracle?"

With this, my composure broke, and I wept openly, burying my face in my hands.

"I'm deeply sorry, my dear," Dr. Bell said gently. "All we can do now is keep him comfortable. Regrettably, everything else we've tried has been unsuccessful."

Defeated, I slumped in my chair, knowing all too well the truth of his words. Our efforts had proven inadequate, except for the mysterious elixir that once provided temporary relief. Now, comfort was all we could offer my father.

With a heavy heart, it was time to return home.

"Thank you, Doctor," I said softly.

"I wish I could do more for you and your father. He is a good man."

Expressing my gratitude with a nod, I rose from my seat. Dr. Bell escorted me out, and he and his wife bade me farewell.

Weary and heartbroken, I made my way back home, but my troubles were far from over.

Along my journey, I encountered an unwelcome presence. Taking the creek road, I soon crossed paths with Vada.

She turned to me, appearing as surprised as I was. "You are out early," she said. She had not been waiting for me, at least. Knowing I wasn't being followed was some small comfort.

"Hello, Vada," I greeted, maintaining my pace until she stepped into my path, forcing me to stop.

"Have you thought anymore about what I told you?" she pressed.

I touched my neck, troubled. "Yes, I have."

"And?"

"And... I am truly sorry about Louella. The whole incident must have been terrible."

"That is quite an understatement," she replied.

"Truly, I am sorry for her. I had hoped to return her photograph to you, but I don't have it with me. Perhaps I can do so this afternoon?"

A tense silence followed. Her gaze bore into me, and I averted my eyes. Still, she seemed to grasp my thoughts.

"You mean that, in spite of her story, you intend to proceed with this... this violin?"

I looked away. "I know you mean well," I insisted, but she would hear none of it.

"After everything—*everything* I told you about Louella? After what that despicable man did to her?"

"What happened to Louella is a tragedy, there is no doubt about that," I admitted. "However, the simple fact that she had dealings with Cassius does not prove he *caused* that tragedy."

Vada's face blanched. "I can see he has charmed you, but he has fooled you. He *cannot* do what he promises. No one can."

"He healed my father, at least for a while. He was sick, so sick, and Cassius gave me this medication that restored him to health." Guilt tightened around my chest, thinking of the lost treatment.

"This proves nothing," Vada insisted. "All Mr. McCalmont does amounts to magic tricks, only smoke and mirrors. I repeat, he is not to be trusted."

"Have you dealt with him yourself?" I inquired.

"No, but I know enough of his work. I saw the results firsthand."

"If you have never dealt with him yourself, then the possibility remains that you are mistaken. You perceive him as some kind of demon, yet I know he is the reason I have not laid my father to rest." Vada glowered at me, but I was undaunted. "I understand Louella must have suffered greatly when Sophia died. I have great compassion for her, for grief is relentless."

Vada appeared pensive and paused momentarily before speaking again, this time more quietly. "Louella was indeed suffering, but she was managing. She was surviving, at least until Cassius appeared." She spat the name like a curse.

"All I know is that to live without my William is death," I declared.

"Maybe that would be preferable."

I balked, feeling a surge of anger within me, yet I responded with restraint. "I appreciate your concern, but I have made my decision."

"You are a fool."

"I must try."

"You must do nothing," she insisted, her voice rising. "Abandon this pursuit. Renege on the deal. Do not move forward. Only misery awaits. Louella is proof."

"I am sorry," I replied. With nothing more to discuss, I turned and headed home.

This is not to suggest that I was untroubled by Vada's concerns, only that if I ceased my work now, everything that had led to this moment would be for naught. That was unthinkable.

For better or worse, whether it guided me to heaven or hell, I had to see the creation of the violin through to its end.

Chapter Thirty-Two

My interaction with Vada faded to the back of my mind as my father's health rapidly deteriorated. My attempt to save the spilled elixir had been futile. Cassius remained unaware of its loss, as I hoped to finish the violin before such confession became necessary. With frayed nerves, I finished the violin's scroll and began carving its neck.

By the time I began carving the hard ebony for the fingerboard, my father had fully abandoned work on his own violin. This only propelled me to work faster, and in my haste to finish, I took to carving beside my father's bed.

"Now, Lissie, I am well enough to join you in the workshop," he had protested the first time I did this. "Besides, there is no point getting wood shavings all over."

Despite his objections, we both knew the chilly workshop was no place for him.

"It's nothing to me to clean up when I am finished, Father," I said. "And you need your rest."

Though the work was progressing well, its inverse relationship with my father's condition troubled me. I trembled thinking upon how sick he was becoming, as it meant his time was near; and, consequently, so was mine. The violin was nearly complete, but still required lacquer. This process would largely be a matter of time, and largely outside my control. The lacquered violin would then need a sound post, strings, and a bridge, as well as any last-minute adjustments.

Still, it was difficult to find satisfaction in my progress, knowing my marriage to Abel was soon at hand.

One afternoon, however, all came to an abrupt halt.

There was a knock at the door during lunch, and I went to answer it.

"Abel, how are you this morning?" I asked, admittedly with more interest than usual, given his stooped posture and furrowed brow. "What is wrong?"

"I know your secret," he said, folding his arms.

"Excuse me?" I asked.

He arched an eyebrow and said, "Your secret plans for the violin."

My heart thrummed. *Oh no.* "Abel, what do you mean?"

"Raising the dead, or so I hear."

I drew a sharp intake of breath, panic rising as I struggled to find words to explain myself. Then Abel let out a laugh. "Oh, Elise, I apologize. I did not mean to vex you," he said. "You know, I had the strangest visitor yesterday. A mad woman, completely batty. She suggested this violin you're making is intended to revive the dead."

I managed an uncertain smile. *So Vada had attempted to intervene with the Sinclairs.* "How utterly ridiculous," I replied, my heart slowly resuming its usual pace.

"Indeed," said Abel. He rolled his eyes. "I confronted my mother about it, for I presume it was her idea to discourage my marriage to you, but such an obvious ruse... You would think she could invent something better."

"Yes," I agreed, nodding slowly.

"She insisted she had nothing to do with it, but I know how she is. But enough about my mother, for I have come to call upon your father."

This, by contrast, was a statement I was prepared for. "I don't believe that would be wise. He is not doing well and needs rest."

"I will keep it brief," Abel insisted.

For selfish reasons, I wished to curtail Abel's visit, but granting him this small favor seemed harmless enough.

"I'm sure he will be happy to see you," I said, then guided Abel to my father's room, rapping on the open door. "Father, you have a visitor."

"Oh?"

Abel and I entered the room. My father closed the book in his hands and shifted to a more upright position.

"Sir," said Abel with a respectful bow. "It's good to see you. I am sure Elise has been taking good care of you, but I wished to come and ask if I could be of service to you. And Elise, of course."

My father paused, contemplating his hands for a moment. "If I am to be honest, I only desire one thing from you," he said.

Oh no. This was no doubt coming, but I had hoped it could be delayed with sufficient progress on the violin. Perhaps indefinitely. My heart dropped when my father proclaimed, "Elise, it is time."

Not wishing to be cruel to Abel, I desired to have the conversation outside of his presence, but there was nothing to be done.

"Father, the violin—" I began, but my father would hear none of it.

"*Enough*, Elise." he said, his tone so final that no response was warranted. The great exasperation in his voice suggested this had been a long time coming. "It is time." He gestured for me, and I moved closer to him. Taking my hand in his, he said, "Darling, you have done excellent work on this violin."

Tears clouded my vision. Abel touched my back gently, perhaps mistaking my emotions as solely related to my father's impending demise.

"You have exceeded my expectations," my father continued. "At this point, I am confident you can finish it on your own. You have strung a violin before. There is not much more to do, and I will assist as much as I can before I pass. However, before I go, what I need most is assurance of your wellbeing."

As I stroked his hand with my thumb without speaking, my lip trembled with the effort to hold back my tears.

"Abel is a good man. The Sinclairs are a good family." He coughed a few more times then recovered, though still rubbed his chest, wincing. "And you know I am not long for this world."

"Father, I cannot bear to lose you."

"I know," my father replied, pulling me closer and embracing me. "It is not within our power to decide when we are called home, darling."

"I cannot lose you," I repeated shakily.

"Abel will be good to you. He will take care of you. Please, Elise. I know your grieving has been cut short, and you must now bear another loss. I recognize the unfairness of that. However, you must now consider the future, not the past, which cannot be changed."

My gut tightened. *If only he knew.*

"But I must be here to care for you," I insisted. "You deserve as much."

My father had no time to respond, for Abel did first. "Then I shall help you," he said, stepping beside me and resting a hand on my shoulder. "If we are to be husband and wife, to be together in sickness and in health, allow us to begin immediately."

"Please, my darling," my father implored.

I touched his hand, looking at it. His ring, still on his finger, pledging fidelity to my mother, who had passed nineteen years ago. Did he not understand? He would if he knew.

Tears stung my eyes at my awful situation. In that moment, my father and Abel had backed me into a corner. My only course of action was to reassure my father as best I could.

"Okay," I said finally. "I will agree." My stomach twisted into knots even as I said it, even knowing my agreement was conditional, with terms I intended to explain further. His face relaxed as he lay back on his pillow.

"Then it is settled," my father said contentedly. Turning to Abel, he added, "We shall inform your family that you two will be married at once."

No, this cannot be.

"Tomorrow," Abel added.

Incredulous at the synchronization with which they spoke, I wondered briefly if they had planned this conversation without my knowledge. Abel's grin was far removed from the expression of a groom delighted to marry his love. It bore greater resemblance to that of a predator who has finally caught its prey.

"Perfect," my father said.

Chapter Thirty-Three

Shortly thereafter, I insisted Abel return home to allow my father to rest.

"I am delighted our marriage is finally coming to fruition," said Abel as we parted ways, grinning that same devilish grin once more, one which said, *You are mine and there is no escape.*

I closed the door behind me, leaning against it as I gazed up at the ceiling. It felt as if it had lowered, and the walls seemed to draw closer.

Cassius's face swam before my mind. What solution might he have? I knew not, only that I needed to speak with him.

"Father, I could use some fresh air," I called, "I will see you later." Before he could respond, I left, my feet instinctively finding their way to the familiar creekside path once more.

The wagon remained in the same place as before. I stepped up to the door of the wagon and knocked, and after some bustling within, the door opened.

"Cassius." My lip trembled. "I need your help." I bowed my head and squeezed my eyes shut, but to no avail; my tears spilled forth anyway.

"Oh, dear," he said softly, consolingly. He cast a quick glance behind me, then beckoned me inside the cramped space of his wagon. Once the door was closed, I gathered myself as best I could. He turned around, looking at me with some measure of confusion.

"Is it your father?"

"Yes," I began, then added, "and no." My panicked mind struggled over the words, unsure where to start. "He's dying. My father is dying, and he wants me to marry another. *Tomorrow.*"

Cassius sat on his makeshift bed at the end of the wagon with a thoughtful expression. "While I empathize with this sudden turn of events, I find I am confused," he said softly. "The elixir worked, did it not?"

"It did," I said, biting my lip before speaking again, "It worked wonderfully. I could hardly believe it. But... oh, Cassius—it fell. It broke. I spilled it,"

"That is unfortunate," he said, his face impassive.

"But I have been working tirelessly to get the violin completed," I added quickly. "And it really is so close to being done. *So* close," *So close*, and yet I found myself stuck in this hopeless predicament.

"How close, exactly?" asked Cassius.

"Only the lacquer remains," I explained. "Once that is set, the strings, the bridge, and the sound post need to be installed—a few weeks at most. But with this situation with the Sinclairs, I find myself at a loss."

Watching Cassius ponder this new information without revealing his thoughts only heightened my panic. What if there was nothing more he could do? Perhaps Cassius could hide me away until it all blew over...

"I am disappointed to learn of the fate of the elixir, naturally," said Cassius with a hint of irritation. "And as you must realize, I will be unable to get you more."

I nodded in acknowledgement.

"This situation with your father and this marriage no doubt complicates things. It obviously weighs on you heavily. Of course, it seems the simplest solution would be to explain you are too distraught over the death of your betrothed to move forward with another, would it not?"

I let out a brief, bitter laugh. "If only it were that simple. The problem is that the Sinclair family is wealthy and well-connected. It is sheer bad luck that their son is so intent on marrying me, leading my father to believe that, should I decline, I might never encounter such an opportunity again."

"That is indeed unfortunate," Cassius remarked.

"I know my father has the best intentions, but under these circumstances, I am at a loss for what to do. I simply need time— just a bit more time to show my father that I will be well cared for. With William."

Cassius fixed his piercing green eyes on me, tilting his head slightly as if pondering deeply.

"I understand you've already helped me immensely. I'm willing to do anything," I insisted. "Please—please help me."

Seconds felt like hours in the silence which followed. When Cassius next spoke, I listened intently.

"Before I answer you, Elise, I must know. Do you, or do you not trust me?"

He referenced our recent argument, of course, with the unpleasantness of Louella and the question of stealing the elixir. Despite this strife, I answered truthfully, "Yes, I do."

"Are you certain? I desire no further unpleasantness between us."

"Yes, I am sure. I am sorry for doubting you before. And I'm so sorry I lost the elixir."

Cassius seemed to weigh his thoughts before he replied, "I hold no malice against you for your shortcomings."

"Thank you," I said, feeling a weight lift.

"I also confess that I am as invested in the completion of the violin as you are." He glanced at his collection thoughtfully. "I believe I can offer you more time."

A spark of renewed hope ignited within me. "You can? Oh, Cassius, thank you. How can I ever repay your generosity?"

"It may be wise to hear the conditions before you thank me.."

"Why is that?" A gnawing developed in my gut at his solemn countenance.

"Because this solution is not so simple."

"In what way?"

Cassius did not answer immediately. Instead, he stood, turned away, and crouched down to lift a threadbare quilt. From beneath his bed, he produced a dark wooden cigar box. He opened it and withdrew what looked like a brightly colored child's doll, brushing a hair from its face as he gazed upon it.

"As I told you before, I have traveled to many places, including remote places where magic is still practiced. Dark magic. This," he said, presenting the doll to me, "is a relic which is reputed to cause death in a selected target."

"Death?" I echoed, recoiling slightly. When he nodded, I whispered, "No."

"As I said, this solution is certainly not easy." He handed me the doll, stitched together with crude purple fabric and looking no more threatening than a child's toy. It had two black buttons for eyes, but no mouth.

"The process, however, is reportedly straightforward," Cassius continued. "From my understanding, if you choose to use this, you must have something personal from the target; preferably blood or hair—something from their body, or at the very least, an object which has some connection to them."

"But… Who?" I asked, feeling repulsed.

Cassius looked from the doll to me. "I suppose that would be up to you."

"But…" My mind raced, unable to grasp such a notion. "I couldn't. I could never."

"That decision, too, is yours," Cassius replied with an air of dismissal. "Though given the current situation, I see little choice."

I gazed at the frighteningly orange carpet on the floor of the caravan. *Murder.* How could such a thing even be considered? Yet, Cassius had a point. What else could be done?

But who to use it on? *Abel?* Flawed though he was, such drastic action was hardly justified.

Could this, however, represent a fair exchange for William?

"How does it work, exactly?" I asked.

"You will take the doll, then perform a short ceremony in honor of the spirit within, then do to the doll that which you wish to be done to your selected target. There are a number of methods for this, I would imagine. Holding the doll under water, for instance, to cause drowning, perhaps. Or a pin, stuck into the area of a vital organ; say, the heart."

The *heart.* To stop Abel's heart from beating. So quiet a death. *Like William's.* William's face entered my mind, his face during those three days when I was so sure he would reawaken. William's face was then replaced with Abel's, sending a sick reverberation down my spine.

"The key element, as I understand, is your intention. Do you intend it to cause death, or merely an illness which causes discomfort? It seems you must be quite specific in your intentions." At the uncertain look on my face, Cassius continued speaking. "As I said, this is only the solution if you are truly as desperate as you say—if you have no alternative."

Abel's predatory grin hovered before my mind's eye.

Kill Abel? To be sure, it was murder, whether it was by my hand or by the powers of dark magic, something one could, perhaps, not heal from.

Yet could I bear to officially, legally become his wife—to vow before man and God that I would honor and obey him to the end of my natural life? Such a lie, told before God. I knew I could not.

But *murder*?

Yet, what more could be done at this point? We were so close to completing the violin. When confronted with two unimaginable situations, perhaps one must choose the path which appears most survivable.

An idea sparked within my unsettled mind, gradually growing brighter and offering a sliver of clarity to my soul. The dark cloud overhead momentarily parted as I contemplated this possibility.

"Elise, I realize this is not an easy choice to make," said Cassius.

My eyebrows lost their tension as I looked at him with determination. "You are sure this...doll...that it will work?" I asked.

Cassius nodded with assurance. "I am sure."

"Then I will do it."

He handed me the doll, which I took hesitantly, gazing upon its still face with new hope as Cassius explained how to use it. Before leaving the caravan, I tucked the doll within my bag, thinking hard about what I must do to set everything right.

To tarnish my soul in this way, to commit such a sacrifice in pursuit of creating the violin, would imbue it with greater power. Perhaps power enough to restore more than one life.

If done correctly, perhaps Abel's death would represent only a brief diversion, one that would enable me to bring my William back to me. Such a thing could be forgivable, so long as it was reversible.

Before I left for home, Cassius had explained the ritual by which the doll would be employed. As I neared home, I glanced toward the place where my father rested. The day was still young, and much remained to be done before the artifact could serve its purpose. Uncertain how long this might take to work, I hoped that it would fulfill its mission by morning.

Abel had surely returned to his home filled with the joy of our impending marriage.

The sky overhead was so far away, so indifferent. Was there truly a God above, one who cared about the predicament I faced? Would He judge me harshly in the end? I hoped for understanding from such an entity.

Without further delay, I made my way home.

Chapter Thirty-Four

Considering the events that were about to unfold, I had little desire to see my father; nevertheless, he was there to greet me at the door upon my return. My face felt flushed, and I avoided meeting his gaze.

"Elise, please understand, I only want what is best for you," he said gently.

I continued toward the stairs, hoping he would perceive me as too upset to discuss the matter.

"Please, darling, speak to me."

My steps faltered, and I turned to face him, briefly meeting his eyes before averting my gaze. "I know, Father. I know you do." I longed to end this conversation as swiftly as possible.

"I hope you will not harbor any resentment towards me," he implored.

"I could never. Only..." I hesitated, searching for the right words. "I am not angry with you, Father, but please, allow me some solitude before—before what I must do."

He crossed his arms, his brows knitted with concern, looking up at me with heartfelt sincerity, which stirred a nervous anticipation within me; yet he merely said, "Of course, darling. All the space you need."

He appeared so frail, so unwell. The thought that my discontent could further burden him was unbearable to me.

"I will join you for dinner this evening," I offered, this seeming an appropriate olive branch.

"I will look forward to it," he replied.

With a tight smile, I turned and swiftly ascended to my room, shutting the door firmly behind me. The door felt like an inadequate barrier against the impending task. To ensure I wouldn't be disturbed, I pushed a writing desk against it, then sat on my bed.

Beside me lay my bag, containing the doll. I took it out. The doll was hardly larger than a book, slender, scarcely stuffed, with no features aside from its black button eyes. One might have assumed it was simply a child's toy. Could such an object truly possess the power Cassius had promised? I had little choice but to trust that it indeed did.

Curious about its other characteristics, I brought the doll to my nose and inhaled. A strange, unpleasant smell emanated from it. It was an earthy aroma, like garden soil, perhaps.

Or grave dirt.

I shivered. Perhaps it was best to leave my questions about the doll unanswered. Instead, I focused on finding a personal item of Abel's. Cassius had suggested hair or blood from the intended target, but I had neither. I believed the ring Abel had given me upon our engagement would suffice.

Retrieving the ring from my dresser drawer, the gravity of what I was about to do weighed heavily upon me. This was Abel's ring, a symbol of my promise to marry him. What I intended to use it for amounted to the worst of betrayal.

I could only hope that, in the end, it would be worth it.

Digging through the sewing box that once belonged to my mother did nothing to alleviate my guilt. The pin I selected was flat-headed and well-worn. My mother would have used this very pin for innocent tasks, never imagining what her daughter would later do with it. Would she look down from Heaven with disappointment or understanding? I hoped for the latter as I pressed the pin into my bed quilt before taking a spool of thread from the box. After cutting a length sufficient to wrap around the doll twice, I closed the sewing box and put it away.

My fingers trembled as they threaded the string through the ring and securely tied it to the belly of the doll. Upon lifting the doll, the ring drooped. I returned to the sewing box to cut another length of string, looping it through the ring once more, determined to tie it more securely this time.

Holding the doll with both hands, I tried to steady myself. Cassius had instructed me to clear my mind before attempting to use the doll. Slowly and deeply, I inhaled and then exhaled, striving to disperse all distracting thoughts. It was easier said than done, but my focus narrowed until only the doll and I remained.

With one more breath, I finally spoke in a whisper, "I offer this doll up as a proxy for Abel Sinclair." I paused, as if waiting for a response. There was none, of course—who would respond? I continued, "I declare that what I do to this figure shall be done to him." Then added, despite myself, "So let it be, amen."

I paused momentarily, assessing the air around me, searching for any sign of change, perhaps akin to the static before a lightning storm. No perceptible change occurred.

Regardless, it was time for the next step, for which I needed the pin: the casting of the final curse. The absurdity of this notion struck me as nearly comical, and a harsh laugh escaped my lips as I glanced at the doll. How ridiculous I would appear if interrupted at this moment, clutching a child's plaything with my supposed engagement ring attached. If anyone became aware of my plans this afternoon, they would surely—

Send me to Kirkham.

All humor drained from me.

This would indeed feel ludicrous if not for the fact that its success or failure held significant sway over my future. If it failed...

No, I chided myself. It was of no help to think that way. Cassius had told me my state of mind was of the utmost importance, so I refocused on the doll. My gaze wandered over its fabric, the four holes of each flat, coal-black button eye. Its purple fabric was tightly woven, smooth beneath my thumb as I brushed the surface. The ring, fastened by three lengths of thread, resembled one being carried down the aisle by a ring bearer.

That groom took the form of Abel. My thoughts lingered on his image, the look of greedy anticipation on his face, then shifted to the heart beating beneath a purple dahlia boutonnière, its color identical to the doll's fabric.

My left hand held the doll gingerly as my right held the pin, positioning it over the approximate area of the heart.

"Prick the heart," I murmured. "Weaken it. Let it beat no more."

The pin slid deftly into the fabric, causing my breath to catch.

My mind conjured the image of Abel lying utterly still in his home's parlor, much like William had. Unbidden, the tears of his parents joined my mental image. I tried to banish the scene, fearing my resolve would weaken in the face of their misery.

"I can undo it," I whispered, perhaps more to myself than anyone else, placing the doll beneath my pillow to avoid raising questions with my father. The pin remained embedded in the fabric. I rested my head against the pillow, staring at the ceiling above, wondering what, if anything, I had done.

Much as it may have been preferable to lock myself away within my room, it was not to be. Descending the stairs to see my father for supper, my racing thoughts were soothed with the repeating thought. *I can undo it.* The smell of ham wafted in my direction, a surprise, but upon rounding the corner to the kitchen, it was clear that the meat, along with fresh buttered pole beans, mashed potatoes, and an intricately latticed apple pie had just been delivered. It hardly needed to be asked on behalf of whom.

Affixing a smile on my face, I took my place at the table, doling portions enough to be polite without troubling my unsteady stomach. *All of it can be undone,* I reminded myself, taking small bites of each item, angst accompanying each tidbit like a bitter condiment.

My father's plate mirrored mine, with small samplings of each dish. Despite our mutual lack of appetite, the meal passed in near silence. What more was there to say?

Despite the impulse to suggest he eat more to keep his strength up, it was difficult to break the silence. Each glance between my father and I was as though we were each attempting to assure the other that all was well, but it was a ridiculous façade. Nothing was all right, in fact, not with my father's illness stubbornly sitting between us as a third, uninvited guest.

Once dinner had been put away, the table cleaned, the silence broken only by the occasional perfunctory *excuse me, please,* or *thank you,* I asked whether my father might like some tea that evening.

"No, darling. I think it will be an early night for me."

Though tempted to press the matter, I reminded myself that it was of little importance. I simply agreed, "Me too," kissed my father on the cheek, and headed upstairs.

My bedroom door closed behind me with a soft thud, and I was left once more alone with my thoughts. No, more than that:

I was left alone with the doll, still stashed under my pillow. The reminder made the food in my stomach shift uneasily.

A deep breath in, a deep breath out. *I can undo it. It can be undone.*

Yet, the doll's very presence heightened my unease, so I moved the thing from beneath my pillow to one of my drawers, buried beneath undergarments. I intended to return it to Cassius as soon as possible, for I didn't wish for it to remain near me longer than necessary.

As the light outside my window dimmed, my thoughts turned restlessly.

What might the Sinclairs' evening be like at present? The servants were likely doing the nighttime chores, preparing meals for the next morning and evening, banking coals in the fireplaces, tending to various things around the house and also preparing the family for the wedding which they believed would take place the next day.

A vision of Abel with his parents swam before my eyes. What moments might they be sharing? Surely, they had no inkling it could be their last as a family. The more I pondered, the more firmly I believed: *I can undo it.*

Still, the thought of their impending heartbreak was more than I could bear. My thoughts turned back to the violin.

Although I did not desire Abel as a husband, I did not wish him dead—not permanently.

Suppose the residents of Chapel Grove simply believed a great miracle had taken place. Surely, people were unlikely to question the source of such a blessing as the return of two of their own from what they believed the ultimate end.

But what if the violin didn't work as I had hoped?

I could hardly entertain the thought and cast it away. What was done was done, and the prospect of failure was hardly worth entertaining.

As I settled into bed, the mantra cycled through my mind.

I can undo it, I thought, loosening, brushing, and loosely re-braiding my hair for sleep.

It can be undone, I thought, extinguishing the light.

All can be made right. I sunk between the covers. *It need not be forever.*

My brow furrowed in realization that, whatever happened, nothing would be the same after this day.

It can be undone.

A raven croaked through the trees, and I fell into a restless sleep.

Chapter Thirty-Five

My father and I said little to one another that morning beyond the usual chit-chat. Perhaps he mistook me for an anxious brideto-be, or simply felt it wise to tread lightly. Either way, he was happy to leave me to tending to various chores around the house, without which my feet would have restlessly paced while I awaited news of Abel's fate.

We soon learned of it.

A knock at the door told me the time had come, and I steeled myself accordingly. The news had seemed likely to come from one of the Sinclair's servants, or perhaps Reverend Willard. Instead, Sheriff Crogan was at the door with his hat in hand.

All had, very evidently, not gone as planned.

"Luther," greeted my father. "What brings you here this morning?"

The sheriff raised his red-rimmed eyes to my father, whose jovial demeanor dropped.

"What is it?" he asked.

Sheriff Crogan's met my gaze. His mustache twitched. "Elise may prefer not to hear this," he said quietly to my father.

"I wish to know," I interjected, rejecting any attempt to shield me from the truth.

"Really, Miss, this news is not suitable for sensitive ears. Your father can tell you later."

"Please, Sheriff, what has happened?"

Sheriff Crogan looked upon my father, eyebrows raised as if to ask permission.

"What has happened?" my father asked, granting it, "Please, come in."

Sheriff Crogan entered, the door closing with a creak. "Please, have a seat."

A knot of dread formed in my stomach as my father and I took our seat at the table.

The sheriff remained standing, bowing his head, and closing his eyes. "Abel Sinclair was arrested this morning," he announced.

Struck as with a blow, I balked. "For what?"

"Murder." He answered quickly, as though wanting to distance himself from the word as quickly as possible.

A ringing began in my ears. I must have misunderstood. "I beg your pardon?"

"Last night, it appears that Abel and his mother had an argument which turned… well, violent."

Abel's mother. How had the spell gone so awry?

"His mother?" I echoed, then my mouth dropped open. The ring. *Of course.* Oh, how could I have been so foolish? The ring had not been Abel's, not really. It had belonged to his mother before it was given to me. "Oh, my God."

"How *awful*," my father said.

"His mother," I repeated softly. My stomach turned. *What have I done?* The question demanded an answer, though I dreaded its implications. "How?"

"Unfortunately, I—I am not at liberty to give the details. It is… to say the least, quite the mess. My deputies and I are still sorting out the details, but a servant informed us of the planned nuptials for today, and—" He broke off, wiping a tear from his face. "Miss Knight, you have already been through so much. I am so sorry for this tragedy."

In stunned silence, I shook my head, staring at the ground. *What have I done?*

My father rose to his feet. "Thank you, Sheriff, for letting us know. It can't have been easy." He extended a hand, which Sheriff Crogan accepted.

"I appreciate that," the sheriff replied.

My father led him to the door. Their muted conversation faded as the door shut behind the sheriff, and my father returned to where I sat, his complexion ashen.

"Father…" I began, but what could be said? My dalliance the night before had at least given me time to prepare for the bad news, even if I did not anticipate this result.

My father buried his face in his hands, his shoulders shaking with silent sobs.

His anguish is my fault. I placed a comforting hand on his shoulder and quieted my own thoughts until the worst of the storm had passed. His sobs gradually diminished, and my father dabbed his eyes with a handkerchief.

"Lissie, I am so sorry," he said.

"For what, Father?" He owed me no apology, of course. Had he forced Abel to commit such a despicable act? *No, that was my doing. My despicable act.*

He coughed into the handkerchief, then wiped his mouth. Blood was visible upon the surface of the cloth. "Lissie, if I had known... Oh, Lissie. I had no idea I was pushing you to marry such a monster."

"Father..." *You do not realize this, but I am the monster.* "Father, this is not your fault. None of it is."

I embraced my father, a blackness seeping into my heart as I consoled his weeping form.

Only one thought reverberated within my head: This could not, in fact, be undone.

Chapter Thirty-Six

As word of Abel's crime spread, it shook the weary world of Chapel Grove irrevocably. A kind of innocence was lost as the town discovered that even seemingly noble hearts can harbor dark impulses.

It could all be undone, I had convinced myself; yet, Abel's mother had not simply passed away, as William had. Instead, she had been stabbed by her son. With multiple retellings, the kind of knife used changed, as did the number of wounds, but the fact remained that she had died a terrible death. It had evidently been done in a fit of passion, for Mrs. Sinclair had suffered no fewer than seventeen stab wounds.

This was not something which resurrection alone could undo.

Appalled by Abel's actions, the town sought justice for Mrs. Sinclair with such fervor that Abel's execution was set for only later that week. With great remorse, he did not contest the charges against him. I visited him once before this, for such a thing was owed to him. When asked, he said only, "I loved my mother. I know not what happened, only that—something came over me. In that moment, I could hardly control myself."

He reportedly expressed the same sentiments before his execution, though I could not bear to witness it. Perhaps in my infirmity,

I would rush the gallows and place the noose around my own neck where it truly belonged. A black filthiness pervaded my heart, one which was impossible to cleanse.

Throughout the week, I contemplated what had gone wrong with the ceremony. *Make the heart stop*, I had requested, having no idea of the collateral damage such a request would incur. Though far from a resolved matter, it appeared to me that the ring had belonged to Abel's mother, lent to him on the condition of marriage to me, thus binding them both to it. There was existing discord between the two, so when the time came for the doll to stop Mrs. Sinclair's heart, it did so in a manner that irrevocably affected both owners.

In that sense, the heart did indeed stop, though not as I had envisioned.

The insidious doll was returned to Cassius at the earliest opportunity. Though briefly considering burning the damned thing, I placed it face-down upon his doorstep, neither knocking on the door to announce my presence nor leaving a note to explain its return.

What more needed to be said, for how devilishly had the doll failed? But, as I say, it had not failed but worked cruelly well—more devastatingly than could have been dreamed.

I chose to believe that included Cassius, the one who had placed it in my hands in the first place, promising a solution. He could never have known it would grant only further misery.

Perhaps the murder would have happened anyway, even without interference. Abel had a dark side, there was no doubt about that. Yet, no matter how I attempted to absolve myself, it was of no use. Deep within, I knew better. Had I not meddled, whatever argument Abel and his mother had on that fateful evening would not have escalated to bloodshed.

Despite the sullied state of my soul, my guilt remained hidden, a fact further underscored by an unexpected visit from Mayor Sinclair in the days following Abel and his mother's funerals.

He arrived on a day when my father felt well enough to join me in the kitchen for a meal, the last of its kind. I invited the mayor inside, but he politely declined, choosing instead to stand on the front porch.

"Mr. Knight, Miss Knight," he greeted us, looking considerably older than the last time we met. There was a heaviness to his posture, a grayness in his eyes. "I apologize greatly for this turn of events." His apology was punctuated by the gift of a large sum of money, enough to pay off our outstanding debts, as well as upcoming funeral expenses for my father.

"It is the least I can do under the circumstances," he said as my heart sank under the weight of regret.

"Mayor, while Elise and I are grateful for your generosity, we cannot accept this money," my father insisted, shaking his head. "We have sufficient funds to meet our needs." It was a slight bending of the truth, nearly to the point of breaking, but I was relieved by my father's refusal, for it was blood money, extorted from the Sinclairs because of my actions.

Nevertheless, the elder Sinclair was undeterred. He shook his head and pressed the envelope into my father's hand again. "I see little use in keeping the money, and I know it could assist you."

I averted my eyes quickly.

"Mayor, this must be a difficult time for you," my father remarked.

"It is indeed," the mayor replied, a slightly ironic smile playing at his lips. "I only hope this can alleviate some hardship for you and your daughter."

My father looked at the envelope again, pressing his lips together as if pondering his words. "Thank you," he said finally. "This is a kind gesture, and we appreciate it."

Mayor Sinclair bobbed his head in dull acknowledgment.

"If - if there is anything we might be able to do for Ida's funeral, please... Perhaps Elise could play a song for her?"

Mayor Sinclair's expression hardened. "That will not be necessary."

Of course. The whole thing had begun with the violin music enticing Abel to seek after making me his wife.

"Once again, I truly apologize," Mayor Sinclair said, turning to leave. But I stopped him.

"Wait," I called out, extending my hand. "Just a moment." I dashed upstairs to retrieve Abel's ring and returned it to him.

The mayor looked at it, his eyes beginning to glisten, then took it with a silent nod of gratitude and made his way back down the path to his home, a now desperately lonely place. His wife's new residence was the Sinclair mausoleum. His son's, the potter's field beyond the gates of the cemetery without even a stone to mark his name. This final cruelty weighed heavily upon me, for he would never have done it, had I not interfered.

Still, desperate hope remained that the violin would, indeed, bring William back – for what else could I do? In the chaos of these disastrous events, I found solace in the fact that it was nearly complete. All that was left was to varnish the wood and give it voice with a bridge, strings, and tuning pegs.

My father's health had only taken a more severe downturn since Abel's crime. I tried in vain to convince him he had done nothing wrong, but he would hear none of it.

He lay in his bed as, with heavy heart and little fanfare, I applied the varnish to the violin.

I could only hope enough had been done, enough power imbued, to do whatever was necessary, and set the violin aside for its varnish to set. Perhaps, in spite of his rapid deterioration, my father would survive just long enough to see the violin's completion. Perhaps then, he would have the opportunity to rest in peace, should all go as planned. Such was an outcome which could only be hoped for.

Without much enthusiasm but having little else to do, I buried myself in household chores, caring for my father, and assisted with some of the preparations for Chapel Grove's Harvest Festival, which was just around the corner. The town was in a markedly subdued mood during preparations, unlike previous years. There was talk of cancellation, but ultimately it was decided that the town needed a bit more cheer in light of what Abel had done.

"Now is the time to celebrate our bounty, more than ever," declared Mrs. Stanway at a town meeting, her statement met with murmurs of agreement. "We need each other all the more."

Indeed, though an air of mistrust lingered, Mrs. Stanway's speech rallied the residents of Chapel Grove to unite once more for the grandest Harvest Festival the town had ever seen. With the demands of preparation and my father's decline, there was little time to consider what to do with the violin in earnest.

In the end, it was hardly a question. Surrounded by such misery, I became increasingly desperate for even the slightest chance to restore William's life.

And perhaps, with such a miraculous return, even without the reappearance of Abel and his mother, it would lift the town's spirits as well. Perhaps they would believe, genuinely, that William's return was as Lazarus.

Chapter Thirty-Seven

The varnish was just about set on the day my father died.

Rain pounded on the roof as he lay in bed. I sat in a chair beside him. As in days past, we each held a cup of tea. His gray complexion was ominous, yet I found solace in his relaxed posture and increasingly heavy eyelids. I took the cup from his hands.

"Before it spills," I explained.

His lips moved in an indiscernible mumble.

"What?" I brought my face closer to his.

"Please, play for me, Elise."

It was a request which could hardly be refused. "I will, Father."

Thunder rumbled in the distance as I fetched the violin—the one he had given me after William's passing. Tenderness filled my heart as I carried it back to his room. He smiled at me, despite his evident exhaustion.

The song choice came to my mind unbidden: an old church hymn, 'Abide With Me,' had always reminded him of my mother and was well-suited to the somber peacefulness of the day.

As I began to play, gazing upon my father, serenity washed over him, confirming my choice. After the tumultuous months that had preceded, he deserved all the tranquility he could find.

"I wish your mother had lived to hear you play," he said after the final note had been played.

I gently placed the violin at the foot of his bed. "Me too."

He reached out a hand, which I took. "She would have loved you."

"I do, too," I replied. "But at least I had you."

The room was permeated with a peaceful spirit, insomuch that my father and I seemed to exist in a kind of protective bubble, a special place away from the rest of the world where we could reminisce safely.

"Elise, I'm so tired," he mumbled, his eyes beginning to drift shut.

"Then sleep, Father. Can I bring you anything else before you do?"

"No, Anna, I will be okay," he said, his eyes unfocused.

Anna had been my mother's name. I leaned in closer, certain he had misspoken. "Father?"

Yet, my heart understood long before my mind could accept it.

"Anna, oh Anna," he said, his eyes glistening. "Oh, I have missed you, my darling,"

"Father, it's me, Elise," I said, desperately hoping for him to recognize me and return to our conversation.

His gaze met mine, unusually bright, once again locking onto me. As his eyes filled with tears, he smiled. "I love you, darling," he uttered. "Now please, let me rest."

Words failing me, all I managed was, "I will."

As his eyes closed, I squeezed his hand. Something deep within urged me to stay, and so I did. I believe I held his hand long after he had passed on, his last words echoing in my mind, the realization of his departure only dawning on me when I felt the limp weight of his hand.

Desolation hardly described the state of my soul with the prospect of another death, another funeral, another burial, even after raising myself from my spot and calling Sumner Philpot, the undertaker, to the home. Unreality superseded the urge to cry, a blank numbness reigning instead.

Dry-eyed, I watched as Sumner and his assistant—perhaps the same one who had handled William's remains—carried my father's body away. When Sumner returned, he informed me that his wife would handle the arrangements for my father's funeral, to take place on the second of November.

"If I may say, my dear, you have endured tremendous sorrow and tribulation." He cleared his throat. "Under the circumstances, I wish that your only worry may be to grieve your father and handle his estate. That is plenty, I believe."

"Thank you, Mr. Philpot."

I shut the door behind them, gazing around the house which now belonged to me alone. The house, the shed, the workshop, and...

My father's unfinished violin was still in the workshop.

It would never be finished.

Upon this realization, this largely inconsequential thing which nevertheless seemed thoroughly, pathetically depressing, only then did I fall to my knees and weep.

Chapter Thirty-Eight

A daughter often longs to make her father proud, a desire I know all too well. As my father approached the twilight of his life, my hope was not only to make him proud but also to ensure his peaceful transition from this life to the next.

Neither of these pursuits had been successful.

My father had died with my future in great tumult, a cloak of guilt around his shoulders due to his belief that his daughter had nearly married a man who murdered his own mother.

The heaviest of shame settled down to my bones, desolation as deep as the marrow in the wake of my great failures.

After William's death, it seemed impossible life could become worse. How wrong I had been, for my anguish hardly ceased with what I had done to my father. The Sinclair family, too, had been torn apart by my actions.

The days following my father's death passed in a haze of affliction, debating what I would do next.

One might question why I didn't strive to restore my father's life, as I had desired to with William's. It would certainly have been more challenging, given the frail state of his body compared to William's robust health, imperiled only by a minor flaw. Likewise, reviving Abel's mother seemed unlikely; would the violin heal her injuries along with restoring her life? I did not know. As for Abel, he would remain forever stained as a murderer, and his resurrection would only extend his suffering.

Yet, Chapel Grove had become a broken place, aching for healing. The idea of leaving it all behind for the allure of France or Italy seemed unthinkable.

Perhaps my near-marriage to Abel had only caused my heart to yearn more fervently for William, whose smile swam before my mind, the warm, dimpled sun-bronzed cheeks from his work in the fields, his eyes warm like the sun descending below the horizon. Had he not been lost, all would have been well.

The thought of using the violin, attempting the miracle of resurrection, seemed suddenly foolish.

And yet, what more could I do but see through the plan already set into motion? The violin, as I saw it, represented my best chance to set things right.

Perhaps Abel and his mother could not be brought back. The burden would weigh heavy on my heart for the remainder of my life. Yet, should those in Chapel Grove witness a commensurate miracle, might it not set to work healing their hearts, as well?

If it was successful, perhaps all could not be undone - but it could represent a start, a renewal for all involved. It seemed likely that it would be, as well, for Cassius had been unfailingly correct.

Had the vial not worked?

Had the doll not worked?

Both, indeed, had been tremendously effective.

I wrestled with the question of where I had gone wrong. Perhaps it had been in my specificity, that in asking the spirits to prick his heart, it had been insufficient. They had provoked the anger which already resided in his theoretical heart. My thoughts had drifted to his parents during the ceremony, of their reaction upon finding him dead.

During this time of mourning, my mind settled upon the idea that it had come down not to an inherent evil in the doll, but an unwitting error by its user.

Perhaps all could not be undone, that was true. If one thing could be made right, perhaps that was enough.

With the violin as my last opportunity, I could afford no reservations. The deaths seemed relentless. But perhaps, in my fervor, at least one, the source of this anguish, could indeed be undone.

If only I finished the violin.

Finding a semblance of steadiness within, I rose from my seat in the hallway, making my way to the workshop. The space offered a comforting retreat from the hollow echo of the house, filled with the specters of memories. My finger caressed the violin's surface gently, gliding across it. The varnish had set. By the next day, I could string the violin and deliver the completed instrument to Cassius.

There was one more detail I wished to add before that time.

I reached for the drawer where my father stored his scalpels—tools reserved for the intricate work involved in crafting the scroll, f-holes, and purfling. Their blades, razor-sharp, were kept separate from other instruments to avoid accidental injury, making a scalpel the perfect choice for my task.

Light danced across the blade of the scalpel I selected, its edge pristine.

My right hand would be best, to retain greater flexibility in my left hand for fingering notes upon the violin's neck. Such mattered more than my penmanship at the moment.

If the violin's power could be amplified by infusing more of myself into it, then I resolved to hold nothing back.

I pictured William's face as it had been, how I wished to see him once more. Then, before I could convince myself otherwise, I thrust the scalpel into my right hand, squeezed hard, and pulled with my left. Pain exploded through my palm as the scalpel sliced from the base of my little finger to the pad beneath my thumb.

Stars flashed in my mind as blood gushed from within the closed fist and crimson droplets fell upon the violin's surface.

My mind screamed with the intensity of the pain, awestruck as the viscous red liquid pooled onto the varnished surface. The cut hand pulsed in time with the beat of my racing heart, but still, I needed more.

"William must return," I said aloud, squeezing my fist as one might juice a lemon. Fresh waves of pain radiated from my hand, but it mattered little to me. Shortly, the pain was replaced with a kind of satisfaction as I observed the blood spattered throughout the lacquer, a bit of my life-force sacrificed in order to restore William's.

My right hand was absolutely coated with blood, enough that, to make my point clear, I wiped more blood along the ribs of the violin. *As Eve, being created from the rib of Adam.* The pain had, by this point, given way to satisfaction.

It hardly mattered if the blood's coagulation altered the vibration of the wood, not when it imbued it with so much more personal sacrifice in pursuit of William.

My work sufficient for now, I retrieved an old rag my father had on the worktable and wrapped my hand in it, then made my way back into the house. More could be done once the wound had been cared for.

A cabinet within the kitchen held some gauze. I placed a fresh towel, a washcloth this time, upon the wound and secured it with the gauze, thinking about my next step as I made my way back to the workshop.

While the blood flow in my hand slowed and the pain ebbed, I retrieved a bridge blank from another drawer in the workshop. The bridge would not go on the violin until the following day, when I also installed the strings, giving the blood upon the body time to dry.

Until then, the bridge needed work, as well.

The bridge rested on my bandaged hand as I spoke aloud, "Let this bridge represent the link by which the soul of William may return to his body once more."

A vision filled my mind of William crossing that very bridge, draped in gold, surrounded by the vivid blues and greens of spring, rejoicing, and embracing me with ecstasy as the devastation was undone.

What more could be done? I pondered this question when a particular turn of phrase returned to my mind. *Of course.* The sound post of a violin was sometimes called its soul, or, in French, its âme.

Placing the bridge beside the violin on the workbench, I searched for a dowel for the violin's sound post. It would need precise shaping to fit within the violin, but for now, I cut it slightly longer than required. I held the piece tenderly, as one might a child, bringing it near my lips and speaking in a mere whisper, "Call to William. Translate the song played into the irresistible call to rise from his grave, to reunite his soul with his body once more."

I laid the sound post on the workspace beside the bridge and the violin itself.

My stomach protested with hunger, but its demands were ignored in favor of the vital work ahead. I returned to the house to collect the violin my father had given me, the one which had raised me from my oblivion.

Standing beside the components of my creation, I raised my father's violin and began to play. I played 'Abide With Me' as my father had heard on his last day of mortality, the Vivaldi piece which I had played for William during my first visit to the cemetery, then a medley of various other pieces, partial and whole, which I had in my repertoire. In so doing, I hoped the fledgling violin might be nourished, infused with an echo of the violin whose magic had resurrected me not so long ago.

I lowered the violin from my chin and let it rest at my side. I gazed upon the nearly finished one, knowing it had, indeed, been infused with a piece of myself, within each fiber.

By the time I entered my father's workshop the following morning, the sun had just begun to rise over the horizon.

The sound post was installed first, with the careful shaving of either end to ensure a tight fit. This task was rather difficult with my bandaged hand, but the residual pain from the scalpel's cut reminded me of the sacrifice I had made, encouraging me all the more.

The sound post setter, a bent tweezer-like instrument, guided the post through one of the f-holes. An initial attempt saw one end of the post slipping against the belly plate, but on a second try, holding the instrument more firmly, I secured the post snugly between the belly and back plates. With a moment of trepidation, I withdrew the tool, and the post stood firm.

It was then time to shape the bridge, filing its feet to ensure an exact fit against the belly plate. Once all four strings were installed, the bridge was held firmly in place by their tension.

Improper as it seemed to play the violin before strictly instructed, I did a rough job of tuning it by plucking the strings, using only the force necessary to hear the note before being at ease with the level of tuning I had achieved.

Each note emerged as a prelude, a sensation like the first kicks of an infant within its mother's womb.

But then...

My breath caught, taking in the violin as the sun crested the horizon, casting golden light into the workshop.

Finished.

It was finished.

The instrument was not a glory to behold, but still held an intrinsic charm, created not only with my hands, but also imbued with my heart, my soul. It was mine, and I belonged to it in equal measure, for within, it held the brokenness of my heart in the aftermath of William's death. It quaked with the rage which had welled within, contemplating life's desperate injustice. It softened beneath wonderful moments my father and I had enjoyed within his workshop. It ticked away my time with Abel, and the crime which had stained my soul. It mourned the lost vial of life-restoring elixir. It contained the horror of the purple doll and all the devastation it had wrought.

Every bit of myself was threaded into that violin, igniting a sense of pride. I would later come to realize I had underestimated how powerful it had become, but in that moment, I reveled in the knowledge that the time had come to inform Cassius that it was finished.

Now—a cold shiver traced my spine with the thought—it was time for him to keep his end of the bargain.

Chapter Thirty-Nine

Under cover of darkness and with violin in hand, I made the journey to deliver the news to Cassius. My heart delighted at the prospect that my William was on the brink of return, and we might be reunited once more—perhaps even this very evening.

Main Street was adorned with the quintessential decorations for the upcoming Harvest Festival. Shop windows had been decorated inside and out with pumpkins, gourds, leaves, cornucopias, while several whimsically dressed scarecrows stood guard at the entrances.

A tractor perched atop Matby's hat shop brought a smile to my face as it reminded me of the long-standing tradition of playful pranks leading up to All Hallow's Eve. I found comfort in the persistence of such normalcy in spite of the surrounding darkness.

I mused briefly on what other trickery may be afoot in town but focused my thoughts as I drew near Cassius's wagon. My heart thrummed as I stepped up to the door and rapped upon it. The sound stirred Osiris from his slumber, his large, ebony eyes meeting mine with a displeased look at the interruption.

"Apologies," I whispered, stepping back and crossing my left hand over the bandage on my right. Osiris continued to gaze at me with a sense of distrust.

After a moment's bustling within the wagon, Cassius emerged, looking bleary-eyed and clad in a flannel nightshirt and pants. "Elise, good evening," he said, stepping out and closing the door behind him.

"Good evening to you." A smile teased at my lips.

Osiris chuffed his indignation. "Return to sleep, this does not concern you," Cassius chided, before turning his attention back to me. "To what do I owe the pleasure?"

"It is finished." My tentative smile blossomed into a full one. Finished.

His eyebrows rose in surprise. "The violin? Indeed?"

I extended the case as proof.

"*Indeed.*" He sat upon the steps of his wagon. "I confess I had my doubts, having heard little from you after the appearance of the doll upon my doorstep."

"It has been a trying time," I acknowledged.

"I had hoped for the best, but did not wish to cause more harm, nor to interrupt your last days with your father." He paused, folding his hands. "I am sorry to hear of his passing, Elise. He seemed a good man."

"The very best," I replied.

"I am sorry for the loss of the elixir."

"That was my mistake. Given what happened…" I trailed off, unable to complete the thought. "Suffice it to say, the violin holds greater significance now than ever."

"Such is understandable. I should have known better than to doubt you," he said with a note of admiration. "Still, I apologize about what happened with the Sinclairs. Such misery could hardly have been foreseen."

Thoughtfully, hesitantly, I inquired, "Is that indeed the case?"

He nodded solemnly. "If I had known," he began, "then I—"

"Surely you would not have given such a thing to me," I said.

His eyes narrowed, head bobbed momentarily from side to side, then he said, "You would have, at least, had fair warning." Before the implications of this statement could be fully appraised, Cassius gestured toward my bandaged hand. "Did the violin give you trouble?"

"No trouble, exactly," I replied.

Cassius raised an eyebrow.

"Perhaps I can show you?" I made to hand him the violin, but he declined.

"Tomorrow night would be preferable," he advised.

I held the case close to my chest, my disappointment evident. "Why not now?"

"Certain preparations are necessary on my part." He glanced skyward at the nearly full moon. "Tomorrow night also seems more auspicious for our undertaking. Given the delicacy of the matter, we must leave nothing to chance."

Disappointed though I was, a day's delay was hardly worth the fight. "If that would be suitable for you. After the Harvest Festival, of course."

"Indeed, after dark would be best. Does midnight suit you?"

"Yes, it does." My heart fluttered with anticipation. The meeting was set for just over twenty-four hours from now.

"Meet me in the cemetery tomorrow night, then, near William's grave, and we shall make the exchange."

"I will," I promised, yet a lingering concern remained. "I still don't understand how the violin will work. Is there anything more I need to do to prepare?"

"*Elise*," reassured Cassius with a dismissive wave of his hand. "It is late. We shall address one matter at a time. Rest assured, I will instruct you regarding this tomorrow."

Momentarily reassured, we bid each other farewell, and I returned home with the violin tucked securely under my arm.

As I followed the creek road, partially hidden by half-barren trees, the path was surprisingly well-lit by the overhead moon. Though not fully illuminated, its light felt exceptionally close. The stars twinkled, casting their final gleam upon a world devoid of William—for tomorrow, we would dance beneath them once more. The thought was so profound, I nearly wept with joy at that moment. Instead, I hugged the violin tightly to my chest once more, the relic which would bring my love back to me.

The house was dark and silent, and upon crossing its threshold, a heaviness fell upon me once more. The void left by my father's passing resonated as a tangible presence within these walls. How cruel it felt that he should depart this world so near the completion of the violin.

I closed the door behind me with a decisive press. Without my father's vibrant presence, the house seemed cloaked in an oppressive shade of gray, unrelated to the mere darkness of night. William's arrival would be nothing short of joyous—a testament to life renewed, paving the way for creation: children, dear and innocent boys and girls, who would once again fill the home with love, laughter, hope, and perhaps, dare I say, happiness?

Indeed, in the bittersweet dawn of my existence, marked by the pain my father endured following my mother's death, this house had long seemed devoid of such treasures. Navigating through the darkness, I ascended the stairs and made my way to my bedroom, where I undressed and slipped beneath the covers. My gaze drifted to the trees and sky outside the window.

Tonight would be the final night I slept alone, I mused, for the following day—All Hallows' Eve of 1871—was destined to herald a transformation.

One way or the other.

Chapter Forty

Upon waking the next morning, every fiber of my being was alight with nervous energy. As it would only be proper for William to return to a comfortable, well-kept home, I used this energy quite productively instead of stewing on what might happen that evening. After all, what was meant to happen would be revealed soon enough.

So, I set to work: the logs behind the house were transformed into a neat stack of firewood. The windows gleamed, their sills freed from grime and cobwebs. With the help of a broom, I chased cobwebs from the high corners of the rooms, places otherwise difficult for me to reach. I dusted behind picture frames on the mantle.

My heart stilled at the discovery of *Robinson Crusoe* tucked into the edge of my father's chair. Moving it seemed a shame, yet something stirred within me, encouraging me onward. My fingers traced the edges, finding a bookmark on the last page he had read. I settled into his customary seat and opened the book to the marked page, which read:

> *It was now that I began sensibly to feel how much more happy the life I now led was, with all its miserable circumstances, than the wicked, cursed, abominable life I led all the past part of my days; and now having changed both my sorrows and my*

joys, my very desires altered, my affections changed their gusts, and my delights were perfectly new...

Tenderness pricked at my heart, wondering whether the passage might be a sign from the beyond, suggesting that though my father found no joy in our separation, he was at peace in his newfound heavenly abode.

Tears welled up in my eyes at the thought that even in death, his greatest concern might be my well-being. I felt undeserving of such care. If my father knew the truth of what had befallen Abel and his mother, perhaps he would have left a very different message—or left me entirely to my devices.

I hoped that this evening would set things right.

Not yet ready to return *Robinson Crusoe* to its place, I replaced my father's bookmark and nestled the book back into his chair. There was still much to be done. My arms ached once the final rug had been beaten clean, but my mind felt cleared once more in the aftermath of the labor. After a thorough sweeping of the floors, the rugs were laid back down. Following this, I refreshed the linens on my father's bed. A light layer of dust had settled in his room, which I carefully wiped away, avoiding drawers or ledges where personal artifacts might be stored, planning to leave them for discovery another day.

With the house largely in order, the time came to prepare myself for the evening. Though I hadn't decided about attending the festival, I chose to dress in a way that would allow me to go.

Sitting in front of the mirror in my bedroom, I parted my hair in the middle and braided it into two long plaits.

It was then time to retrieve my dress.

Several months ago, I had hidden the dress away, as it was a painful reminder of what should have been. Tonight, that lovely blue gown, lovingly sewn by Mrs. Miller to be my wedding dress, was the only outfit suitable for greeting William.

As I pulled it from the back of my closet, I couldn't help but feel compassion for the Elise who had tucked it away, her presence emanating from the fabric—the woman who had hidden it, not wanting a reminder of a future that never came to be.

If only that Elise had known what was to come.

My night clothes fell to the floor, then I slipped the dress over my head and buttoned the front. It was significantly looser than the last time Mrs. Miller had checked the fit, but it was still the best choice for the evening. The dress had a sash around the waist, which I tied into a bow.

I wore a pair of thick stockings to keep warm, then chose the sturdier of my shoes to allow for an easier walk across uneven ground.

Once dressed, I felt a desire to visit the violin before joining the town for the Harvest Festival.

I returned downstairs to where my violin still rested against the wall by the door. I picked up the case and set it upon the kitchen table. I opened the case, and oh, what a sight it was.

I traced my finger along the violin's edge, from the top of the scroll, along the neck, down the ribs, over the belly, and finally to the chin rest and tailpiece. The blood spilling over the varnish created a slight tackiness. Would it affect the sound, I wondered? But it mattered little, given how much more important its spiritual essence was compared to its aesthetic or acoustic qualities.

Looking upon the instrument, its success seemed certain. My soul pacified once more, I clasped the case shut and left the violin there until the time came to meet Cassius in the cemetery.

Until then, it was time to attend the Harvest Festival, at least for a short stint. I made my way to town, where the distant sounds of revelry echoed.

A row of tables had been set up along Main Street, the place where the meal would be shared among friends and neighbors. The familiar sight brought levity to my soul, which was jolted by a roar somewhere to my right, followed by a commotion.

"*Boys*!" an adult voice roared, followed by peals of youthful laughter. "This is no laughing matter! *Thatcher*!"

I proceeded cautiously, my footsteps tinged with trepidation. One of Crogan's deputies, Riley Duncan, was kicking dirt over a small fire in some bushes while two of the Thatcher boys and freckle-faced Dirk O'Callahan stood aside, laughing hysterically.

A harassed-looking James Thatcher hurried to the scene. "Boys, for crying out loud. That's enough pranks for this year." This admonition was met with only more howling laughter, after which the boys ran off. "So sorry, Deputy. I will put a stop to them at once."

"I should *hope* so," said Duncan, brushing his sandy-blond hair from his sweaty face, leaving a bit of ash behind as he did so. The smell of burnt underbrush hung in the air.

"How many fires does that make?" I asked.

The deputy was momentarily startled. "Miss Knight," he said, recovering, "How are you?"

"Well enough, I suppose. You, however, seem to be having quite the day."

"Indeed. The pranks this year are out of control. Did you see the tractor? On Matby's?"

Suppressing a smile. I nodded. "I did."

"Unbelievable. Just absurd. If these pranks worsen, I shall propose their abolition. They're a nuisance at best." He seemed eager for an opportunity to vent his frustrations. "I, for one, can hardly believe we've let them go on as long as we have. It's utter nonsense, if you ask me."

"I would likely feel the same if it were my hands that were singed."

"Miss, what happened to *your* hand?"

"Oh, nothing," I replied, tucking it behind my back. "The slip of a knife."

He eyed the rather conspicuous bandage. "If you're sure, then." He seemed to drop it but added quietly, "Really sorry to hear about your father."

"Thank you."

"You know, if you need any help around the house, anything a man might assist with, please let me know," he offered. His tone was innocuous, yet a glint in his eye suggested more than mere friendliness.

"I will, thank you," I said. "Best of luck firefighting."

He softened a bit and laughed then. "Sure will. Thanks, Miss."

I then continued to Main Street, where preparations for the feast were in full swing. The festival, as bustling as ever, nevertheless had a somber undertone. As I reached the edge of the table arrangement, the air was still lively but somewhat subdued, lacking the full-throated joy of previous years.

The celebration, with its smell of apple pie and roasting corn and chicken in the air, existed in the shadow of William's death, of Mrs. Sinclair's murder, of the execution of Abel Sinclair, and, of course, of my father's death.

This shadow made the familiar sensations all the more comforting.

The Purcells, lugging cartons full of freshly pressed apple cider to just outside the general store, where it seemed most everything had been set up.

Mrs. Miller approaching me, commenting on the dress. "It seemed a shame not to wear it," I said, then thanked her once more before she parted to assist with the setting up.

Elmer Matby, laughing drunkenly about the tractor on the roof of his store.

Dr. Bell sitting next to his wife, who was busily crocheting a baby blanket while chatting with Mrs. Stanway.

Children, running, playing, their rosy-cheeked faces as joyful and carefree as ever.

I noticed Mayor Sinclair sitting alone at one of the tables, a shadow of his former buoyant self. His discomfort tugged at my heartstrings.

I approached him, then asked, "Is this seat taken?"

He looked up with red-rimmed eyes. "No, it's not."

Though he had not formally invited me, I sat beside him. "It's good to see you here," I said.

He offered me a weak smile. As I glanced at the crowd, I spotted William's parents, with one of his brothers close behind. They seemed better than during our last meeting. I waved but was met with a disinterested look.

When William had returned, whether they knew I was the cause or not, perhaps things could be different, I thought.

I hoped all could be set right. I gazed past the current scene to Cassius's wagon, where only Osiris's back legs and hindquarters were visible. The wagon was packed and ready to depart in the morning. His departure saddened me slightly, as I had grown accustomed to seeing his wagon at the road's end.

Shortly thereafter, Reverend Willard rose, calling everyone to attention. A hush fell over the crowd.

"Welcome, residents of Chapel Grove, to the annual Harvest Festival. I am so glad we have come together on this day to rejoice in the many blessings the Lord has granted us, especially as we mourn the things which have passed away. It is times like these when we must come together, and I have never been more heartened to see everyone united."

I noticed Mayor Sinclair's shoulders begin to tremble, and I gently placed a hand on his shoulder.

The dinner commenced in earnest shortly afterward, and though my nerves dulled my appetite, I knew I needed to preserve my strength for the night ahead.

As the festival drew to a close, I bid farewell to Mayor Sinclair in particular, as well as to others, then returned home to await the arrival of nightfall.

My feet paced the house restlessly, my eyes fixed on the clock until finally, blessedly, the time turned to a quarter to midnight.

Adjusting my hair in the mirror by the entryway, I donned my coat, picked up the violin case, and stepped into the night to meet Cassius.

One last time.

Chapter Forty-One

Clutching the violin case protectively against my chest, I made my way to the cemetery. The full moon on this chilly evening illuminated the path before me.

The construction of this violin had taken much from me, sacrifices which had only been tolerable with the understanding that the return would be far greater.

My love, restored to life once more.

Perhaps it was because of that promise that this night was full of an electrified kind of excitement, such that, though I wore no overcoat, the chill in the air was scarcely noticeable on the way to the cemetery.

A calm assurance filled me as I drew near. Tendrils of fog swirled along the edges of the cemetery, obscuring the most distant gravestones. Among the closer rows stood the figure of a man.

Cassius.

My heart fluttered at the sight of him. I navigated the aisles between the headstones, which appeared like politely waiting guests, fall leaves strewn on the neatly trimmed grass resembling flower petals left by a rosy-cheeked flower girl. If only I had a bouquet, the comparison would be complete, for this was indeed the evening I would reunite with my husband-to-be.

Cassius waited beside William's grave, shovel in hand. A considerable pile of dirt lay beside him. It occurred to me that, naturally, the dirt should be removed from atop William's casket—it wouldn't do to restore his life only to leave him buried. One of my old nightmares resurfaced, of desperately digging through stubborn grave dirt as my William screamed beneath. But such fears were unfounded now.

"Good evening," greeted Cassius. Despite having dug the grave, his suit was quite clean. I supposed he must have changed before this meeting. He was as dapper as ever, though my attention was drawn to the purple dahlia in his pocket, a sight that momentarily dampened my spirits. I quickly set aside both the flower and the nightmarish vision of a buried-alive William.

"Good evening," I replied. "You have been busy." I gestured to the mound of dirt beside him.

"Indeed," he said, leaning upon the shovel. "My show has been packed away, and it seemed the best use of time to complete the task before your arrival."

"Well, thank you," I said.

"My pleasure."

We shared a smile which slowly grew, eager as we both were for the culmination of this pursuit.

"Are you ready to see the violin?" I asked.

Cassius fixed his gaze upon the case, his eyes shining with hunger. "I am," he replied.

I knelt to open the case beside William's newly reopened vault. One latch stuck slightly before yielding. The others followed without issue, and the lid opened. I removed the violin, cradling it against my shoulder with the strings facing out, and stood to face Cassius, whose breath caught audibly.

"Elise, *what*…"

"You instructed me that the more of myself was imbued within the instrument, the more powerful it would be," I said.

Cassius looked upon my bandaged hand, then stepped forward, reaching for the bloodied surface of the violin.

"I have held nothing back, Mr. McCalmont."

"*Indeed*," he breathed, his Adam's apple rising and falling. He paused before touching the violin. "May I?"

I nodded, savoring the satisfaction gleaming in his expression. He took the violin gently, reverently, his left hand on its neck, his right supporting the tailpiece as he slowly turned it, inspecting every inch.

"There is more within," I explained. "The bridge, for instance." I hesitated, feeling that my alterations to the bridge were too esoteric to put into words, and decided to continue. "The f-holes, too, have had details of personal significance added. There are Bible passages written within the body, as well."

Cassius turned the violin to look at the bridge from an oblique angle, able to see some evidence of these alterations. "You have done a truly exceptional job," he remarked, caressing the violin's surface with his fingertips. "Better, even, than I had imagined."

Though much of its workmanship was no doubt of amateur quality, especially in comparison to my father's abilities, I agreed. My creation was indeed a thing of great beauty in my eyes.

Impatience must have shown on my face, for Cassius then said, "I imagine you're anxious to test its power." His green eyes glittered.

"I am." He held the violin out to me, but I shook my head. "Please, it is yours."

"No, truly, I insist."

Perplexed—and, confessedly, a bit hurt—I asked, "You do not wish to try it?"

He declined with a raised hand, the other resting behind his back. "Not only are you the superior violinist, but it seems only fitting for you, its creator, to play it first."

Of course, this connection between myself and the instrument. As prioritized as it had been, this should hardly have surprised me. "If you are sure, then," I said. I retrieved the bow from the case, then took the violin from Cassius.

"It needs tuning still," I explained.

"By all means," he replied.

Settling the violin under my chin, I got into playing position with a touch of awkwardness, unaccustomed as I was to having an audience besides my father. And William, of course. I reminded myself that he would be listening, too, that the violin would be calling out to him more than any other.

I drew the bow along the G string, which, despite being out of tune, resonated with loveliness. As the knob was turned to adjust its voice, the resonance within the body of the violin stirred within my heart, as well. A dark richness swelled within which I had never before experienced. With a look at Cassius, it was apparent he could feel it, too.

It was more than the simple pleasure of the lovely voice of a well-voiced violin, but something deeper.

It will work. In my father's workshop, something incredible had been crafted, an object powerful enough to raise my love from his grave.

As I continued tuning, tears welled in my eyes, my heart stirred with longing as G was brought into its correct tune, then D.

I was reminded of what I had pleaded for the sound post, its soul, to do; what I had impressed upon the bridge it must represent.

Then A. I recalled the golden bridge adorned with spring flowers and vibrant life. The trees surrounding the cemetery rustled.

Then, finally, the highest string, the E string, was brought into tune. I drew the bow over all four strings, resulting in the ideal progression of sounds. Then, I allowed both the violin and bow to rest at my side as goosebumps rose on my arms and legs.

"There is nothing I want more than what this violin is intended to bring back," I said quietly.

By this time, the power which buzzed in the air centered around where Cassius and I stood, swirling in the air like the gathering of a lightning storm. Indeed, the night had dimmed with the clouds collecting in the sky. Though the bow had ceased stroking the violin strings, there remained in our surroundings a distinctive hum, an energy which caught my breath short.

"I imagine that is true," said Cassius.

I nodded. With much effort, I drew a deep, steadying breath, preparing to finally speak the words which had been so eagerly anticipated. As though the energy in the air could be dissipated if one spoke too vigorously, my voice was hushed as I spoke.

"It is ready."

"Wonderful," Cassius said, his wide green eyes alight despite the dim conditions. "If that is so, let us begin."

Chapter Forty-Two

The cemetery lay in an eerie silence, the only movement the wisps of fog curling around the gravestones. The violin and bow hung by my side as I awaited further guidance.

"Now, then—play," Cassius instructed.

I tilted my head to the side. "Simply play?" The simplicity seemed contrary to my previous complex efforts.

"Simply play," he confirmed. "When you are ready, of course."

I nodded, then raised the violin to playing position and flexed the fingers of my left hand. My gaze swept over the cemetery once more, and I shivered. *Had it been so cold before?* The fog seemed to gather, becoming denser. Casting aside the thought as a mere figment of my imagination, I settled on 'Abide With Me', for a song I knew well would be easier to play despite my nerves.

With one last look upon William's body, where only the pine lid of his casket was visible, I drew the bow across the strings, ringing out the first note. The sound reverberated deeply, trailing up my arms, causing my breath to hitch. I looked to Cassius, dipping the violin from its playing position.

Cassius stood with his arms folded, a contemplative fist beneath his chin. He nodded, silently encouraging me to continue.

I raised the violin back into position and resumed playing. As the song unfolded, a tingling sensation coursed from my arms through my chest, radiating through my stomach and down to the soles of my feet. This excitation, pleasurable as it was unnerving, strengthened throughout the song. It seduced me, calling upon the whole of my being to cease resistance, to embrace it. I closed my eyes, yielding to that strange tingling, swaying slightly with the movement of my bow. My mind's eye conjured the image of the bridge over which I had imagined William returning to life.

Upon playing the final notes of the song, two phenomena occurred simultaneously. A flash of light shone even through my closed eyelids. At the same time, a blast like thunder, which originated from the violin itself, rumbled throughout the landscape. The combination elicited a gasp from me, and I opened my eyes. They were briefly unfocused on the scene before me. A ringing remained in my ears.

"Elise," Cassius said. His voice seemed oddly far away, as though we were separated by a long tunnel.

My eyes readjusted to the darkness of the graveyard. The ringing subsided.

"*Elise*," Cassius repeated, his voice heard nearer this time, his tone more insistent. "Look."

I followed Cassius's pointed gesture towards William's grave. To my great astonishment, there was a disturbance in the dirt covering the casket's lid. My breathing became shallow as the lid first shifted, then raised, revealing the being beneath.

"Oh, *William*," I breathed. There, emerging from the grave, stood William—my William—rising to stand. His eyes cast around, bewildered, his lips parted slackly. "Darling, it's me. It's Elise."

William looked up at my words. His eyes—the lovely, honey-brown eyes I had so desperately missed—met mine. He seemed to recognize me, at least vaguely.

"William," I repeated, falling to my knees and setting the violin and bow aside. My hand stretched out to meet his, to assist his rising from the grave. The hand which met mine was cold as the surrounding night. *How awful,* I thought. *We must warm him at once.*

With my support, William stepped from his earthen bed.

We gazed upon one another. He looked just as I remembered, just as he had been buried, in a nice suit which, in life, had been reserved for church services. Or weddings.

What a vision we were, adorned as bride and groom, just as we had been intended.

I fell into his embrace. "Oh, my love," I said, overcome with joy, breathing in his smell, that sweaty, smell of grass and corn which had the scent of safety to me.

Tears fell unabated, for the violin had worked, just as Cassius had promised.

My love had returned.

The world around us faded into insignificance as we clung to each other, allowing time to pass unnoticed through our fingers. The atmosphere was almost enchantingly simple in its magic.

I stepped back to look at Cassius, to thank him for all he had done. My eyes then took in an unexpected sight: that of a shadowy figure looming behind him in the fog.

Had we been discovered?

"Cassius," I warned but my fear waned upon my recognition of the figure. "*Father?*"

My father had not been buried yet, but had been in the funeral parlor until a proper service could be conducted. And yet, there would be no need. He had returned! I stepped toward the figure, for indeed, it *was* my father; but confusion soon replaced joy.

Something was wrong.

"Father?" I asked again, and the figure grinned. It was not my father's warm, welcoming smile but its counterfeit, the bared teeth of a demon. My blood turned to ice at the sight.

"What—" But my thought remained unfinished.

Looking back upon William, a change had overcome him as well, for his eyes were no longer filled with love. Instead, they were dark, blackened. A similarly ferocious grin was stretched upon his skin, which now appeared dry, leathery.

"Oh *God.*" The whisper escaped my mouth.

"Elise, the violin." It was Cassius, still beside me. My eyes, briefly stuck on the horrid scene before me, tore away to look at him. His hands were outstretched. "Give me the violin, Elise."

I looked upon the violin beside William's grave.

"I will take care of it," Cassius assured me.

Nodding, unable to speak, I stooped to pick up the violin and the bow and handed the set to Cassius. I then stood beside him, gazing out at my father.

A fetid odor assaulted my nostrils, replacing the scent I had imagined was William's in life, perhaps a fabrication of my unstable mind, desperate to believe he could somehow return. The air was thick with the aroma of decay, so much so that I could almost taste it. It called to mind the night of the raven's reanimation, that display of power with the resurrection flute, only intensified: a blend of old, abandoned farmyard, forgotten meat, mold, fecal matter, rot, and corrosion. I instinctively covered my nose and mouth, but it made little difference, so pervasive was the stench.

A silent scream rose in my throat as I took in the scene. Movement caught my eye in the distance. Someone was approaching.

No, I thought, we must not be discovered before this situation is resolved. No one else should witness such horrors. Let our eyes, our minds, be the only ones tainted by bearing witness to this event, having orchestrated the entire debacle.

Such thoughts turned out to be unwarranted, for it was not the residents of Chapel Grove who lurched in the distance—at least, not its current residents. An entirely new kind of fear overrode the former.

Instead of the living residents of Chapel Grove coming to discover the source of the commotion, it was those who now called the cemetery home. All along the graveyard, from just behind them to the farthest reaches, restlessness ensued. Whether buried beneath the ground, in crypts, or in mausoleums, it seemed all were moving, every place of rest yielding its dead.

Old Mrs. Landon, the sweet old woman who, in life, had made little knitted handcrafts for children many years ago, now lurched toward me amid the throng. She had been a good woman—my friend, even.

"Mr. Wilcox?" I said sadly, recognizing, too, one of my father's former friends. He had died before I had even turned ten if I remembered correctly, but he showed no signs of recognizing me, only blankly staring as he continued wandering.

Oh God, what have I done?

This was precisely what Vada had warned me about, of course; oh, what had Louella seen, what had become of her little Sophia in light of this dreadful power? The vision of that tiny body amidst all this horror flashed through my mind, my eyes welling with tears.

There was little time to ponder this point while all the formerly dead were shuffling unsteadily but persistently toward Cassius and myself.

My hand reached my chest, a wave of nausea churning my stomach, and I glanced at Cassius. His face betrayed none of the disgust, shock, or misery I felt. Instead, his expression was that of a biologist observing an unusual yet not entirely unexpected phenomenon. He appeared not horrified by the scene, but rather intrigued.

How could he respond in such a way, if not just due to the smell emanating from the bodies walking around us?

I looked once more at the resurrected dead, frozen in place with fear. "Oh, God," I murmured, my hands covering my mouth, for it seemed even more of my sins had come to haunt me.

Abel stood with the dead, his face contorted with rage upon the sight of me.

His mother was beside him. The dress she had been buried in was stained by dried blood from her mortal wounds, her fair hair darkened by grave dirt.

"No, oh no," I whispered. "This cannot be real."

But alas, how real it *was*.

My mouth opened and my face froze in a silent scream as I took a step back. Cassius had said the more of myself I poured into the violin, the stronger it would become. It seemed unlikely even he could have anticipated the strength it would wield once completed.

I looked at Cassius, whose eyes were fixed on the throng of undead gathered around the violin. His inquisitorial expression had transformed into something else entirely.

He looked, of all things, *pleased*.

"What have you *done?*" I said, launching myself at him. In doing so, my foot caught upon something unseen, perhaps a stone or root, causing me to lose my balance. Wedged as my foot was, the fall caused my ankle to twist painfully beneath me. Pain surged from the joint, I screamed as stars exploded before my eyes.

Slow though the dead may move, I was acutely aware of my vulnerability in this moment. I scrambled to a seated position and looked upon the dead once more. A whimper escaped my mouth. I attempted to force myself up, to rise from where I sat, but my ankle crumpled uselessly beneath me.

The time had come to reap the consequences of the evil I had sown, for the dead would soon exact their retribution.

As the scene before me came more fully into focus, my mistake became apparent. Though dozens of reanimated bodies were, indeed, making their way toward Cassius and myself, their eyes were fixed upon neither Cassius nor me. Instead, like a guiding light, the dead were interested wholly in one thing.

The violin.

Chapter Forty-Three

The violin.

Lying upon the ground, I called out to him, "Cassius!"

Cassius slowly turned his gaze from the advancing mob to look at me, but his face had transformed. The remaining moonlight glinted upon his forehead, nose, and cheekbones, leaving the hollows of his face darkened; a visage like a skull.

It was a face like death itself.

"Cassius, give me the violin," I entreated, my voice heavy with unease and devoid of certainty that he would comply. Yet, a fleeting hope lingered within my heart, soon extinguished by the slow shake of his head from side to side.

"No," he replied softly. "I do not believe I shall." His eyes were no longer an entrancing green but dark, empty, and black. "You have received your end of the deal, Elise, and I have claimed mine."

"No," I whispered. "You cannot... Cannot possibly—" The correct words danced beyond my reach. In my stunned silence, Cassius smiled what would otherwise have been an endearing expression.

"Farewell, love." Cassius grasped the brim of his hat, sweeping it down into a deep, performative bow. The violin was still tucked beneath his arm as he turned on his heel, a grand maestro leaving the stage after the performance of a lifetime.

Rage blazed within me, seeing my blood, sweat, and tears walk away in the arms of one so callous, so cruel. The violin, my great sinful object of desire.

"*No!*" Getting to my knees, I attempted to stand once more, but my shattered ankle refused to cooperate in pursuit of Cassius.

The violin must be destroyed.

I attempted to hobble after him as best I could, it was futile. Even with a final desperate lunge, Cassius pulled easily out of my reach. Instead of capturing him, I toppled to the ground once more.

"Cassius, please," I said from the ground.

He turned to face me again, a maddening lack of emotion on his face.

He is enjoying this, I realized. "Can you not see what an evil thing we have created? It must be destroyed."

He paused before responding. "It is, indeed, powerful. Evil? That is up for debate. Alas, this violin is my rightful property, and I shall do with it as I see fit."

"You—You are a monster. You are a *demon*." But no matter what I said, his expression remained unmoved. "How *could* you?"

He placed a hand over his heart, feigning contrition. "What more shall I say?" Then, gesturing at the oncoming crowd, he said, "I did consider returning them to sleep, for your sake." He shifted the violin slightly beneath his arm. "But if that is what you think of me, then I wish you the best of luck until morning."

With that, Cassius lifted the violin from beneath his arm, settling it comfortably beneath his chin, and drew the bow across the strings. His posture was that of an expert violinist. He played a short piece, containing a combination of dissonant chords. I glanced behind me to the oncoming throng, who paused, appearing thoughtful.

"Cassius, what are you doing?"

He said nothing, continuing to play. He held the final note for a moment, then ended the piece. I looked back at the undead, who remained still.

"As I say, Elise," said Cassius, tucking the violin beneath his arm once more, "Farewell."

With that, he walked away, without so much as a backward glance.

"*No!*" I shouted, but he departed as casually as one might leave a social event, his figure soon vanishing into the dense fog that now cloaked the graveyard.

With Cassius gone, my attention shifted to far more pressing matters: the crowd of the undead. I turned to face them once more, finding that they had been diverted from their pursuit of the violin. They now hungered for me.

Raw, primordial fear coursed through my veins as I looked out upon this congregation, led by those I had loved most: William and my father.

"Please, no," I said, my voice quivering as I looked upon my pursuers. This well-dressed, foul-smelling mob had evil in their eyes and a look of intent which was inescapable. Fearful, desperate tears slid down my cheeks. "I am so sorry," I said, slowly dragging myself through the graveyard. "I'm so sorry."

Clinging to a gravestone, I attempted to pull myself up.

"I did not know what would happen," I said, but my pleas fell upon deaf ears. Perhaps too little humanity remained for them to hear me, their bodies driven by instinct, giving the chase as much thought as a moth seeks light.

How long might they pursue me? Cassius had wished me luck until morning. Would that be the end?

Desperately, I cast my gaze around, searching for something—anything—with which to defend myself. The shovel Cassius had used to remove dirt from William's grave lay a long way off. Retrieving this weapon pushing past the dead or going around them. It seemed unthinkable with my injured ankle, and yet, perhaps I would need to find a way.

It was then that I became aware of a noise cutting through the shuffling of the dead, above the knocking, scratching, and muffled screaming of those trapped below the ground. It was a haunting yet familiar croak—the call of a raven. I spotted the outline of its dark form, faint against the distance above the fog.

The raven perched proudly upon a mausoleum, not just as a mere visitor but as a harbinger of hope. The mausoleum might offer the much-needed haven I sought, its door a barrier from the advance of the undead. Assuming, of course, that it was no longer occupied by its previous residents, but given the throng of bodies surrounding me, this seemed probable.

The mausoleum stood on the far side of this terrifying assembly—the macabre crowd closing in from every direction as more of the undead emerged from the fog that had cloaked Cassius's departure.

With few options before me and time slipping away, I steeled myself for what lay ahead, scarcely comprehending any alternatives. I pulled myself upright on a gravestone with quivering legs, casting a gaze over the bizarre tableau. These well-dressed men and women, in suits and dresses, yet decaying and full of ill intent. Stripped of their humanity, they behaved with animalistic ferocity.

These figures before me, monstrous as they appeared, had not always been so. A kind of desperate sadness overtook me.

I created them. I created this.

Banishing these thoughts, I propelled myself forward despite pain flaring from my injured ankle, a visceral scream tearing from my throat as I navigated the writhing sea of bodies, inhaling the stench of decaying flesh that threatened to suffocate me. The fabric of their burial attire brushed against my bare arms, the contact with their rotten flesh making my skin crawl.

Midway to the mausoleum, I tripped and fell.

Panic coursed through me such that my bladder released. In desperation, I crawled the remaining distance with frantic determination. *They will catch me,* I thought, *they will be upon me before I can shut the door.*

As if in answer to this fear, a hand closed around my leg. A shriek tore through me as I glanced back to find the hand belonged to what was once William.

"Get away from me," I cried, shaking my leg free from his grip and pressing onward. As I crossed the mausoleum's threshold, I took a cursory look around, hoping fervently it was empty.

Attempting to close the door, I encountered stubborn resistance, the obstacle unseen but unyielding.

"Please!"

I pushed harder, then there came a soft, gooey *pop*, and the door shut firmly, plunging me into near-total darkness, save for the faint light filtering through the mausoleum's high windows.

My back pressed against the door, I slid to the floor and collapsed into uninhibited, unabated sobs.

Chapter Forty-Four

The morning after was a tumultuous scene. Once the chaos had subsided, I managed to drift into a light slumber, my back still propped against the mausoleum door. The first sign of life beyond the mausoleum came from the morning songbirds, their melody a welcome sound of hope. It was a refreshing change from the noises of the dead.

Outside, a new noise—a more comforting one—emerged: the low murmur of conversation, unmistakably the speech of the living.

"Hello?" I called, attempting to rise, only for my injured ankle to give way beneath me. "Please, I need help."

A brief pause was followed by a response. "Who's there?"

"Elise," I replied, moving away from the door. "Elise Knight. Please, I need help."

There was a sound of shifting outside the door before it swung open, revealing the caretaker, Rowan Mackenzie, and Sheriff Crogan.

"What in the name of God happened here?" asked the sheriff.

Faced with the ghastly sight before me, I shook my head, unable to articulate the horror. A jumbled mass of bodies lay by the mausoleum's entrance, lifeless once more. They resembled discarded marionettes, left in disarray with their limbs splayed unnaturally.

Closest to me was my beloved William, resurrected only to meet an unceremonious end. Tracks of tears marked his blood-streaked, decaying face. His eyes, cloudy and unseeing, appeared too small for their sockets. The feet that once chased me were now gruesome stumps, his shoes lying far from him. They had been secured so tightly that the flesh tore before the shoes could be removed.

The obstacle that had blocked the door the previous night was revealed to be William's hand, which now lay severed within the mausoleum. I retched, then vomited beside the door.

"She shouldn't be here," Mackenzie said, addressing the sheriff. I wiped my face with a trembling hand.

"Best get her home," the sheriff agreed. "Let Dr. Bell know she'll be needing his care. Christ, I might be needing him as well."

Mackenzie gently wrapped a sturdy arm around me, guiding me out of the graveyard, avoiding the pile of bodies as I hobbled on my good leg.

Though I scarcely wished to witness the scene of destruction again, I cast one last glance at the heap of bodies. The raven, dead once more, lay at the top of the heap like a flag.

―――――――――――――――――――――

As the town of Chapel Grove awoke on that fateful All Saints' Day, word of the graveyard desecration spread quickly.

"This is the work of a devil," Reverend Willard proclaimed. "The consequence of sinful desires. We must repent as a community, or risk inviting this evil again."

Others had a different view.

"I warned you all, didn't I? I said these pranks were spiraling out of control," remarked Deputy Duncan, throwing a stern look towards the boys he had reprimanded for lighting fires the previous night.

Mrs. Stanway sniffed disdainfully. "I notice someone missing from this whole thing," she said, gesturing towards the field where McCalmont's Curiosities had previously been, the grass still flattened by its wheels. A murmur of agreement rippled through the crowd.

"A warlock!" someone shouted. "Let him never return to darken this town with his sorcery."

Meanwhile, efforts to clean up the graveyard were underway. Dr. Bell treated my ankle as best he could, muttering, "What a mess." He wrapped my ankle in a bandage and gave me a rudimentary set of crutches, which I used to return to the cemetery. Helping with the task felt like my duty.

Mackenzie and Sumner Philpot were there, separating the bodies and lining them up in neat rows. As I approached, they were carefully moving Abel's mother to rest beside her son. They laid her on the grass, and both looked up simultaneously.

"Miss, this is no place for you," said Mackenzie.

"I wish to help," I replied.

Sumner's gaze lingered on my leg, securely bandaged and propped in a boot, then shifted to my crutches. He asked gently, "With what, my dear?"

"With the dead," I responded.

Chapter Forty-Five

Life in Chapel Grove went back to normal thereafter with a few notable exceptions.

Upon the restoration of the last desecrated grave and the re-consecration of the cemetery, there was an unspoken but resolute never to speak of the catastrophe again. All Hallows' Eve was no longer celebrated in Chapel Grove, especially activities involving pranks. Anyone caught indulging in such behavior faced steep penalties.

An All Saints' Day celebration took its place. Where All Hallows' Eve would pass unremarked upon, the following day would mark the annual Harvest Festival, a tradition which continued, but with the addition of a special service held at the church in honor of the dead, followed by a candlelit Remembrance Walk through the cemetery.

It was on the first of this kind, the first anniversary of the harrowing incident, that I began to make peace with what had happened. It became a day of remembrance not only for my beloved William but also for my father, Ida Sinclair, Abel Sinclair, and Sophia, along with Louella, whose photograph I carried with me to the graveyard. We had all been pawns in the bizarre game played by Cassius.

For what purpose he desired such a thing, I could never imagine.

As for me, I seemed to have somewhat of a gift for working with the dead. After assisting with the cleanup of the cemetery, I began an apprenticeship alongside Sumner Philpot. Reluctant though he was at first, his last assistant had quit, and I was willing. Thus, he taught me to prepare bodies for wakes and burials and arranged memorial services.

Distasteful as some may consider such work, death no longer terrified me as it once had. Following the events in the graveyard, handling the remains of the dead did not unsettle me. Considering my involvement in those events, it was only fitting. Counseling those who had lost loved ones served as a form of catharsis for me.

Using my position, I advocated for the reburial of Abel Sinclair with his family. After the indignities his body suffered, he deserved no less. The town was convinced it was necessary for our collective healing, and I am grateful for that. Although his death could not be undone, this gesture allowed me to offer a modicum of restitution.

Whatever one might say about the cruelty of death, it was infinitely preferable to the chaos that unfolded in the cemetery that night; yet, had I never sought William's return, my talents might have remained undiscovered. But perhaps this is just how I rationalize the penance I underwent for my sins.

I could only hope that, ultimately, my service was enough to make my father and William proud, and possibly regain my place in Heaven, having already endured the torments of hell.

Epilogue

Chapel Grove, 1923

The conversation Lucy had initially planned never came to fruition, utterly captivated as she became by Ms. Knight's tale. When the story eventually concluded, Lucy's eyes softened with empathy as she regarded the elderly woman.

I can't just abandon her, she thought. *This poor woman. Perhaps she's sensed my intentions and crafted this tale to draw me closer. How lonely she must truly be.*

Despite her advanced age, Ms. Knight did not appear senile; yet, such a story seemed implausible.

The hour had grown late. After tidying up following their meal, Lucy bid farewell to Ms. Knight, promising to return the following week. It was the first promise met with something akin to excitement, as if Ms. Knight appeared to sit taller, her spirit somewhat unburdened by sharing her story.

Could it possibly be true? Surely, life cannot return to the dead.

Yet, as Lucy walked home, the narrative clung stubbornly to her thoughts, especially as elements from the tale manifested along her route.

First was the overgrown entrance to the creek road near Ms. Knight's home, the site of much of the story. Could this path truly have been where she encountered Vada and learned about Louella?

Perhaps there is evidence, like a newspaper clipping at the library, which can corroborate part of the story, Lucy mused.

So outlandish was the tale that it seemed beyond belief, but Ms. Knight had recounted it with unwavering conviction. In relating the incident, she appeared to find a peace that had obviously long eluded her.

Beyond the creek road lay the old cemetery. Lucy hesitated, contemplating whether she should explore the headstones there, but ultimately chose not to and continued on her path.

Could the dead have indeed risen in that cemetery half a century ago, or was it merely the product of an aged mind's fantasies?

Crossing Main Street, Lucy noted several stores that Ms. Knight had described, such as Nash's Deli. Others, like the hat shop—a site of one of the last All Hallows' Eve pranks in Chapel Grove—were no longer in existence, casualties of time.

Could there really have been a traveling showman with his wagon at the edge of that road, where new houses now stood? Could Cassius have truly existed, with his strange creatures and macabre relics?

As she walked home, Lucy noticed purple dahlias blooming in a nearby garden, triggering memories of the Sinclairs. Had Ida Sinclair truly existed, tending to those very flowers, only to be murdered by her son? Surely a record of Abel and his mother's tragic ends existed somewhere.

Perhaps this story warrants further investigation, Lucy considered upon arriving home. Ms. Knight had provided ample details; if true, they could potentially be verified through the Chapel Grove Historical Society. Surely, the group would possess newspapers from that era, journals, or other documents that could confirm or refute Ms. Knight's account.

Indeed, All Hallows' Eve celebrations remained subdued in Chapel Grove to this day. Was this tragedy the root of such muted, solemn observances? Reverend Bell, after all, was planning an upcoming All Saints Day celebration with the choir. Lucy pondered whether "Abide With Me" might be an appropriate selection— should Ms. Knight attend, would such a song heal or distress her? Lucy was unsure.

As echoes of these tragedies lingered in Lucy's mind, she prepared supper, contemplating what she might share with Neil about her visit to Ms. Knight.

If she chose to mention it at all.

By evening's end, Lucy was exhausted from the lengthy and emotionally taxing visit with Ms. Knight. She brushed her teeth, changed into her nightgown, turned off the light, and nestled under the covers.

Perhaps it was a trick of her imagination, but just before falling asleep, Lucy could have sworn she heard a violin playing somewhere in the distance.

Acknowledgments

I wrote the first draft of The Violin in 2020. I challenged myself to complete 50,000 words during the month of October and was proud of myself when I achieved this goal in just 15 days. After this initial accomplishment, however, I put the first draft aside for several years, unsure what should be done with it. It was a terrible first draft.

In mid-2023, I resolved excavate what I had written and try to finish the book. It's been quite a journey.

I began whittling away at it shortly after the birth of our fourth child, who was only 19 months younger than our third. This meant I was incredibly sleep-deprived, short-tempered, and swamped with responsibilities, especially because we had (and still have) a quite limited income. Investing money for editing, cover design, and other publishing expenses seemed, frankly, insane.

Sleep-deprived as I was, maybe I was a little bit insane.

However, since I was a child, I have wanted to become a writer. Seeing my children grow and make sense of the world motivated to proceed, to be an example to them that they, too, can do hard things. Although balancing work, home, and family life was sometimes a challenge, I wished to make them proud.

To my children, thank you. Each of you inspires me to be a better person, and I would never have been brave enough to pursue my dream without you.

On a related note, I must acknowledge those who helped watch my children, allowing me to write, edit, and, occasionally, cry in peace. Thank you for keeping me grounded and allowing time for basic necessities like sleep and meals.

My husband deserves heartfelt thanks for his unwavering support of this ambitious project. Despite sometimes working up to 80 hours a week, he came home to a distracted wife absorbed in her laptop, often greeted only with a brief, "Hey, welcome home." He also was on the receiving end of many phone calls where I cried, wondering whether it was time to throw in the towel. He wouldn't let me give up.

My mom and several friends, who know who they are, received similar phone calls. Thank you for listening and encouraging me.

A huge thank you also goes to Madeline Dyer of Book Butchers, who meticulously edited this book and helped transform it into the story it became. Your knowledge, hard work, and patience have been invaluable. Thank you for being a teacher in addition to an editor.

I regret that I will inevitably overlook some vital mentions in this note of gratitude, for I could not have finished this book alone. I am profoundly grateful for all the assistance I've received.

Finally, to you, dear reader, who chose to purchase and read this book: thank you for taking a chance on my story. I sincerely hope you enjoyed it. There will certainly be more to come.

Could You Do Me A Favor?

If you enjoyed this book—or even if you didn't—I would be immensely grateful if you could take a moment to leave a review on Amazon, Goodreads, Apple Books, BookBub, or even your social media platform of choice.

For self-published authors, reviews are vital to connecting the right readers with our work, granting it a chance in a competitive market. Your feedback, whether praise or constructive criticism, helps the right readers find the book.

Thank you wholeheartedly for supporting independent authors.

About The Author

Odella Howe is a former ghostwriter and full-time mother of four who's now taking "ghostwriting" literally, crafting supernatural stories that both terrify and thrill her readership. Her debut novel, The Violin, combines her lifelong passion for dark fiction and her obsession with Saint-Saens's haunting composition, "Danse Macabre." When the writing desk isn't holding her captive, Odella enjoys hiking the stunning foothills of Utah, sewing, and spending time with her family. To connect and get updates on her next releases, follow her on Instagram @odellahoweofficial or visit odellahowe.com.

www.ingramcontent.com/pod-product-compliance
Lightning Source LLC
Chambersburg PA
CBHW050148120726
47903CB00002B/543